# BETHANY J MILLER

# A Whole New Playlist

*This story is dedicated to everyone who sings to the music in their heads.*
*You keep the world interesting.*
*\*\*\**

*To Creamery Station and Parsonsfield,*
*two amazing bands who have inspired me*
*with their creativity, passion and dedication.*
*\*\*\**

*Thank you to Linda Fausnet, Tara L Roi,*
*and the Greater New Haven Writers Group*
*for making sure my my singing isn't too off key*
*and my lyrics are lyrical.*
*\*\*\**

*And to Mike, because you're always number one on my playlist.*

# Chapter 1

The '68 Camaro hugged the road as Macy maneuvered effortlessly around the other cars. She watched the speedometer creep steadily toward a hundred, the rumble of the V-8 engine sinking into her bones. She knew her friends would laugh at her for wanting to drive a car twice as old as she was, but with adrenaline pumping through her veins and all the power of a big-block Chevy at her fingertips, what other people thought didn't matter.

Wylie gave her total freedom to photograph his cars anywhere, but in the middle of winter her options were limited. The areas closest to the dealership were covered in new-fallen snow and, without a cloud in the sky, it would be nearly impossible to balance the intense brightness of sun on snow with the glossy black of the car.

She'd opted to head north of Hartford, to the old tobacco barns that lined both sides of the highway. They'd create plenty of shade and their weathered red paint, rough and peeling, would contrast the smooth lines of the car perfectly.

Anticipation mingled with the adrenaline; she couldn't decide if she was more excited about driving the car or photographing it.

The road straightened in front of her. She glanced to the passenger's seat and tapped the play button on her phone. Drums, then guitars, filled the air as Steppenwolf began singing about being born to be wild.

The sound wasn't as full as she'd get if she could stream through a sound system, but the car's previous owner had kept everything original and in 1968 that meant the vehicle had come equipped with an 8-track player. *I could probably get Steppenwolf on 8-track, on eBay.*

She didn't mind listening through her phone, though. Most of the time she had no choice. The bulk of Wylie's inventory were big classics; if they had radios at all they were only AM. Plus, streaming music meant she could design a playlist for every era, every car she photographed.

"Born To Be Wild" ended and "Magic Carpet Ride" began. Macy settled into driving. *I could buy this car. Then I could drive it every day.* She caressed the steering wheel. *That'd be amazing.* She brushed that idea aside; she thought that about at least half the cars she photographed. It was a ridiculous notion anyway. At 23 years old, still living at home and only working freelance, she wasn't in the position to buy any car. *Someday, though.*

She crested a hill, saw a sedan at the bottom veer erratically left, then right, into the snow.

*Shit! Ice!* She hit the brakes, desperate to slow down before it was too late.

The Camaro began to slide.

*Don't lock the brakes! Left— no right! Stop stop please stop.* She downshifted, pumped the brakes. *Shit shit please don't—*

The squeal of metal on metal drowned out everything else.

She sat, gripping the steering wheel, her feet jammed on the brake and the clutch, even after the car had stopped. Blood pounded in her ears. Her whole body shook.

*You're okay. Breathe. Just breathe.*

The frantic pace of her heart began to slow as she acknowledged that she was unhurt. She forced her fingers to uncurl from the steering wheel and opened the door. Ignoring the snow that filled her shoes, she made her way to the front of the car. A new wave of panic welled in her chest.

She'd gone off the shoulder and through the snow before sliding, the side of the car against the guardrail, for a good twenty feet. The front bumper was hanging, the headlight dangling from its socket, and the whole passenger side of the beautiful classic Camaro, a car that didn't belong to her, was wrecked.

She might have been better off dead.

*** ***

Work was never steady for Macy, but this was the third week in a row she hadn't had a single job and she was really starting to worry. Wylie had been her only regular client. She'd destroyed the trust he'd had in her and any chance of working for him again. And since all her other clients had been his friends, wrecking the Camaro had wrecked those jobs, too.

She replayed the accident over and over in her mind, as she had since it had happened. It had been so stupid to drive like that in a car that didn't belong to her. *Dad always says you drive too fast.*

She flopped to her back and stared at the Imagine Dragons poster she'd hung on the ceiling when she'd still been in high school. She and Logan had seen them in Boston, back when they'd still spent every day together. Before he'd met Jennifer, who didn't want her boyfriend hanging out with another woman. It didn't matter that they'd been friends for their entire lives. According to Logan, Jennifer felt threatened by Macy and therefore they were only allowed to hang out in a group. *Ridiculous. He's never been interested—*

The knock on her door broke into her thoughts. Wishing for about the millionth time that she didn't still live at home, she called, "Come in."

Her mom poked her head around the door. "I'm going shopping. Dad needs a tie to match the shirt Grandma just bought him, and I'm going to look at shoes. Why don't you come with me? We'll have lunch at Panera."

Not bothering to sit up, she said, "I hate shopping."

"They're having a sale at JCPenney's. I thought we could see about buying you some new outfits."

Even if she'd wanted to go someplace, shopping with her mother was not the slightest bit appealing. "I've got too many clothes already." She pointed to the piles of concert t-shirts stacked on top of the dresser because they wouldn't fit in the drawers.

"I was thinking of something... nicer. Slacks, a blouse or two, maybe even a dress."

Appalled at the idea, she said, "A dress?"

Her mom came all the way in and sat on the edge of the bed. "Aunt Holly was just telling me they're looking for an office assistant where she works. It's not glamorous, but it's full time."

*What the hell?* "I'm a photographer."

"I know that. And Aunt Holly knows that. But it's been a while since you worked, and we thought this could be something to do. While you wait for your next job."

Disbelievingly, she asked, "You want me to get an *office job*? With Aunt Holly?"

"It's a great opportunity. You'll have benefits, holidays off, and there's room for advancement. You've already got a semester of QuickBooks, if you went back to community college and finished—"

"I sucked at that. I suck at everything except photographing cars, remember?"

Gently, her mom said, "It just might be time to try something...else."

"Mom, sitting at a desk all day? Doing paperwork?"

"It's not as bad as you think." She added, "Emma loves it."

Macy snorted at the mention of her best friend. "Yeah. Because where she works there's a bunch of women who spend all day gossiping and avoiding doing any actual work. I'm not into that. At all."

"Maybe not, but you need a job. You've got school loans and your cell phone, and with a totaled car on your record your insurance premiums are going to go up."

"I've got it under control."

She raised her eyebrows. "So you've got jobs lined up?"

Not willing to admit she didn't, Macy stayed silent.

"I'll tell Aunt Holly you'll send her your resume."

As soon as she was alone again, Macy rolled over and hugged her pillow. She didn't want to do something else. Especially not something her mother wanted her to do. That's how she'd ended up taking that semester of QuickBooks in the first place, which she'd hated. And why she'd tried going to school for nursing. And a million other things her mother had "suggested" that hadn't worked out.

Photography was the one thing she'd chosen for herself, and she'd had to go through her father because her mother had insisted it was a waste of time. When Macy had asked, she'd laughed it off, 'How are you going to make a living at that?'

Maybe she wasn't raking in millions, but she'd been working really hard, building a reputation and a client base. *Until you wrecked it.*

An overwhelming feeling of helplessness welled in her chest. She knew her mother was right. This was her fault. She didn't deserve to get to do what she wanted.

But it was the only thing she wanted. And she wasn't about to give up something she loved because she'd made a stupid mistake.

She'd just have to change her focus. Maybe contact Ford. They had car photographers, probably on staff. Although that might not be the best fit. Once she'd proven herself, Wylie had let her shoot cars any way she wanted. She doubted Ford would give her that kind of freedom.

She could offer "car sittings," like family portrait sittings except she'd photograph people's cars. Even as she thought it, she knew that was ridiculous.

There were tons of other uses for car pictures besides dealer advertising. Calendars, postcards, mouse pads. She could do a whole line of car-themed products and sell them online. Maybe on Etsy? Or she could—

The phone rang, interrupting her musing. It was an out of state number, most likely "Rachel, from Card Services." Robo-call or not, she answered, "Macy LaPorte."

A man's voice, deep and smooth, said, "Hi, Macy. My name is Gage Dawson. I hear you photograph cars."

"I do."

"Great. If you've got time I'd like to sit down and see if we can help each other out."

Hope mingled with nerves. She went to her desk and moved random papers around, trying to make it sound like she was really busy. "I'd love to. I've got an opening," she fluttered the papers once more, "Thursday at eleven."

He cleared his throat. "I'm on a bit of a tight schedule. Is there any way I can swing by today?"

Sweat broke out on her back. *Stay calm. And don't sound desperate!* "Um, I think I can re-arrange my schedule. I work strictly on location, though, so either I can come to you or I can meet you somewhere." No matter how badly she wanted this, there was no way in hell she was going to meet someone at her mom's kitchen table.

"How's noon? You pick the place."

She glanced at the Hello Kitty clock her oldest brother had given her for her eighth birthday. *It's ten-thirty. Crap, that's soon. I can make it, if I hustle.* "Where are you coming from?"

"Branford."

Her mind raced. *Branford, okay, so not out of state. Maybe an old cell number. Irrelevant. What's between here and... New Haven.* "There's a coffee shop, Book Traders?" She gave him the location and told him to look for someone with long, curly blonde hair, knowing that was the first thing people noticed about her.

As soon as she hung up, she texted her mom to let her know she was going out. She kept it purposely vague in case this turned out to be nothing. *Last thing I need is Mom reminding me that I don't have a real job.*

She began putting things together for an interview; her laptop, price lists and contracts, trade magazines and catalogs that her images were in, copyright information, a list of referrals. *Maybe not the referrals.* Gage Dawson hadn't told her where he'd gotten her name, or what kind of cars he had. If he was a hot-rodder or raced street cars there was a chance he wouldn't know Wylie, or any of his friends. *Branford, though. There's car guys there. Guys I've worked for.*

She pushed a pile of clothes off her desk chair, ignoring that they landed on the floor, and sat. "Yeah, okay. So maybe he knows about the Camaro. But he still called. So even if he does know, it doesn't matter to him. And," she put the list aside, "if he already knows, then he probably knows the people on my referral list."

With her bag set and time slipping away, she pulled on black dress pants and the blue button-down shirt her mom had bought her specifically for interviews because it matched her eyes perfectly. The outfit didn't suit her, but her mother had insisted that it was vital she presented a professional appearance when she met with prospective clients. Macy didn't think the guys she worked for cared what she wore, or that her eyes and shirt were both blue, but she'd booked every car job she'd interviewed for, so she figured it couldn't hurt to wear the outfit. At least for the initial interview. When she was shooting she wore jeans and t-shirts; photographing cars was a dirty job.

She paused to collect herself. She'd never liked interviews. And there was a lot riding on this one.

As soon as she was dressed and calm, she climbed into the driver's seat of her mom's old minivan. Her parents kept the van for her, and she appreciated that she could take it any time she needed to, but she still hated driving it. *No matter how loud you crank the music, it's still a minivan.*

Someday she'd choose her own car. One that suited her. There were so many she loved. Classic Mustangs, the new Challengers, Jeep Wranglers, vintage Firebirds with the decal on the hood. She checked out cars on the highway, sometimes wrinkling her nose, sometimes nodding appreciatively.

There was always a ton of traffic in New Haven and she almost missed her exit because she couldn't get over to the right lane. She finally cut off some guy in a blue BMW, ignoring the blast of his horn. Driving wasn't any better off the highway. Between city busses, college students crossing the street, and a zillion people trying to get where they were going, she started to wish she'd chosen a different meeting place.

The calm that she'd worked so hard for evaporated as she hunted for a parking space. She couldn't be late; she had enough stacked against her already. It took twenty minutes of driving back and forth on side streets to finally find an open spot, two full blocks from where she needed to go. She slung her bag and purse over her shoulder and tried to think through her sales pitch as she hurried down the sidewalk, head bent against the frigid air.

Outside the coffee shop, she pulled herself up straight, pushed her shoulders back, and reminded herself that she was a damn good car photographer. Stepping inside, she glanced around, not sure who she was looking for. The guy behind the counter looked up and smiled in welcome; she knew that wasn't Gage Dawson. She moved into the room off to the right, ignoring the book lined walls as she scanned the studious-looking people typing on laptops or talking quietly to each other. The guy at the table right inside the door stood and asked, "Macy?"

He was probably little older than she was, maybe late twenties, and had the look of a car salesman. It was more than the slicked back hair and red power tie. It was the confident attitude she could feel from across the table. Smiling nervously, she held out her hand. "You must be Gage."

He shook firmly, his hand soft and warm against her still cold fingers. "It's a pleasure to meet you." He gestured for her to sit and asked, "Can I get you something? A cup of coffee or something to eat?"

"A coffee would be great."

"Be right back."

While he went to get her drink, she settled into a chair. She'd taken sales classes in photography school and knew his welcoming smile was supposed to put her at ease, as much as his blue shirt was supposed to make her trust him.

Once he was back with her drink, she let him start. "Macy, I'm glad you could fit me into your schedule." When she didn't say anything, he continued, "You come very highly recommended."

It was amazing how fast her hands went from freezing cold to clammy. "You've seen my work?"

"You did those pictures of the '38 Packard 12 in last month's *Old Car Spotlight*, right?"

"I did." She relaxed a little. That was Wylie's car, but he always gave her photo credit and lots of people read that magazine.

"I thought you did an excellent job. It can be tough to photograph a barn fresh car. I appreciate that you didn't gloss over the effects sitting in storage for forty years had."

"My clients are trying to sell their cars. My job is to provide an accurate representation of the vehicle. So, if a car needs new upholstery, or there's rot or whatever, I'm going to show it." She shrugged. "I'd hate for a buyer to come back and say the dealership misrepresented a car based on my pictures."

He pointed at her. "That is exactly what I need."

He gave her what she thought of as a 'trust me' smile, which only served to put her more on edge. She smiled back, although she didn't feel at all like smiling. All she really wanted was for Gage to cut to the chase and tell her what he needed. "Gage, why don't you tell me about your cars."

He smiled a little before he began. "My dad owns an auction house, and four times a year he holds an auction for classic and special interest cars. We post pictures to our website and print a catalog for all registered bidders. For the most part we have the owners submit pictures, which means we never know what we're going to get. A snapshot taken in front of a garage, a picture of the car from twenty years ago." He shook his head slightly. "Something that doesn't look remotely like the car they deliver."

She nodded. "And you're on the hook for that."

"We are. And it's not just owners who do it. We've had professional photographers retouch pictures, or fail to show a major issue. At Dawson's Auctions, we pride ourselves on presenting the cars we sell exactly as they are." He kept his gaze locked on her. "Macy, I like what I've seen of your work. The creativity, the eye for detail, and the honesty in representation."

Her heart beat harder. There were auction houses where they had staff photographers, people who made sure every car in their catalog looked amazing. If this was something like that, it was literally her dream job.

He continued, "I understand that you have a very casual arrangement with the dealers around here. What I'm looking for is a more formal arrangement. Someone willing to work exclusively for Dawson's Auctions. I'd want you full time, to shoot whatever comes in."

*Full time! Holy shit!* Clasping her hands tightly in her lap and working to keep her voice steady, she said, "Just to clarify, I've got a number of regular clients. You're saying I wouldn't be able to work with them if I accept your offer?"

He folded his hands on the table. "Even if continuing to work with your previous clients was an option, you'd have to refer them to someone else. Dawson's Auctions is located in Arizona."

*Arizona? Shit!* Heat rose to her face and she desperately wanted to break eye contact. *You can't look away.*

"And, just to clarify, you won't be driving any of the cars."

The heat in her face drained, replaced by cold. *He knows I have no other options.* Gage waited; his icy blue eyes locked on hers. She swallowed, "Can I think about it?"

"I can give you until Monday morning."

*** ***

Macy stood at a table by the dance floor, trying to shout over the thumping of house music. She wasn't into clubbing at all, but it was the only thing Emma ever wanted to do. "I don't know. I mean, Arizona?"

Emma tipped her drink in Macy's general direction. "Why don't you take that job with your aunt?"

"Because it's not photography."

"Who cares? It's a job." Emma grinned. "And maybe there's a cute mail room guy or something."

It annoyed Macy that Emma wasn't taking this seriously. "Mail room guy?"

"Would you rather get with one of the accountants?" Emma snickered, "Maybe he can check your balance?"

Logan leaned over, sloshing his drink in the process. "Mace, babe, you don't gotta take that from her."

She hated when Logan called her 'babe'. She turned away, watched people on the dance floor. Behind her, Emma and Logan started going through a list of Macy's old boyfriends and how she'd met them. *What the fuck? Why do they even care?*

"Hey, there!" Emma grabbed the arm of a guy she apparently knew as he walked past.

"Hey." He smiled, obviously happy to see Emma. "I was on my way to get a drink. You wanna come?"

"Sure." Emma let him lead her towards the bar.

Logan picked up Emma's nearly untouched beer. "Think she'll mind?" He didn't wait for an answer before he drank.

Macy half-listened as he talked about some party he'd gone to with his girlfriend, his words becoming less clear as the night went on. *I should've expected this.* Since Emma's last relationship had ended she was totally desperate to find the next one. And Logan... things just weren't the way they used to be.

The worst part was that Macy had, as usual, ended up as the designated driver so she got to deal with all of this stone cold sober.

After a while Macy texted Emma, asking where she was. When she didn't answer, Macy called.

Emma answered, yelling into her phone. "Hey, Macy!"

"Where are you?"

"Down the street."

"What the hell, Emma!"

Laughing, she said, "Don't wait for me. I'll call you tomorrow."

Macy snapped back, "Whatever." She hung up and shoved her phone back in her purse. "Logan, let's go."

He protested when she grabbed his arm and began pulling him through the crowd. She didn't care. All she wanted was to go home.

In the car, he talked incessantly. She tried her best to ignore him, but when he started talking about when they'd been kids she couldn't take it anymore. "Logan, I don't give a shit if my hair was pink when we were fourteen. It was a goddamn phase."

"It was cute." Drunkenly, he added, "You're cute. 'Specially your freckles." He reached for her, as if to run his fingers over her freckled skin.

There had been a time she'd have given just about anything to have him touch her. Now, she pushed him away.

"Hey, remember how we used to sneak out? Go to the graveyard in the middle of the night."

"Yeah. I do." *Don't encourage him. Maybe he'll just stop talking.*

"All of us from the neighborhood. Me 'n you, 'n that chick I was with and that dude, what was his name? You and him had a thing."

"Stop."

"Come on, you remember."

"Just stop." It didn't matter if she did remember. She did not want to talk about this.

"Man, those were— Ryan. That dude was Ryan." He laughed, "Come on, right? He was the guy—"

"Logan, you can either shut up or you can walk home from here."

His head lolled against the seat. "You wouldn't do that."

"Wanna try me?"

"You looooove me. You'd never leave me like that." Leaning towards her again, he added, "You," he pointed at her, "will never leave again."

Not wanting to be reminded of any more of her mistakes, she turned the radio on. Some woman, probably Taylor Swift although Macy wasn't sure, was singing about how shitty some guy was to her.

*Practically my theme song.*

"How can you listen to this shit?"

"Emma left it on." Macy had given up on trying to assert her musical tastes years ago.

Logan reached forward to change the station. The heartsick woman's voice was replaced by Twenty-One Pilots' instantly recognizable blend of rock, rap and anything else that caught their fancy. It wasn't what Macy'd have picked in her current mood, but at least it was something she liked.

Logan tried to sing, making up the words he couldn't remember and laughing hysterically at himself. Macy didn't find it funny at all and she wished she hadn't turned the radio on. *This is you, Macy, all day long. Always doing shit you wish you hadn't.*

It was a relief when she finally pulled into Logan's driveway. He sat in the car until she opened his door. She pulled him up and half dragged him into his apartment. Once she'd gotten him to his bed, she yanked his shoes off and left him lying on top of the covers.

As she turned away, he slurred, "Stay with me."

She hated that she hesitated, hated even more that she turned back. If he hadn't started talking about all that shit from when they were kids she probably wouldn't have. Tears welled in her eyes. "You don't want that."

"Yeah, I do."

For a moment he seemed completely sober. She knew better. "Logan, I have to leave before Jennifer gets home. We both know she won't appreciate me being here." Quietly, she added, "Besides, when you wake up you're going to wish you'd never said that."

"How'd'ya know?" He squinted at her blearily, unable to hold focus for that long.

"Because I do. And if you weren't drunk you'd know, too." She watched as he leaned over the side of the bed and puked into the trash can. When he was done and she was sure he was okay, she whispered, "Bye, Logan."

*You don't need this shit. None of it.* As she closed the door, she knew it was the last time she'd walk out of his apartment. First thing in the morning she was going to call Gage Dawson.

# Chapter 2

Of all the possible places to be, his father's office was not the one Talan would have chosen. Ideally, he'd be home working on the song that had been circling in his brain for days. Or at a bar, drinking a beer and checking out the next up and coming band. But at this point he'd take his own office, where he could sit in peace and listen to music while he worked on the pile of papers that had accumulated seemingly of their own accord on his desk.

Instead, he sat swiveling back and forth in one of the black leather chairs normally reserved for the big-wigs his father dealt with himself, idly staring at framed posters of million-dollar cars adorning the otherwise boring white walls.

His brother, Gage, was going on and on about contracts, reserves, commission; things that were irrelevant to what Talan did at Dawson's Auctions. He researched the history and validated the specifics of every car that came through the classics division, regardless of what kind of deals Gage made.

His father began asking a series of questions. Talan tuned him out and instead listened to the music in his head. He'd been hearing the same riff for days, had actually worked out the lead guitar already. The problem was, in his head he heard something he didn't personally own. "Piano."

"What?"

The sound of his father's voice pulled him out of this thoughts. Trying to pretend he'd been paying attention, he said, "Piano black."

Glaring, Nate leaned forward. "The car is maroon." His sharp blue eyes narrowed. "And there is no such thing as piano black."

Leaning casually on the arm of his chair, Talan said, "There should be."

"If you're not going to take this seriously then get out."

He sat up quickly. "Yeah?"

"No. Sit your ass in that chair and listen. How the hell else are you going to know what's going on?" Nate turned his fierce gaze back to Gage. "The paperwork was completed this morning. The car will be here by the end of next week."

Gage nodded. "Excellent."

"When is that photographer starting?"

"Monday."

Running a hand over his military-cut grey hair, Nate said, "You better know what you're doing."

Gage assured him, "It's under control."

The conversation moved on to the estate of a car collector who had died recently, a line of discussion Talan didn't care to follow. He'd worry about the cars if they handled the deal.

After what felt like hours, their father dismissed them. Outside his office, Gage grabbed Talan's arm. "What is your problem?"

Yanking his arm away from his brother's grip, he kept his tone cool. "I have a ton of shit to do and these meetings are a waste of my time."

"This is your company as much as it is mine."

"Not by my choice."

Staring intently into his face, his blue eyes an exact match to their father's, Gage said, "You agreed to this."

"I agreed to help you not go to jail for fraud. Not work for Dad for the rest of my life."

"Because you've got something more pressing to do?"

Not into arguing the point, Talan didn't say anything.

"Come on, Talan. Playing dive bars wasn't exactly a solid career path."

The dig hurt. He considered firing back, reminding Gage that *he* was only there because he'd screwed up *his* life so badly he didn't have any other options. Instead, he said, "I don't play bars at all anymore, remember? Because you need me here." He turned and headed down the hall, leaving Gage staring after him.

He wasn't even five steps away before the guilt set in. Gage had gotten his now ex-girlfriend pregnant, flunked out of college, and with no other options had begged his father to hire him. But he'd also worked hard to rebuild his life and to be there for his daughter, and Talan respected that.

He also respected what Gage had accomplished at Dawson's. Since their father had shifted his focus to dealer auctions, he'd let the classics division slide. Gage had come in and revived it.

Except that had almost cost Gage, and their father, everything. Talan couldn't forget the fear that had radiated from his brother the day he'd come to beg Talan to work for him. *Travis is in jail, for falsifying paperwork. Half my fucking inventory came from him. I gotta figure out if we sold cars with faked titles, and I have no idea how.* Talan had spent his first months at Dawson's researching retroactively.

He knew, no matter how badly he wanted to, he wouldn't leave Dawson's unless there was someone he could trust to take his place. Someone who understood that, although selling cars was vital to Dawson's success, making sales based on lies could land them in jail. And regardless of how he felt about his family, he didn't want them in that kind of trouble.

As he stepped into his assistant's office, he briefly considered if Keira could replace him. It was a fleeting thought. Keira was great at completing the exact tasks he gave her, but she wasn't motivated to do the kind of in-depth searching he did. *Not unless what she's searching for is a deal on shoes.*

She smiled her too-polished smile as she greeted him. "Hi, Talan. How'd your meeting go?"

"Fine." He tried getting past her desk without saying more. Talking to Keira was always risky. He'd learned the hard way that she could take the simplest comment and turn it into gossip, which would land him in his father's office, which was something he avoided as much as possible.

"Fred called back about that Cadillac that supposedly that actress took to the Academy Awards. I didn't want to bother you so I took the information down and put it on your desk. He said if you need anything else to call him back. And that book I ordered for you from eBay came in. It's on your desk, too."

"Thanks." He walked the rest of the way to his office. Finally alone, he dropped into his chair, pulled the elastic out of his hair and shook his head. He hated that his father forced him to wear his hair in a ponytail at work. His hair wasn't even that long, and the rule was just stupid.

He picked up the note Keira had left him, read the message from Fred. *Has seen a pic of actress Dorothy Fulton in a 1953 Eldo, can't verify beyond that.*

If Dorothy Fulton had been driven to the 1953 Academy Awards in this Cadillac Eldorado, it would increase the value of the car. If the story told by the current owner of the Eldo was false, and they included it in the ad, the buyer could sue them for misrepresenting the vehicle. If he was going to include that piece of trivia, he'd have to do better than that Fred had seen a picture.

There were other people he could call. Car aficionados he'd met over a lifetime of being dragged with his father to car shows and meetings with both buyers and sellers. People like Fred, who housed massive stores of car history in their brains. That's how his father had pieced together histories of the cars he'd sold.

Now, though, the stories from the old-timers needed to be backed up by proof. No matter how many people "said" they'd seen that photo, or that they "knew" what had gone down, if Dawson's was going to include the story in the ad for the car Talan needed to find the photo himself. Then he'd need to prove the car in the image was the same car currently sitting on Dawson's lot.

He turned to his computer and began searching.

*** ***

Talan definitely felt like he deserved a night out, far away from cars and paperwork and anything having to do with Dawson's Auctions. He paid the cover charge at the door of Foundry 41 and stepped into the old brick building. He never minded paying to get into a bar. He knew the money went to the band and they deserved to be paid for what they did. He hadn't appreciated his brother reminding him, but Gage had had a point. Very few musicians actually made a living playing music.

The sheer number of people milling around the open area in front of the stage confirmed that the band playing that night, Shuffle, already had a very strong following. That was a good sign.

He made his way to the bar, got himself a beer, and found an empty table at the edge of the room. He sat in the shadows and watched the band tuning. They bantered back and forth, the kind of easy camaraderie that came from working together for countless hours.

He'd had that once.

Gage's words resurfaced; *playing dive bars wasn't exactly a solid career path.* Talan hadn't been playing dive bars when Gage had appeared at his door, begging for help. He hadn't been playing anywhere, because his life had just turned to shit and he hadn't even begun to pick up the pieces. *If Gage hadn't shown up on that exact freaking day, there's no way I'd have said yes.*

That wasn't true, though. Gage was his brother, and Talan would have done what he could to help him no matter what. The only difference was, if he'd had something to go back to, he wouldn't have stayed at Dawson's this long.

Lately, he'd been thinking it'd been long enough.

The seemingly random sounds from the stage coalesced into an actual song. The chatter from the audience morphed into cheers. Rock and roll, leaning towards bluegrass, filled the room. Talan pushed aside all thoughts of Gage and what could have been and let the music carry him away.

During the set break he checked out the band's merch table. He picked out a t-shirt and bought their CD. *Another thirty bucks in the band's pocket.*

Back in his spot he nursed his beer and looked over the flier that had been tucked inside the CD case, listing upcoming shows. None of the venues were local, but he was happy to see Shuffle would be playing the Sounds In The Sand Festival he was planning to go to that summer.

"Holy fuck. Talan Dawson."

He looked up, to a guy he didn't recognize.

"James. James Camp?" When he didn't get a response he added, "From high school?" The guy grinned. "You don't remember me."

"Sorry, no."

"Not surprising. We didn't travel in the same circles. I was friends with Gage."

A very vague memory surfaced of a face in the crowd that had always surrounded his older brother. "Hey, James. It's been... a while."

"How is Gage? I haven't seen him since graduation."

"He's fine."

Giving Talan a curious look, he said, "I'm surprised to see you here. I thought your tastes were more... metal."

He smiled a little. If the last time James had seen him was when they'd been in high school, he'd remember a very different Talan. "Not so much these days."

"Ya know," he paused, glanced up to the stage. "I was just telling Roland about you this afternoon. Being back in Arizona, you were the first person who popped into my head." James gave him a look, the kind of look Gage got when he was working out a deal with a client. "You still play piano?"

"No." He shook his head. "Not for a long time."

"Any interest in going back?"

"No."

"Too bad." James indicated the stage. "Roland, the front man, is working on some new material." He smiled apologetically. "It doesn't matter, since you don't play anymore." Holding out his hand, he said, "It was good to see you."

Talan took the offered hand. "Yeah. You too."

"Tell Gage I said hello." James started to walk away, then turned back. "I've always wondered. Why'd you leave?"

"Sorry?"

"Cyanide Suicide."

"How'd you—" He stopped dead. His old band was not something he talked about. Ever.

"I didn't keep in touch with Gage, but when your name started to come up I paid attention. It's too bad shit went down the way it did."

Talan had no idea what James had heard, but it was obviously inaccurate. He hadn't "left" Cyanide Suicide. He'd been left *by* them. Just days before signing a recording contract.

James held out a business card. "If you change your mind about going back to piano."

Talan took the card and watched as James maneuvered through the crowd, greeting people here and there as he went, until he was out of sight.

The card was nice. Thick card stock in matte black, with 'James Camp, Talent Manager' in crisp white type. He stared at it for long moments before he stuck it in his pocket. He had no desire to go back to piano, or to join another band, but it didn't hurt to keep the card.

# Chapter 3

Absently pushing his hair behind his ears, Talan scanned the information on his screen. He mumbled, "Come on. Where are you?" He retyped his search criteria and clicked a different website. The one single piece of information that held the entire story of the car together seemed to be non-existent. It wouldn't be the first time someone had invented a story to make a car more interesting. *Fabricated stories, fabricated cars, you straight up can't pull that shit anymore.* There were still guys out there who tried, though.

He sang under his breath, The Lumineers playing softly enough that no one outside his office would be able to hear it.

Then, it was there, just like the owner had said. Relieved, because he never liked having to tell his dad when a story didn't pan out, he scribbled the source on scrap paper. He shut off the music, grabbed a clipboard and headed out. He stopped at Keira's desk on his way. "I need you to get a copy of this for me."

Reading the note he handed her, she raised a perfectly shaped eyebrow. "You want an original copy of a car club newsletter from sixty years ago?"

"Yeah." He left her to it and went out to the lot. Squinting against the glare of the sun, he scanned the cars out front for the Hemi 'Cuda he was doing next.

It was parked near the road, so passers-by could admire it. A woman, her blonde hair a mass of curls falling halfway to her waist, wearing a Weezer concert t-shirt, jeans, and purple Converse, walked slowly along the side of the car.

The way she moved, the sultry glide of her fingers down the bright red hood, had his head spinning. *Damn. And she's into Weezer.*

He asked, "Can I help you?"

The woman looked up, her startlingly blue eyes intense in contrast to the dreamy smile lingering on her lips. "Sorry, I was just admiring this car. The contrast of the matte black stripe against high gloss red, the curve down the side," her smile turned quirky, "I find it so appealing."

Thinking he found *her* so appealing, he moved closer. "This is a great car. They made just," he knew without looking but he glanced at his clipboard anyway, "two-thousand seven hundred twenty-seven of them."

"That's a damn shame."

The way she said it, he had to agree. Trying to keep her talking, he said, "This one's for sale, if you're in the market."

Her eyes found his and held them. "Maybe, someday."

He held out his hand. "Talan Dawson."

"Macy LaPorte." Taking his hand, sending a wave of heat shooting through his veins, she said, "You must be Gage's brother."

Disappointment dampened his reaction. "I am."

Gage appeared from behind him. "Macy, glad you made it. Come on in."

"Talan," Macy tipped her chin down and, looking up at him, smiled a tiny bit before following Gage to the office.

Talan watched her walk through the lot. He was about to turn back to the car when Macy paused, one hand on the door, and looked back at him. Her blue eyes caught his and his gut clenched. Then she was gone.

*** ***

The heat in Macy's face had nothing to do with the Arizona sun. She paused, her hand on the door, and looked back at the Hemi 'Cuda. It wasn't the car that caught her attention, though. It was the guy next to it. Her skin still tingling from Talan's touch, she turned away and hurried across the foyer.

Gage waited at the receptionist's desk, tapping his fingers impatiently until she caught up. "Macy, this is Celeste."

An older woman, looking very professional in slacks and a tailored shirt, her grey hair cut stylishly short, held out her hand. "It's a pleasure to finally meet you. We've heard great things."

Startled that someone besides Gage would care that she was coming, she didn't know what to say. She settled on, "Thank you."

Gage immediately set off down the hall. "I'll give you a quick tour, then we can get started."

She tried to remember the things he pointed out as they made their way through the building. Where the bathroom was, that the foyer was at the center of the building, what office belonged to whom.

It was all much more formal than what she was expecting. Gage introduced her to the people in the financing and accounting departments, where the women were dressed like they'd just stepped off the set of the talk shows her mom watched. Then there was the woman Gage identified as the research assistant, who looked Macy over so obviously, her eyes narrowed critically, it made Macy want to hide behind the door.

And there was Gage's father. Technically Nate would be her boss, which she wasn't too thrilled with. She felt like she understood Gage already, and that they wanted the same things— great pictures of beautiful cars. Nate, on the other hand, took their first meeting as an opportunity to tell her he was taking a chance hiring her. And he gave her a look that said he didn't have much confidence in his choice. Everything about Dawson's already had her feeling less than adequate and Nate's obvious lack of confidence didn't help.

The only person who made her feel welcome was the graphics guy, Paul. When Gage introduced him, he turned in his chair and greeted her warmly. "Macy. It's a pleasure. You and I will be seeing a lot of each other."

Gage elaborated, "Paul manages our website, designs our catalogs, does basically everything Dawson's puts out for the world to see. You'll be giving the pictures to him."

She smiled weakly. She'd never worked with a 'graphics guy'. She'd always just given the files to her clients and let them do what they wanted with them.

Paul indicated her shirt. "Weezer fan, huh?"

"Yeah." She hadn't given her shirt any thought that morning, but now she desperately wished she'd chosen something different. Like her blue interview shirt, which she'd left back in Connecticut.

Gage said, "We've got paperwork to fill out, then we can get started on shooting cars."

As he led her to the other end of the building, she was acutely aware of the click of his dress shoes on the white marble floor, and of the fact that she didn't own shoes that clicked. The fear she'd tried to squash since she'd said yes to this threatened to engulf her.

*I'm so far out of my league.* The guys she'd worked for in Connecticut had sunk all their money into cars. They didn't care about fancy offices or personnel who looked like Wall Street executives. And they didn't care if their photographer wore concert t-shirts to work, as long as she took spectacular pictures.

And no one had ever given her an employee handbook, or required a W-4. The knots in her stomach tightened as she filled out forms, using her parent's address. Soon enough, though, it was official. She was a Dawson's Auction employee.

Back in the foyer, Gage asked, "Do you want to grab your camera?"

*Oh shit.* He'd expect her to have a plan, to know where to take the cars. But she'd been distracted on her way in and hadn't paid enough attention to the grounds. She said, "I'd like to see the rest of the facility first."

"Sure." He set out into the yard, leading her through row after row of cars.

Dawson's inventory included everything from rusted out barn finds that probably didn't run to near-new cars that must have been just off lease. Fords sat next to Studebakers parked next to Volkswagens. There were some of her favorites, and some she secretly despised. She paused at a Chevy Nova SuperSport, its pristine paint gleaming in the sun. "This car looks fantastic in orange."

"It's for sale, if you're looking."

It took her a second to respond. He'd said almost exactly the same thing Talan had said earlier, but it sounded so different. When Talan had said it, he'd sounded cute. Like he was fishing for something to say. When Gage said it, he sounded like he was ready to start negotiating. "As much as I'd love to, I'm not ready to start building a collection." She felt her face flush. "I don't even have a daily driver. In Connecticut I was driving my mom's old minivan, and here I just have a rental car."

"If you see something on the lot that you like, for your daily driver, let me know. I'm sure we can give you a deal."

She couldn't help smiling. He really was a salesman. "Where do you usually take pictures?"

"At the front of the lot." He pointed to the four-lane road that fronted Dawson's property.

There was no way in hell she was taking pictures there. She squinted at the strip mall across the street, thinking. "That's not going to work." She continued through the lot, looking for a background big enough to put a car in front of and plain enough not to be distracting.

Dawson's was sandwiched between a busy road and a highway; neither made a decent background. The tan stucco on the front of the office would work in a pinch, but with giant windows breaking the continuity of the wall it wasn't great. She pointed to a line of corrugated stainless-steel Quonset huts along the far side of the property. "Are those yours?"

"They are. We hold auctions in the first one." He pointed. "The second is where we detail cars, then there's the body shop, garage, and the last one is my father's personal storage."

The fronts of the buildings all had bay doors, which she preferred to avoid. Inside might work, but she knew without having to look that neither shops or storage buildings would have room. "What's inside the auction building?"

"Come on, I'll show you."

As she stepped inside, she was reminded of an airplane hangar; a bare metal shell and concrete floor, flanked by garage doors on both ends. Except there were bleachers along one side and an auctioneer's platform in the center of the opposite wall. "Can we use this? It'd be perfect for studio set-ups." She'd been expecting to work exclusively outdoors and hadn't brought lights or backgrounds, but she could have her mom ship all her equipment.

"Besides holding auctions here, my dad uses this as a showroom. It happens to be empty today, but it isn't usually."

"Too bad." Still hoping she'd find something useful on Dawson's property, she went through the building and out the back door.

The back side of the detailing building had serious potential. Unlike the auction building, it didn't have a back door and the uninterrupted corrugated steel made a decent background. But it would only work for a certain type of car. "This is perfect for that Nova, or the Hemi 'Cuda out front. But big classics need open space. Trees, hills.

Photographers call it a neutral background." She gestured to the building. "If you're going to put them in front of buildings they need to be something like Brownstones or graceful mansions. And some of the cars you've got on the lot, like that blue pickup truck? They need a barn."

"We don't take cars off the property."

Thinking about what he'd said he wanted when they'd met back in Connecticut, she said, "If I have to do pictures here you're not going to get the kind of thing I did for Wylie. He let me take cars wherever I wanted."

"That's not happening." He paced a few times, then stopped in front of her. "There's nowhere on our property that'll work?"

"Do you see anything that you want behind your cars? The best I could do, besides this, would be the front of the office. But there's a commuter lot one exit away that's perfect."

Startled, he asked, "How do you know that?"

"That's what you hired me for."

He glanced around once more. "Okay. Let's go see my dad."

As they walked back through the lot, she asked, "So, the cars we're doing are for the next auction?"

"They are."

"You've already got them here?"

"We do."

Curious, because that was unusual, she said, "Whenever Wylie put cars in an auction he sent them so they'd arrive the day before."

Gage glanced at her. "Every car that comes through our classics division is verified, including physical inspections. So, we require that cars be on our property long before the auction. And because we're responsible for representing their condition accurately, they don't leave."

"Huh."

Five minutes later she sat on the black leather couch in the waiting area between Gage's office and his father's, flipping through an auction catalog and listening to angry voices drifting through the closed door. She couldn't hear what they were saying, but she knew Gage was trying to talk Nate into letting her take cars out.

It didn't seem to be going well.

Putting the catalog back on the glass coffee table, she went to the window and looked out at the front lot. Movement caught her attention as Talan made his way between cars, stopping at a Cadillac. He walked around it, made notes on his clipboard, opened the driver's door and squatted to look at the door jamb. He pushed at his hair, despite that it was held back in a short ponytail.

The memory of the heat she'd felt the moment his gaze had met hers was fresh in her mind. She'd looked up and been transfixed by eyes so dark the pupils were barely distinguishable. She'd struggled to sound normal as they talked about the Hemi 'Cuda. That had been the only reason she'd been able to speak at all; she could talk about cars in her sleep.

It hadn't been until he'd introduced himself that she'd realized Talan was Gage's brother. Although their hair was the same sun-streaked dark blonde, they looked nothing alike. With his striking blue eyes, square jaw, and perfectly styled hair, Gage looked like he belonged on the cover of a magazine. Talan's face was thinner, the bridge of his nose slightly flattened as if it had been broken. She could picture him in jeans and a t-shirt, a beer in his hand, kicking back—

*Stop! You're being stupid.* It was too easy to spin an entire scenario in her mind without ever knowing a single thing about a guy.

"Macy?"

She jumped at the sound of Gage's voice from behind her. "Yes?"

"Let's go." As he led her to their first car, he said, "My dad is going to allow us to take cars as far as the commuter lot, under the condition that I drive."

She'd have preferred to drive herself, but she'd take what she could get.

*** ***

The Packard sat at the edge of the commuter lot, sunlight glinting off chrome, the tan paint in harmony with the reds and oranges of a desert background marred only by tumbleweeds and cacti. Macy would have loved to play music, to get in the mood, but she didn't feel comfortable with Gage right there. She contented herself with walking slowly around the car, getting to know it as best as she could.

The square corners of the roof and hood gave it a boxy look, despite the curve of the fenders. The rumble seat was open, breaking the line of the trunk. She could imagine kids, a girl in an ankle length dress and a boy in freshly pressed pants, climbing in for the ride to church. They'd sit nicely, afraid that if they messed around their parents would make them walk next time. Their dad, in a tailored suit and a Fedora, would hold the passenger's side door open for his wife. She would step carefully on the running board, holding layers of petticoats as she struggled to get into the car.

Macy stood on her toes to shoot down into the rumble seat. That wasn't good enough; she stepped on the running board, then finally up onto the rear bumper. There was plenty of room in the compartment, even if the little girl's dress was as fancy as her mom's. The little boy would put his shiny black shoes on the foot rail, making sure not to get mud on his daddy's floor. The chrome bar at the bottom of the compartment was a well thought out touch, something Packard was good at.

Climbing back down, she focused on the other details, things that were just as practical but showed an attention to aesthetics that she appreciated. The radiator arched gracefully at the top, a shape repeated on the housing of the huge headlights, and again on the side mirrors. The wire wheels, Packard 8's in the center of each, gleamed.

A hand painted brown stripe began as a complex pattern of swirls and loops on the flat front of the fenders before it flowed in a long, thin line following the curve of the wheel wells. That would have been done later, the last time the car had been restored. Pinstriping had never been a factory option.

Squatting low to focus on the front of the fender, she adjusted the camera settings to make sure the crisp focus on the swirls would quickly fade to dreamy softness around the edges of the image. Shallow depth of field was one of her favorite techniques for drawing the viewer's eye to the most important element in her images and she also used it on the door handles, the emblem on the grill, and the hood ornament.

Finished with the first side, she asked Gage, "Could you please turn the car? I need it in the same spot, turned the other direction."

"You can't just walk around to the other side?"

She already missed working for Wylie. She was used to doing what she wanted without having to explain herself to anyone. "The light's not good that way. Plus, I want the desert in the background, not the parking lot."

Once he had the car back in the same spot, facing the other way, she repeated everything she'd done the first time, then moved on to the interior. She did pictures of the wood grain dash, its golden veneer glowing in the sun. The buttery soft leather seats had been stitched with brown thread to contrast the tan upholstery and tie in the pinstriping. The interior door handles and window cranks, curved to match the exterior chrome, and the custom shift knob were all details she knew set this car apart from any other, and each detail received her attention.

When she was satisfied, they headed back to Dawson's. Gage spent the ride talking to a client on his cell. Macy was more than happy to let him talk. It gave her the freedom to watch out the window for other places to take pictures. Dawson's had so many different cars, she was going to have to find better locations than a commuter lot and the back side of a warehouse.

*** ***

The timer on Talan's screen ticked away the seconds. If he didn't commit soon the website would reset and he'd lose his order. The cursor hovered over the quantity box. *One ticket or two?*

Some of his favorite indie bands were playing the Sounds In The Sand Festival. If he chose one ticket, it meant he'd get to spend three days completely immersed in music. If he chose two, he'd potentially have someone to share it with.

Part of him didn't mind being alone. But part of him thought it'd be nice to have someone to go with. The image of that girl, the one in the Weezer shirt, flashed through his mind.

*Genius, Talan. Go invite some girl you don't even know to a concert you really want to see. Seriously, what if she's one of those people who talks over the music?*

Definitely a bad idea. Besides that she was into Weezer, he knew literally nothing else about her. *Other than she likes Hemi 'Cudas. That's reason enough not to invite her.* He knew how car people were. They talked about cars all the time. He dealt with that enough at work, he didn't want to continue at home.

Not that he could invite her anyway. He didn't have any way to contact her. *Except that's not true. Her name's Macy LaPorte.*

Not the most common name. He could potentially find her on social media. Or he could try to figure out what car she'd been there to buy and check the records.

34

*Does her being a client put her off limits?* There were rules at Dawson's about employee relationships, but as far as he knew there was nothing about dating a client. *What's Dad gonna do? Take back the car she bought? Fire me?*

If he'd been anyone else, that's exactly what would happen. But he was a Dawson, and he knew damn well his dad wouldn't fire him, no matter what. Gage had slept with their previous receptionist and the only repercussions he'd suffered were a stern talking to and a warning not to do it again. And an immediate end to the relationship, since Stephanie had no interest in continuing to see Gage after she'd been fired for sleeping with him.

Since this woman wasn't risking her job, there was nothing stopping Talan from pursuing her. *Except, do you really want to?*

The seconds on the screen ticked down. Whatever had passed between him and Macy LaPorte had been a momentary blip on his radar, and not something he was actually going to follow up on. But he still liked the idea of having the option to invite someone if he decided to. He left it at two tickets and clicked the checkout button with eight seconds left.

As soon as he'd finished paying, he pulled his hair back and wrapped a hair elastic around it. He needed a cup of coffee and leaving the privacy of his office carried the risk of running into his father. He hoped that didn't happen. His dad would want an update on the cars he was supposed to be working on and he didn't have one. He'd checked out each car, gotten the information he needed— VINs, features, condition— then he'd gone back to his desk to research. But instead of cars, he'd researched concert tickets.

He stepped into Keira's office and stopped dead. Gage was leaning over the spare desk their father had stuck in the corner, looking at a laptop screen. Sitting next to Gage was Macy LaPorte.

Gage straightened and turned around. "Talan, Macy's going to use this desk for now."

Macy swiveled in the chair, her blue eyes just as striking as they'd been outside. *Not cold blue. More like they have their own light.*

Trying to hide that he was staring, he asked, "I'm going for coffee. Anyone want anything?"

Macy smiled, "Coffee would be great, thank you."

All he could think about was his ridiculous attempt to hit on her. Like she gave a shit about production numbers for Hemi 'Cudas. "How do you take it?"

"Regular."

He wasn't sure where she was from, but guessing from her accent it was New England. Remembering their annual trips to the northeast for car shows, and how frustrated his dad got when they put cream and sugar in his coffee every morning, he asked, "Do you want anything in it?"

A puzzled look crossed her face. "Cream and sugar." She swiveled back to the screen.

In the break room, he stood at the counter and stared at the coffee machine. What was Macy doing there? Definitely was not buying a car, or selling one, because those people would never have been at Talan's end of the building. But it had to be work-related. *Shoulda listened in those meetings.*

"Hi, Talan." Celeste opened the refrigerator and started rummaging around. With her head hidden by the door, she asked, "Have you met Macy?"

Hoping he could get through this conversation without Celeste realizing he was clueless, he said, "Yeah. She's using the spare desk in Keira's office."

"Glad Gage found a spot for her." She pulled her lunch from the back of the fridge and transferred it to the microwave. Once she had it heating, she leaned her back side against the counter and looked at him. "We really need a professional photographer. And from what I've heard, she's the best."

He stared at Celeste. The hot girl, the one who had him tongue-tied and thinking crazy shit, was the new photographer. He turned back to the coffee machine. *So much for taking her to Sounds In The Sand.*

"You have to push the blue button, if you want that to brew."

Embarrassed, he mumbled, "Thanks." He knew how to work the machine, he'd just gotten caught spacing out. He pushed the button and almost instantly coffee streamed into the cup.

He added an ice cube to his cup, cream and sugar to the other, and took both back down the hall. He promised himself that, for his own sanity, he was going to give Macy her coffee and go to his office. She was hot, and he could appreciate that, without doing any more than appreciating her looks. The way he'd appreciate a woman in a movie.

He set the cup on her desk and, without speaking to her, went back to what he was supposed to be doing.

*** ***

Macy dragged the comforter off her hotel bed and dropped it on the floor, pulled back the top sheet and blanket and settled on the bed to eat the salad she'd picked up for dinner.

She'd only taken two bites of lettuce when her phone rang. "Mom" flashed across the screen. She swiped, answered, "Hi, Mom."

"Hi, Sweetie. How was your first day?"

That was a loaded question. *Well, there's this really cute guy named Talan who brought me coffee. And there's his brother, Gage, who's all business all the time. And I was supremely uncomfortable and I'm not sure this is going to work out.* "Fine."

"Did you make any friends?"

She nearly choked on a cucumber. "Mom, it was my first day at a new job. Not kindergarten."

"You can have friends at work."

"I didn't have time to make friends."

"I'm sure you will tomorrow."

Time wasn't really the issue. It was that she knew she didn't belong there. She didn't want to get into it with her mom, to give her an opening to mention the job with Aunt Holly again. "Maybe."

"Did you have dinner?"

"I'm eating now."

"What are you eating?"

"Salad. From Panera."

Her mom grilled her about what else she'd eaten, if she'd remembered to check for bedbugs before she'd brought her luggage in, if she'd sanitized the steering wheel in the rental car. She assured her she'd taken care of everything, assured her she wasn't going to starve by rattling off a list of the nearby restaurants, and promised she'd call as soon as she got out of work the next day.

Finally, her mom said, "Macy, if this doesn't work out you can always take the job with Aunt Holly."

*Ignore it.* "I'll call you tomorrow."

In the quiet of her hotel room, she let her mind wander. Maybe her first day hadn't been great. But she'd gotten permission to take the cars someplace decent, even if she wasn't allowed to drive them herself. And there was the potential of making friends. Just because the women dressed up at work didn't necessarily mean they dressed up at home, too. Her oldest brother, Alex, didn't. He wore a suit to work but at home he still wore jeans and t-shirts any time he could get away with it.

Plus, it's not like work was the only place to meet people. Maybe she'd see what the local music scene was like. Smiling to herself at the idea, she searched "music venues near me" as she finished her salad.

# Chapter 4

It had only been a few days, but already Macy wished she had a private office. Aside from desperately wanting quiet, it was very awkward to eat in front of Keira. She'd never realized before how loud chewing was until she had to do it in an enclosed space with someone she barely knew. She stabbed a piece of chicken and stuck it in her mouth anyway.

The graphics guy, Paul, had asked if she could tweak the contrast on some of the pictures she'd done. Since she was waiting for Gage to finish a phone call, she thought she'd work on it. Once she knew what Paul was looking for she'd be able to give him files tailored to his needs, but it was a learning process.

Keira interrupted her, "Macy, how can you eat Chinese food for breakfast?"

Not turning around, she asked, "What do you eat for breakfast?"

"Fresh fruit. Every day. Then for lunch I have—"

She continued but Macy stopped listening. It had taken all of one day to figure out that Keira talked non-stop. It was annoying as hell. If she thought Gage would okay it, she'd have asked if she could edit the pictures in her hotel room. She did her best to concentrate on work while Keira griped loudly to someone at some dealership in Texas about how much it had cost to have her hair cut.

Macy didn't need quiet to work; she actually preferred to listen to music. It had been a point of contention between her and her roommate when she'd been in photography school. Eventually, she'd agreed to use headphones.

Her headphones were back in Connecticut. She could picture them, on the desk in her room. Maybe after work she'd call her mom and have her ship them to her.

That meant three more days of listening to Keira, though. And there was an electronics store just down the road. If she bought a new pair, she could be listening to music right away.

Abruptly, she shut down her computer and told Keira, "If Gage comes looking for me tell him I'll be back in a little while."

Covering the mouthpiece of the phone with her hand, Keira whispered, "Where are you going?"

"Out."

"You can't just leave."

"Why not?"

"It's 9:30 in the morning."

Wondering why that mattered, she shrugged. "Okay. I won't be long."

The store was huge and it took a couple minutes to find the right section. Then it took a few more to decide which set of headphones would be the best. She wanted them to block all sound, but she didn't want them to cost a million dollars. She settled on a purple pair, partly because when she put them on she couldn't hear the store's piped in music, and partly because they were purple. The fact that they were wireless was a bonus.

On the way back to work she went through a drive-thru and got a cup of coffee. After checking that they'd made her coffee correctly, because no one seemed to understand what "regular" meant, she pulled away from the window. Then it hit her. Talan always brought her coffee, she should return the favor. She drove around the building and went through the line again. The cashier looked at her questioningly but didn't say anything as she took Macy's money and handed her a second cup.

Gage was waiting for her in the lobby when she got back to work. "Where'd you go?"

"Out. Let me put these down and grab my camera." She breezed past him, towards the office she shared with Keira.

Halfway down the hall she realized how stupid the second coffee was. Talan didn't actually buy her coffee. There was a coffee machine in the kitchen and everyone was welcome to as much as they could drink. Under her breath, she said, "Too late now," and continued down the hall. She set her cup on her desk, dropped the bag with the headphones in it on the chair, and went around Keira's desk to Talan's door.

She knocked, heard something that sounded like "come in".

Talan's office had plenty of room, but there were no chairs other than the one he was using. Bookcases stuffed to overflowing lined three walls and an eclectic collection of posters covered the remaining wall space; The Ramones, Nirvana, and Imagine Dragons were interspersed with bands she hadn't heard of.

"Can I help you?" Talan sat behind a big wooden desk piled with folders, books, and magazines.

Embarrassed to realize she was standing in the doorway openly staring at his space, she blurted, "I brought you a coffee." She rushed to his desk and set it down. "I didn't know how you took it, so I left it black. But here." She dropped sugar packets and creamers next to the cup. He was giving her the strangest look, like 'why are you bringing me coffee?'. She wished she could go back in time and not do this. She went for a quick exit. "I gotta go. Gage is waiting."

Ignoring Keira's curious gaze, she got her coffee and camera bag and went to meet Gage. Being in a car, away from the office, with

Gage, was good. As usual, he was on the phone, freeing her from the need to make conversation.

At the commuter lot he parked in the same place they had used for every car so far. This time they had a '51 Pontiac Chieftain. It was basic black with a body style typical of the era; taller than modern cars, with rounded corners, a chunky chrome grill, and lots of useless trim pieces. The coolest thing about it was that the hood ornament, a glass Indian head, lit up. She did all the standard shots and whatever details she saw, but there was no real flair. Especially because she was already bored with doing the same background over and over. In no time they were headed back to swap the Pontiac for a Chrysler, a car with a design remarkably similar to the Chieftain. Its most interesting feature was that it was yellow and the upholstery was red. That probably meant someone had started to restore it and run out of money. Or died.

On the way back with the Chieftain, Gage told her, "We're doing a Buick Hotrod next."

Immediately interested, Macy said, "Cool. Can we take it out behind the warehouse?"

"If that's where you want to go."

Craning her neck to look out the window at the sun, she told him, "We've gotta hurry. Or wait. I want it either totally in the shade, or totally in the sun."

"How long do you think we have?"

"I don't know. The sun's pretty high. If we get it over there and it's not good can we leave it until later and I'll edit the pictures we just took first?"

Gage shrugged. "That should be fine."

Once they'd switched cars, she directed him to a spot at the back of the warehouse. The car had been chopped, bringing the roof down and transforming what had been a non-descript coupe into something undeniably sleek. While it retained the rounded fenders and bulky front end, the lower top flowed seamlessly into the gently sloping back. With shaved door handles and the absence of portholes there was nothing to break the perfectly smooth sides.

Macy thought shaved handles were just about the coolest thing. The first time she'd seen a car with no handles had been when she'd been working for Wylie. She'd stood staring at it, clueless how to get in but not wanting to admit it, until Wylie had popped the doors remotely from the other side of the car. He'd laughed until he could barely stand at the look of shock on her face. Then he'd taken the time to explain that the doors had a gas shock, called an actuator solenoid, operated by a remote called a popper. It was something she still found fascinating.

Glancing at the rapidly climbing sun, she started shooting. She wanted the warehouse in the background of every shot, so after a series of exposures straight on she turned to Gage. "Can you turn the car ninety degrees, so it's in the same spot, facing straight at me?"

Just as he opened the door his phone rang. He sat in the driver's seat until she motioned for him to get out.

While she started on the overall shots, Gage paced behind her. "I can't do anything about the entry fee, but I can see if we've got wiggle room on the commission. Why don't you—" He moved out of earshot.

It wasn't long before Macy needed the car turned. Usually she did all the exterior shots first, but she had to wait for Gage so she concentrated on shooting details- window cranks, headlight trim, the shift knob- until he wandered back over. She motioned for him to turn the car. He did, never once stopping his negotiations.

*** ***

At her desk, Macy took a couple minutes to sync her new headphones to her computer. She opened her music library, clicked to play a song list, and smiled in satisfaction as The Beatles began singing. No matter how many times she heard "Blackbird" it was still her absolute favorite song.

Minimizing the music window, she switched to Photoshop. She opened all the exterior shots of the Buick at once and let the images stack on her screen. Just as they finished, Talan came in and set a cup of coffee on her desk.

She turned to thank him, but he was already stepping into his office. She stared at the door for a moment before she turned back to her computer and started tweaking the first image. She really needed to figure out how he took his coffee, since he knew exactly how to make hers.

"Blackbird" ended and The Arctic Monkeys started singing about whether or not some girl was interested. She wondered if the girl was real, and if she knew the song was about her. Macy had always thought it'd be pretty cool to have a song written about her.

She played with adjustments in the image on her screen. The matte black paint of the Buick was less than striking, and the grey building failed to provide contrast. Neither of those things were a deterrent; she knew the potential of the images. Bumping the black down and intensifying the white gave saturation to the boring paint and depth to the wall. She blurred the corners, leaving the car in crisp focus. Finally, she darkened the edges slightly, gently forcing viewers' eyes to the center. She finished the first image and moved on to the second, then the third.

The song changed to Vance Joy singing about his personal fears. She really liked Vance Joy. All his songs were sweet, about how messy life is and how that's what makes it good. He was definitely someone she'd go see live. Maybe later she'd search—

She was jerked out of her thoughts by someone pulling her headphones off. She spun around to see Talan holding them up to his ear.

"Your phone was ringing," He dropped the headphones on her desk.

Too shocked to speak, she just stared at him as he walked back into his office. As soon as he closed his door, she sat back down and tried to go back to work.

It was impossible to stop thinking about what had just happened, though. Talan had been so rude, and she hadn't done anything about it. She wished she had at least said something about how inappropriate his behavior was.

She glanced at Keira, who quickly averted her gaze. She was glad Keira had the decency to pretend she hadn't seen what had happened.

Macy pulled her phone out of her purse and saw she had a missed call from Emma. Not in the mood to talk, she turned the ringer off, put her phone on the desk, slid the headphones back on and turned to her screen. When Emma called back, predictably and less than a minute later, she ignored it.

When her phone rang yet again she saw Logan's name and answered, "Hey."

Logan said, "Hey, Mace. What's going on?"

"I'm working."

"Oh. Soooo, are you coming Friday?"

"What's Friday?"

Sounding annoyed, he said, "Do you ever check Facebook?"

"No. Why?"

"We're doing a thing. Here. Jennifer sent you an invitation."

"Oh, yeah, sorry. I didn't get it." Even if she had checked, which she hadn't in months, she wouldn't have opened something from Jennifer.

"Are you coming?"

Macy rolled her eyes; she'd known this was going to happen. "No, I'm in Arizona."

Logan asked, "Still?"

"Yes."

"When are you coming home?"

She let out an exasperated breath. "I'm not. I told you that."

"Seriously, Macy."

She could hear the laugh in his voice, knew he didn't believe her. "I'm working. I'll call you later." She put her headphones on and went back to work.

Logan's refusal to believe that she was capable of getting a job and moving away really bothered her. Sure, she'd dropped out of school in Florida because she'd been homesick. And she'd come home every weekend all through photography school. But this was different. This time, she was going to do things, make new friends, be her own person.

She opened the window for her music library and reset her playlist. As "Blackbird" started again she closed her eyes and let the familiar notes calm her. By the end of the second verse she felt better.

She looked at the picture she'd just finished. It had a stark, vintage quality that suited the car perfectly. Her chest swelled with pride. It was good. Damn good.

Although it had been three years since she'd first felt the wonder of seeing an image she'd made and realizing it was spectacular, sometimes she was still surprised that she'd actually taken a particular picture. She hated to admit that it sort of made sense that Logan didn't see her as competent. She didn't usually feel competent.

Not that it mattered. She was here to do a job, and she was going to do it.

*** ***

Macy dropped the remnants of her salad in the trash, brushed her teeth, and got into bed. She flipped channels without really seeing what was on. Her phone beeped and she swiped her finger over the screen. For three seconds she stared at a picture of Emma and her new boyfriend, captioned with, "Wish you were here," before the picture disappeared into oblivion. She mumbled, "Yeah, I'm sure."

After shutting off the TV and shoving her phone in the nightstand drawer, she rolled over and pulled the blankets up to her chin. If she *was* there Emma wouldn't care.

No one had ever cared. Once upon a time she'd thought Logan had, but she'd known for a long time that wasn't true. Since that night in the graveyard.

The oppressive mugginess of an August night in Connecticut, the smell of the grass as she lay looking up at the stars, trying not to hear the soft laughter of Logan and Pamela. Logan's voice murmuring words Macy didn't want to hear, Pamela's moans, starting softly but becoming increasingly louder. Macy had worried that someone would hear and send the cops. Even though they knew they weren't supposed to be there, the old cemetery at the end of their street was a perfect place to hang out, especially in the middle of the night.

She lay on the ground watching the dappled moonlight as it shone on headstones through the branches of nearby trees and wondered if everyone was that loud when they had sex. If she would be, too. She plucked a blade of grass, twirled it between her fingers, wondering if Logan knew everyone could hear them, and if he cared. Maybe he liked that people knew he was having sex. She thought about getting up and going home. It had been stupid to sneak out to meet Logan, to think he'd wanted to see her. It had been even more stupid to stay after Pamela showed up.

Just as she decided to leave Ryan materialized out of the darkness, settling into the grass next to her. He whispered, "Damn she's loud."

Relief at not being alone made Macy smile. "Yeah."

"Those two are always going at it. I swear, Logan gets more ass than the seat on a city bus."

She didn't say anything. It made her uncomfortable when guys talked like that, and she never knew what to say.

Ryan lay back, his hands behind his head. "So, what are you doing here, all alone?"

"I came out with Logan, but, ya know."

"Why do you hang out with him?"

"I don't know. I guess it's just always been that way."

"Maybe you should hang out with someone else once in a while."

"Like who?"

"Me."

The moonlight washed all color from the world, but she knew he had hazel eyes. They seemed to go perfectly with his dark brown hair. Next to Logan's striking black hair and steel blue eyes, Ryan seemed very plain. At that moment that didn't matter. Logan was fucking Pamela. Ryan, on the other hand, was looking at Macy in a way that made her stomach fill with butterflies.

Her eyes popped open, shame surging through her despite all the years that had passed.

Sex always made her feel that way. Not because she thought sex was wrong; she didn't. The problem was, there was something wrong with her.

That night with Ryan had been the first, but most definitely not the last, time she'd faked an orgasm. That night it had been because it had been so obvious that Pamela had gotten off, Macy thought she should have, too.

Some nights, she'd faked it because the guy she'd been with was trying so hard and she couldn't break it to him that it wasn't working. There had been times the guy she was with had been determined to satisfy her, no matter how many times she said she didn't need more, and it had been the only way to end it. And sometimes it was just easier than explaining that she couldn't orgasm during sex. The only way she could, was to masturbate.

That was a conversation she avoided. It meant admitting she'd done it, which was mortifyingly embarrassing. And it inevitably led to the guy trying to prove she just hadn't been with the right guy, which lead to more sex she didn't enjoy.

For the most part she'd accepted that she'd never enjoy sex, but there were still times she wished she was normal. *Why the hell would you be normal in bed? You're not normal anywhere else.* It was easier, though, to have her own tastes in music and clothes than it was not to like sex. Because not everyone liked hip hop, but *everyone* liked sex.

She whispered to herself, "Think about cars, Macy." She squeezed her eyes shut and concentrated on remembering the first car she'd ever photographed. A '57 Mercury, its red paint shimmering with metallic flecks, the fins that ran from the back to—

Her phone beeped in the drawer, disrupting her thoughts. Most likely that was Emma. She didn't have it in her to look at another picture of people having fun without her. Alone in the dark, two thousand miles from home, she cried herself to sleep.

# Chapter 5

Talan drummed his fingers rhythmically on the desk. He concentrated on his screen. "I already know the friggin history of Cadillacs. I just need..." he mumbled to himself, "the first year for AC. Shit." He leaned back in his chair and threw his pen on the desk. "Shit."

He was going to have to tell his dad there was a discrepancy. The owner of a 1939 Cadillac had indicated in their auction registration paperwork that the car had factory air. The problem was that Cadillac hadn't started installing air conditioning in cars until 1941, meaning the air conditioning in the car had been installed later.

Someone knocked, interrupting his thoughts. "Yeah?"

The door opened and Macy stepped in. "Talan? I'm sorry to bother you. Gage is in the middle of some big deal." She smiled crookedly, "He's got a phone in each hand and he's trying to send emails."

Unable to resist her smile, he smiled back. "That would be Gage."

"He told me to ask if you'd drive for me. I guess he's going to be a while."

"Yeah, okay." Talan's brain went into overdrive. Walking past her desk, saying hi if they happened to see each other in the hallway, was one thing. Being in a car with her was something completely different. Suddenly, he felt like he was back in high school, trying to make conversation with the cheerleader who sat next to him in Biology. "Now?"

"Yeah, if you're not doing anything."

*Idiot. Of course she means now.* He stood up and banged his knee on the desk. "Oomph." He stifled a swear and limped out behind her.

Outside she said, "We're taking the Willys, over there." She pointed at the predecessor of the Jeep, a military vehicle that looked like it had come straight from the set of M*A*S*H, and held up keys. "Gage told me to tell you to be careful."

She dropped her camera bag on the floor in front of the passenger's seat and climbed in. By the time he'd walked around to the driver's side she had her seatbelt on and was pulling her hair into a ponytail.

He buckled and started the vehicle. "Where to?"

She gestured up the street, "One exit that way, to the commuter lot."

Taking a Willys, with no top or doors, on the highway wasn't all that appealing. "You sure you want to go there, in this?"

"Do you know someplace else we can go?"

Realizing he didn't, he agreed. "You might want to hold on."

She gripped the seat. He put the car in gear, took his foot off the brake and stepped on the gas.

He let the clutch go too fast. The car jerked forward and stalled. He started the engine again and made sure he gave it a little gas first. It didn't help, he stalled again. He glanced sideways. "Sorry."

Trying really hard not to stall, he stepped on the gas too hard, making the engine rev, but managed to let the clutch go slow enough that he finally got the car moving. He inched towards the exit of the parking lot in first gear, trying to time it right with the traffic so he didn't have to come to a complete stop. As he got near the road, he looked both ways then stepped on the gas, and chirruped the tires. He pulled onto the street and shifted into second. The gears ground horrifically; sweat started to run down his back.

He felt like a moron, like he couldn't drive a stick. He turned onto the entrance ramp to the highway and shifted into third, lurching again. This was ridiculous. His truck, that he drove every single day, was a fucking five-speed. At least they were on the highway and he didn't have to worry about grinding gears again.

Although, even on the highway he was aware of her next to him, wisps of hair blowing around her face as she stared straight ahead. *Stop looking.*

"The exit, Talan."

He jerked the wheel, barely in time. She didn't say anything.

Once they were in the commuter lot she told him where to park. He followed her instructions, praying the whole time he wouldn't stall; the clutch in this stupid car was so difficult. She went to work and he sat on the guardrail, trying to stay out of her way.

He was glad she ignored him. It didn't seem to matter that his rational brain screamed that she was a car person, or that she was a Dawson's employee. Every other part of him thought she was so damn sexy that nothing else seemed to matter. She stood on her toes, walked around the car, squatted. After a few minutes he got up and walked away, wandered around the other side of the parking lot, intentionally not looking at her.

He knew, *knew*, he had to get this under control. Hitting on someone who worked for his father was not a good idea.

Macy called, "Talan?"

Startled out of his thoughts, he snapped, "What?"

She flinched. "I'm sorry. I just need the car turned around."

He silently cursed himself for snapping at her. This wasn't her fault. She couldn't possibly know what was going on in his head. "How do you need the car moved?"

*** ***

Macy braced herself for another nerve-wracking ride. It wasn't that it had been painful to watch Talan struggle with the Willys. Old cars, many without the benefit of power steering or self-adjusting clutches, were hard to drive.

It was being with him. He was just so impossible to read. Sometimes was so sweet. Like when he brought her coffee. And she couldn't forget the way he'd smiled at her the first day they'd met.

She snuck a glance at him, his features serious with concentration as he drove. She liked the contrast of his blonde hair to his dark eyes. It was unexpected. She wondered if he always wore his hair pulled back, and what it would look like if he let it down. Her eyes wandered to his hands on the steering wheel, his long, thin fingers on the crossbar. She remembered how it had felt to shake his hand, how her skin had tingled for long minutes after.

*You're being stupid again. He's not into you. He never even talks to you. And just now he snapped at you for no reason.* There'd been those few moments, though, like when he'd taken her headphones. At the time she'd been annoyed. But maybe she'd misread that. Maybe he'd been flirting, like when the boys in high school snapped the girls' bras.

They were off the highway, and the wind wasn't as loud. Hesitantly, she said, "It's too bad there's no radio in this."

"I don't think it was an option. These were pretty basic."

"I can't imagine having a car with no radio."

Pulling into a space on Dawson's lot, he shut the car off. "What do you listen to?"

Nerves immediately tightened in her stomach. Everyone she knew, except Logan, listened to Top 40, which she just couldn't get into. "Whatever's on the radio, mostly." In her head she added, *on the alternative rock station.*

"They don't play much Weezer on the radio." He pointed at her shirt. "Or Beatles."

Heat filled her face. "No. I guess not." Wanting to escape the conversation, she undid her seatbelt and stepped out of the car. "Thanks for driving."

"No problem."

She was relieved that Gage was done with whatever he needed to do and was able to drive the next car. She was also relieved that even away from his desk he was always on his cell. She wasn't really into talking.

Working easily together, she and Gage got through the rest of the cars for that day. Once they were done, she headed to the office she shared with Keira. The closer she got, the more nervous she was. Her desk was in Keira's office, but Talan had to walk past them to get in or out of his office. And she still felt ridiculous about buying him coffee. *What if he thinks I was flirting with him? Wait. Was I? Oh my god, I was.*

She wasn't even through the door when Keira started. "Hi, Macy."

"Hi, Keira." *At least I don't have to talk to Talan.*

Her eyes alight with curiosity, Keira asked, "So, do you have any plans for this weekend?"

"No." Macy had found a list of places that had live music, but the idea of going to a bar alone made her nauseous. She'd shelved the idea, hoping she'd meet people some other way.

Keira's already big smile got bigger. "A bunch of us are going out for drinks tomorrow night. Do you want to come?"

Relieved at not having to face a Saturday night alone, she immediately answered, "Sure!"

"Cool. I'll text you the address of the bar."

# Chapter 6

As soon as Macy saw Keira waving from across the bar she knew she'd made a terrible mistake.

Usually Emma told her what to wear when they went out. Without the benefit of instructions from her best friend, she'd asked Keira. Her response had seemed simple enough; just wear jeans. Macy thought that meant jeans and t-shirts, so she'd grabbed a clean pair of jeans and the top t-shirt in the pile, which happened to be from a Twenty One Pilots concert she'd gone to with Logan.

That had been a bad choice. Keira *was* in dark blue skinny jeans, but she wore an emerald green blouse with a ruffle along the top. It was shiny fabric that made Macy think of a prom dress, and it left her shoulders bare. She looked even nicer than she did at work.

Macy forced herself to cross the room, weaving between dark wood tables where people in cowboy hats sat in chairs upholstered in black and white faux cow-hide. Laughter erupted from a table in the far corner, loud enough to be heard over the country music playing on the bar's sound system.

When she reached the far side of the room she smiled nervously at the group of women with Keira, trying to meet all their eyes at once. "Hi."

"Ladies, this is Macy. Macy, this is Hailey, Lee Ann and Zoe." Keira pointed to each woman in turn. "And you know Vanessa and Sandra from work."

Zoe, who was closest, indicated the empty chair next to her. "It's a pleasure to meet you."

"Nice to meet you, too." Macy held out her hand.

A look of distaste flitted across the other woman's features, fast enough that Macy questioned whether she'd actually seen it. Zoe shook briefly, her hand slack, and began talking to Vanessa about a TV show Macy had never seen.

Keira looked Macy over questioningly. "Did you work today?"

"No. Why?"

"You're dressed like it."

A wave of heat rushed to her face. "This is all I have." Trying to cover her mistake, she added, "Once I'm settled I'll have the rest of my things sent."

"Oh, you should have said something! I'd have been happy to loan you an outfit." Excited, Keira added, "Or we could go *shopping*. Moving to another place is a perfect excuse to buy a new wardrobe, right Hailey?" She glanced at Hailey.

Hailey smiled slightly, her dark pink lipstick glistening in the dim light. She wore a black sequined top. The kind with a skinny strap over just one shoulder. Not something Macy would even attempt to pull off.

Keira continued, "Hailey's a fashion vlogger. She takes you through stores and explains exactly what styles flatter each body type, and how the same piece of clothing can look completely different depending on who's wearing it. She has a whole series on what colors to choose for each season based on your skin tones, and how something as simple as wearing turquoise instead of teal can completely change your look."

Macy wasn't sure there was that much difference between turquoise and teal. She looked over at Hailey and tried really hard for a natural-looking smile. "I'll have to check it out."

Coolly, Hailey handed her a business card. "Please, do. And if you mention my vlog at any of the stores I feature you'll get 10% off."

Keira said, "Oh! And if you sign up for her newsletter she sends a list every week of what stores have sales or coupons. Honest to God, it's the most useful tool. I never go shopping without checking it first." Excitement bubbling in her voice, she started to tell Hailey about a pair of boots she'd bought and how she'd combined discounts to get an amazing deal.

Macy wasn't even slightly interested in shopping. She went when Emma dragged her, or when she absolutely needed something. She listened to the other conversations around the table, hoping she'd be able to join in somewhere. Sandra and Zoe were swapping stories about their kids and Vanessa and Lee Ann were across the table talking about golf. With sinking certainty she realized it wasn't just her clothes that were different, it was her. She wished she hadn't been so quick to accept Keira's invitation.

When the waitress came over she listened closely to what the other women ordered; she wasn't about to order a beer if everyone was doing shots. The other women didn't order beers or shots. They ordered cocktails, which Macy knew nothing about. When it was her turn she said the first thing she could think of that wasn't copying anyone else and sounded adult. "I'd like a Mojito, please."

"Sure thing." The waitress smiled as she wrote it down.

As soon as their orders were placed Sandra turned to Macy. Her hazel eyes, enhanced by smokey eyeshadow, were alight with curiosity. "Macy, I'm so glad you came out with us tonight. I can't believe we haven't had time to have a single conversation at work!"

Being ignored had been uncomfortable, having everyone focused on her was worse. She tugged at the hem of her shirt, feeling too hot, as she desperately tried to think of something to say. Sandra hadn't asked her anything, but she obviously expected Macy to respond.

"Gage has her playing catch-up." Keira said. "They've got a ton of work to get done."

Vanessa leaned in, her long blonde hair hanging perfectly straight around her shoulders, and said, "If I had Gage to myself as much as Macy does, we wouldn't be getting any work done."

All the women agreed, nodding, snickering, and making "Uh huh" noises.

Vanessa continued, not hiding her curiosity. "What's he like?"

Macy had no idea how to answer. "Um, he's, nice."

Incredulously, Sandra said, "Nice?"

Vanessa raised an eyebrow and pressed, "You're alone with him for hours every day, and that's it?"

All Gage ever did was talk to clients and look annoyed when she asked him to move cars. Wracking her brain to come up with some other answer, she said, "He's a really good salesman."

"No shit." Vanessa rolled her eyes.

Sandra said, "Seriously. The only thing we ever hear him talk about is cars."

"We want to know about him. What does he eat for breakfast? What did he do last Saturday?" A gleam in her eye, Vanessa said, "Does he have a girlfriend?"

Keira chided her, "Ness, you know damn well it wouldn't matter if he didn't."

"I'd give up my job for that." Vanessa asked Macy directly, "So, does Gage have a girlfriend?"

The women were all looking at her with intense interest, the way the girls back in high school had looked when they stood in the hallways and gossiped. Gage had given her a second chance. Fought for her to be able to take cars off the lot. And he worked hard, which she respected. Even if she knew him on a personal level, she wouldn't tell these women anything.

Before she could come up some way to deflect their questions, the waitress came back with their drinks. Hers had a slice of lime floating in it, and a blue straw that was just long enough to stick out of the glass. Glad for the distraction, she took a tentative sip. The minty sweet liquid barely tasted like alcohol. She took another much bigger sip, wondering why she'd never tried this before.

Everyone started new conversations, seeming to forget about Gage. Macy sipped her drink, wishing she watched more TV, or knew what a Michael Kors bag was and why she'd want to spend a couple hundred bucks on one, or had at some point in the past had a mani/pedi. This was, amazingly, worse than going out with Emma and Logan. Emma always dragged them to clubs, but at least she'd had Logan to talk to.

When the waitress came back she ordered herself a second drink, even though she wasn't done with her first. She wanted to make damn sure she had something to distract herself from just sitting there.

As the waitress left, three guys came in and headed straight for their table.

The tallest one slipped an arm around Keira. "Hi there, beautiful."

Keira grinned, her nose wrinkling. "Hi there, yourself." She kissed him, smiling as she did.

He pulled back and looked around the table, giving a non-specific "hello" to everyone before he zeroed in on Macy. "You're a new face."

She wished he hadn't noticed her. All the women, plus the guys, looked at her again. All she could manage was, "Yes."

Keira rescued her. "Charles, this is Macy. She just started at Dawson's."

"It's a pleasure to meet you, Macy."

His warm smile settled her nerves a bit. She glanced at the other two men and he immediately said, "I'm forgetting my manners. This is Zack and Jim."

She nodded politely, as they were across the table and shaking hands was out of the question, then went back to her drink. One look at their polo shirts and pressed slacks told her these weren't the kind of guys who talked to girls like her. She sipped her Mojito, hoping to make it last until the next one came.

"Macy?"

One of the guys, she was pretty sure it was Zack, squeezed in next to her. "Yes?"

"You work at Dawson's, with Keira?"

"I do." Even though that was obviously a line, because Keira had just said that, she was happy to have someone to talk to.

His grey eyes fixed inquiringly on her, he asked, "What do you do?"

"I photograph cars." She squirmed, unpleasantly aware that that sounded so lame. Not that it mattered, that's what she did.

His lips twitched into a smile. "Huh. You make a living doing that?"

"Yes." She'd heard that so many times, she was sick of it. She turned back to her drink and took a big swallow. All she wanted was not to have to explain that photographing cars was a real job, and to go back to her room and sulk. Alone.

"Hey, I'm sorry. I didn't mean it like that." She leveled a look at him, daring him to continue, which he did. "I guess I never thought about it before, that someone has to do it."

"Yes, someone does."

"Dawson's handles classic cars, don't they?"

"Yes. And they do dealer auctions and they have a regular sales department, too." She made herself stop. *Why are you talking to him?*

"Cool." He glanced away as the waitress came to deliver the girls' drinks and take orders from the guys.

Macy finished off her first drink and started on her second. Zack was still next to her. He was the only person not talking to anyone else. And he'd made an effort to talk to her, even if it had been kind of shitty. *Maybe he doesn't know what to say either.* She took a sip of her drink, watched as the level of the liquid fell noticeably. She'd never used a straw to drink alcohol before. Her friends all said it gave them a headache. Her head felt just fine.

She turned to Zack and asked, "So, what do you do?"

Leaning an elbow on the table so he could look at her more easily, he said, "I'm an actuary."

She snorted. "You're actually a what?"

"I'm an actuary." His expression was stony. "I work for an insurance company, assessing risk probability."

"Huh." That sounded super boring. "My aunt works for an insurance company. She dresses like Keira." Hearing herself, she wondered what the hell she was talking about. But she didn't really care, either. She just wanted this guy to pay attention to her so she didn't have to tell the office girls about working with Gage, and because sitting there was lonely, and partly because he was kinda cute, with his super short hair and nicely trimmed beard.

"Yes, well, people who work in a professional office setting do generally dress professionally."

"I wear jeans and t-shirts to work. Cuz, ya know, I spend all day outside, getting filthy." She looked him over, his light blue shirt covering what appeared to be a muscular build. "You probably don't get dirty at work."

"No, I don't." He cleared his throat. "So, Macy, where are you from?"

She answered his question, and all the others he asked. How many siblings she had, where she'd gone to school, what her favorite food was. It sort of felt like answering a questionnaire on the first day of school.

When the waitress came back, she ordered another Mojito, which Zack insisted on paying for. He was so easy to talk to, and it was so nice to have someone there, she could barely believe she hadn't liked him right off the bat.

Keira interrupted their conversation. "Macy, I'm going to get going. Are you okay?"

"Yeah, I'm great. Thanks so much for inviting me." She grinned at Keira, feeling like she was on top of the world.

"Any time." Keira glanced at Zack and raised an eyebrow.

He assured her, "I've got it."

"Okay. Macy, I'll see you Monday." She left, glancing back once before she was out the door.

Macy had no idea what they were talking about. "Got what?"

"You. I'll get you home, when you're ready."

Giggling, she told him, "I've got a car. I mean, it's not mine. It's a rental. I don't have a car. But maybe, if I stay in Arizona I'll buy one. Gage said he'd give me a deal." She giggled again. "He's always trying to sell cars."

Zack gently took her by the elbow. "I think it's time we get you home."

"No! I want another Mooo—jitooo," she pouted.

"You've had enough Mojitos for one night." He pulled her through the bar and outside. "Which car is yours?"

She looked around the parking lot, dumbfounded by the seemingly simple question. "Ummm…" She wasn't looking for her mom's minivan. She knew, she'd just told Zack, it was a rental car. It was right at the edge of her mind. Maybe if she looked at the keys. She pulled them from her purse and stared at them.

Without asking, he took them and pushed the unlock button on the key fob. There was a beep and the headlights on a car a few spaces away blinked. He pulled her to the car and got her in the passenger's seat. Once he was settled into the driver's seat he asked, "Where do you live?"

"At the hotel."

There was a long moment of uncomfortable silence. She tried to figure out why he was looking at her like that but her mind seemed unable to focus. Finally, she said, "You just gotta tell your phone where you wanna go and it'll take you there. I mean, you still have to drive," she laughed nervously, feeling like something wasn't quite right but not sure what it was, then she continued lamely, "but the guy'll tell you where to turn."

"What's the address?"

She stared at him blankly.

"You use your phone for GPS?"

"Um hm."

"Can I see it, please?"

She handed him her phone. "Just be really careful with it. It cost," she lowered her voice, "seven-hundred dollars." She whispered conspiratorially, "I had to lie to my parents. I told them I got it for free with service. But I didn't."

She stopped talking as he looked at her phone. "What's your password?"

"Draw an M."

He touched the screen a bunch of times and eventually asked, "Is your hotel on State Street?"

"Yup. It's a suite. That means it has a microwave and a fridge." He started driving and she babbled, "I picked that one cuz it's cheap. I mean, all the hotels here are cheap, but that one is less than Emma pays for rent! Can you believe that! And it includes a maid, and breakfast every day, and HBO. I mean, if I had'da get an apartment I'd have'ta pay for all that stuff. And electricity, and..." She continued the entire way back to her hotel.

After he'd parked the car, he slipped his arm around her waist and guided her inside. He stopped at the main desk and asked the clerk to call him a cab, then quietly told him that Macy had had a few too many drinks and could he please direct them to her room.

She rolled her eyes. Like she couldn't hear him. And like she didn't know her limit. She'd only had three drinks. She told the clerk, "Tommy, I know where my room is," and walked away.

Tommy and Zack talked for another second, then Zack caught up with her at the elevator. It was probably a good thing, since the floor seemed to be soft, or moving, or something. She leaned against him as they rode the elevator to the second floor.

For some reason her key card didn't want to work. After three tries Zack took the card from her and opened the door on the first try. Once they were inside, she went straight to the bed, pulled the bedspread off and dropped it on the floor. She plopped down and asked, "Are you staying?"

"I don't think that's a good idea." He placed her keys on the dresser.

She fell back. "'Kay. Thanks for the ride." The door clunked closed and she thought she really should get up and lock it. She almost didn't, then she thought what would happen if her mom found out she'd left it open. She stood, swayed, stumbled to the door and flipped the security lock, then stumbled back to the bed.

*** ***

The room was so bright. Macy pulled the covers over her head in a futile attempt to block the lights she hadn't shut off the night before. Bits and pieces started to come back, and the memories were worse than the pain throbbing in her head.

She'd gotten totally shit-faced drunk. She hadn't meant to, didn't really understand how it had happened, but she had. Groaning, she remembered babbling to Zack about rental cars and automatic pancake makers in hotel breakfast bars and God only knows what else.

Feeling decidedly sick, she dragged herself to the bathroom and vomited. She sat on the floor, her back against the tub and her head on her knees, and wished she'd never gone out.

When she was sure she wasn't going to throw up again she brushed her teeth, shut the lights off and got back in bed. She didn't have to go anywhere, no one cared what she was doing, and she was going to take advantage of it and sleep this off.

*** ***

Macy's cell phone was ringing. She answered it, trying to shake the groggy feeling. "Hello?"

"Macy?"

"Yeah?" There was no way of hiding that she sounded like shit. *Shoulda let it ring.*

"This is Zack. From last night?"

"Zack?" She sat up, relieved it wasn't her mom, or work-related.

"I wanted to make sure you were okay."

Physically she'd live, but knowing she was going to have to go into work the next day and face all those women, after she'd gotten trashed in front of them… "I'm okay." She hesitated, then added, "Thanks, ya know, for bringing me home and everything."

"No problem." He cleared his throat before saying, "I had a good time last night."

Surprised, she asked, "You did?"

"I did. I was wondering if you'd like to go out again."

"I…" She wanted to say yes, but one of the things she did remember clearly from the previous night was how awkward she'd felt with Keira and her friends. But Zack had been nice, so…… maybe.

When she didn't continue, he said, "If you don't want to, it's cool. I just thought we could get to know each other a little better under… different circumstances."

She snorted. "You mean like me not being completely blitzed?"

"If you want to put it bluntly, yes."

"You've got no reason to believe this, but I don't usually do that. I'm not even sure how it happened. I only had three drinks."

"Three Mojitos, if I remember correctly."

"That would be correct."

Kindly, he explained, "The way they make them there, that's probably the equivalent of nine shots."

"Jesus Christ, that would explain the hangover."

"I'm sure it would," he chuckled.

He had a nice laugh. She liked that. And he was willing to give her a second chance. She asked, "You still want to go out?"

"Yes, I do. Maybe we can do something with less alcohol and more conversation?"

"That sounds great. What'd you have in mind?"

# Chapter 7

Talan grabbed jeans off the bedroom floor and slid them on, did his morning bathroom thing, and headed for the kitchen. He needed coffee.

With the pot brewing, he sat at the island separating the kitchen from the living room and paged through a catalog of studio and recording equipment. He didn't need recording equipment, unless he was going to do more than play guitar in his living room.

His eyes shifted to the pile of miscellaneous papers he'd stacked on the counter, and the black business card on the top. James Camp's words echoed in his memory. *If you want to come back.*

That had been the plan, originally. To help Gage get everything straightened out and give himself time to decide what to do next. Even his apartment- filled with hand me down furniture, bed sheets instead of curtains covering the windows, boring white walls- screamed "temporary."

He'd just gotten... stuck.

The coffee pot beeped. He poured a cup, dropped an ice cube in it, and settled onto the couch. He picked up his favorite guitar and strummed a chord; it echoed loudly in the still morning.

He leaned back and closed his eyes, the cold back of the guitar against his bare stomach making him flinch. Keeping one hand pressed against the base of the neck, he plucked at the strings with his other hand, each making a nearly inaudible plink. His fingers slid idly back and forth over the roughness of the 6th string, making a sound reminiscent of a zipper.

Music drifted through his mind. He sat up, moved his fingers up to press between the frets, strummed. Notes drifted through the still of the apartment, becoming fuller, emerging into a full-fledged song.

The problem with this song, what he'd known from the start, was it needed piano. And for that, he needed his mom.

He set the guitar aside and picked up his phone.

*** ***

Talan stared at the house he'd grown up in. Single story, off-white stucco, terracotta tiled roof, nearly identical to every other house on the street. His sister's minivan was parked next to his mom's classic Nova. It made him smile, for a moment, to think that Macy would love his mom's car.

The cars meant that there was a house full of people, though, and that wasn't something to smile about. It'd been ten years since he'd touched a piano and the idea of having an audience while he reacquainted himself with it wasn't the least bit appealing.

He walked slowly to the front door and opened it. It was surprisingly quiet inside. His footsteps on the orange tile floor echoed through the empty house as he stepped over matchbox cars and Legos scattered around the living room. Laughter drifted from the back yard. Through the French doors, he saw his nieces and nephews in the pool, his mom and sister watching them from the shade of the cabana. His mom glanced over and waved. He waved back, relieved that everyone was busy. He had the house, and the piano, to himself.

It had been that way often when he'd been a kid. His dad was always at work and his mom spent her time driving Gage to football practice and Felicity to cheerleading, or to whatever else they were doing. Talan had never minded being left alone. It gave him time to practice in peace. And when he'd decided to pick up the guitar, it had allowed him to figure it out in private.

Until the day Gage, surrounded by the group of friends he always had with him, had caught Talan standing on the coffee table with Slayer blaring from the stereo, pretending he was on stage at Ozzfest. He hadn't been playing the guitar; it had just been a prop in his ridiculous teenage fantasy. And Gage had nearly fallen over laughing. The music hadn't been loud enough to drown that out.

It wasn't the first time he'd suffered ridicule. Gage was popular, athletic, and their dad's favorite. Everything Talan wasn't. And he'd made sure to remind Talan every chance he got.

That time, though, was different.

Maybe it'd been because he'd been truly interested in learning to play the guitar, or maybe because he'd been dealing with the emotional trauma of his parents' divorce. Or maybe it was just because he'd been fifteen and not in full command of his emotions. Regardless of the reason, he'd stepped off the table, walked up to Gage, and punched him in the face.

Gage had gone after him, breaking Talan's nose before his friends were able to pull him back. The pain, and the lump he'd always have on the bridge of his nose, had been totally worth it. After that, Gage had never teased Talan again. And, more importantly, Talan had learned to actually play the guitar. And because of that, his ridiculous teenage fantasy had become reality. For a brief time.

He could be on stage again. If he was willing to call James Camp, and go back to piano.

It wasn't necessarily the piano that had kept him from calling James. The more he thought about it, the more he knew that if he was going to chase a career in music it was going to be on his terms.

At the moment, that meant he was going to write the song he wanted, the way he wanted it.

The piano dominated the back room, in the spot once occupied by his father's pool table. Talan sat on the bench. Out of habit he stretched his back up straight and let his fingers rest on the keys. Silence pounded in his ears.

He started with scales before moving on to pieces he'd practiced tirelessly years earlier. The full, rich sounds of Phantom of the Opera filled the house. His fingers flew over the keys, his mind full of nothing but the sound of the music he created. Then he faltered, unable to remember exactly what came next. "Huh." He'd played the piece so many times he'd been sure he'd never forget it. He plinked out the last few notes again, but the next part eluded him.

"Uncle Talan?"

His head snapped to face the door. Felicity's oldest was standing in the doorway, a puddle of water on the tiles beneath her. "Sonja, you're dripping."

"Oh. Sorry." She wrapped her towel around herself. "I didn't know you played the piano."

"I don't, anymore."

She stepped into the room. "Do you think I could play like that?"

"Yes, if you practiced enough."

"Can you teach me?"

His first instinct was to say no; teaching kids was not his thing. But her expression was so hopeful, he reconsidered. "I can show you something." She took another step forward and he held up a hand. "After you change into dry clothes."

She grinned, her dark eyes sparkling, "Be right back."

While she was gone, he tried to think back to when he'd first learned to play. It was impossible, he'd been three when he'd started taking lessons, which he only knew because he'd heard his mother say it countless times.

In no time Sonja was back. She sat on the bench next to him, looking to him for guidance.

"How old are you?"

"Eight."

By the time he was eight he'd begun working on Chopin. "I guess, well, this key is Middle C. When you sit at a piano you always start with your hands like this," he put his fingers over the keys.

"Why's it called Middle C?"

She listened intently as he explained the names of the keys and showed her how to play a scale. She repeated it, haltingly at first then with growing confidence as he encouraged her.

"You like music?"

Grinning hugely, she said, "I love it. My mom gets annoyed because I sing all the time."

Returning her smile, he told her, "She used to get annoyed with me, too. Do you have a favorite song? Maybe I can teach it to you."

"I like the one about the ring." She began to sing, *"My sugar daddy buys me golden rings. He decks me out in all that bling, every time I shake my thiiinnnng......"*

He stared at her. "That's quite the song."

"My mom always plays that one in the car. Do you know it?"

"No, I'm sorry, I don't. Your mom and I have... different tastes in music." A vague memory of elementary school music class his only frame of reference for basic music lessons, he said, "How about we start with 'Hot Cross Buns.'"

"Okay."

She picked up what he showed her quickly. After a while, he asked her, "You've never played before?"

"No. Why?"

"Just curious." Unless his mom had moved it, there was a beginner's piano book in the bench. He could pull it out, show her how to actually read music. Maybe move on to something a little harder.

She began another round of "Hot Cross Buns".

"Wow, Sonja, that's really good!"

She stopped playing and grinned at her mom. "Uncle Talan taught me."

Felicity shifted her gaze to her brother. "I didn't know you were giving piano lessons."

"I'm not."

Sonja turned to him, hope shining on her face. "Will you, Uncle Talan? I'll practice, like you said."

Feeling trapped, he stared into her hopeful eyes and tried to figure out a way to say no.

"Sonja, why don't you go see if Grandma needs help with lunch." Felicity came into the room and leaned her hip against the piano.

Sonja looked at her mom, then back to her uncle. "Thank you for teaching me."

As soon as she was gone, Felicity said, "She's never expressed an interest in music before."

He snorted. "That's not what I heard." He repeated what he could remember of Sonja's favorite song. "My sugar daddy buys me golden rings?"

She clarified, "Other than singing what's on the radio."

"You let her listen to some pretty questionable shit."

Felicity smiled and, ignoring that, asked, "Will you teach her?"

"I have absolutely no idea how to do that."

"I think you continue with whatever comes after 'Hot Cross Buns.'"

"If she's going to learn, she has to have a teacher who knows what they're doing."

"Yeah, and no one knows piano better than you."

This whole thing had been a fluke. He'd acted on instinct, but that wasn't the way to learn an instrument. Especially not one he didn't even play anymore. "I haven't played in ten years. And I don't know anything about kids."

She crossed her arms over her chest. "Based on what I heard today, that doesn't seem to matter."

Flatly, he told her, "No."

"She'll be crushed."

"And any potential she has will be crushed if you don't find someone who knows what they're doing."

She asked, "Will you think about it?"

Sonja's hopeful expression flashed through his mind. "I'll think about it."

*** ***

The song wasn't perfect, but it was getting there. He set his phone to record and started from the beginning. Not because he intended to actually use the recording, he'd need better equipment if he was going to do that, but because he wanted to hear the whole thing together even if the quality sucked.

After two times through, he was satisfied. He stopped the recording and sat back.

"I miss hearing you play." His mom was leaning against the door frame, arms folded lightly across her chest.

He was reminded of Felicity standing there just a little while before. His sister looked so much like their mom, with long dark hair and deep brown eyes, a thin face and straight nose.

He knew he looked like the male version of his mom. His whole childhood everyone had always said he and Felicity took after her. Except his hair was lighter. That was the only thing he had in common with Gage, who looked like a carbon copy of their dad.

His mom asked, "Did you write that?"

"I did."

"It's different than what you used to write."

"My tastes have changed." The last set of songs he'd written had been death metal. It was a far cry from the folk-rock music he was drawn to now.

"It was beautiful, Talan." She shifted a little. "It made me feel sad."

"It's that kind of song."

Concern in her voice, she asked, "How are you these days?"

He shrugged. "Fine."

"Anything interesting going on?"

"Nope."

"Work's going okay?"

"Yeah."

"How's your dad?"

He snorted. "Same asshole as always."

Her mouth tightened for a moment before she said, "If you wanted to quit, I'd help you."

He shook his head. "I made a commitment to Gage."

"What about making a commitment to yourself?"

The moment he'd decided to call about using the piano he'd acknowledged to himself that he was, in fact, going to start working towards the career he really wanted. But he wasn't ready to start telling anyone. Not even his mom. "This isn't the right time."

She nodded. "Do you want lunch?"

"Sure, thanks." As soon as he was alone again he opened the bench and verified, to satisfy his own curiosity, that the beginning piano book was still there.

# Chapter 8

Talan did not want to be at work.

If he could have called in sick he would have. It was fucking ridiculous that his own father required a doctor's note.

The thought of what that note would say was kind of funny, even through the fog of a serious hangover. "Talan can't come to work today, as last night he tried unsuccessfully to drink his shit life into oblivion." He snorted, and immediately regretted it as pain shot through his head. He never should have polished off that bottle of Jim Beam he'd found in his cabinet.

Resisting the urge to groan, because he figured that'd hurt too, he tried not to remember the day before at his mom's and how good it had felt to sit at the piano again. And definitely not think about James Camp, or the business card sitting on his counter.

Instead, he tried to concentrate on work. He held his fingers over the keyboard, considering. It was extremely tempting to type James Camp. "C-h-e-v-r-o-l-e-t. Enter." *Yeah, typing Chevrolet is going to work. You fucking idiot.* The official website topped the list. He mumbled, "Add the year, moron." Adding 1965 changed the search results drastically. He read the blurbs under the first few links then typed a new search.

"J-a-m-e-s C-a-m-p." *Because I'm obviously a fucking masochist.* He half expected not to find him; typing a name into a search engine wasn't exactly precise. Below a couple mug shots of other James

Camps and links for websites advertising actual campgrounds were links for people named James Camp on LinkedIn and Facebook. He clicked the only guy he recognized on LinkedIn. In his profile was a list of bands, including three Talan had heard of. That was pretty impressive. Most managers were lucky to have one client who made it past dive bars and local Music on the Green shows.

This guy was the real deal.

He folded his arms on the desk, put his head down and closed his eyes, succumbing to the headache. *Fuck work. Gage can look up his own stupid cars.*

One second later there was a knock on his door and he bolted upright, confused. Wiping drool from his cheek, he realized he had no idea how long he'd been asleep. Whoever had woken him knocked again, forcing him to respond. "Yeah?"

Macy came in, another perfect example of how the universe seemed hell-bent on taunting him with what he couldn't have. "Talan?" She smiled nervously. "I'm sorry to bother you. Gage is on the phone and he told me to have you drive the cars today."

*Come on, Talan, let's go for a ride so you can wallow in misery. Instead of being five feet away, with a desk between us, I'll be close enough to touch.* "I can't. I'm busy."

She gently closed the door behind her. Coming closer, keeping her voice very low, she said, "Do you want some aspirin? I have Visine, too."

"No. Just go away." Great, she could tell he was hungover.

She didn't move. "I'm sorry, I can't. I need you to drive for me."

"That's Gage's job."

"He can't take me. He's doing something."

He growled, "*Get out.*"

She stood there for another moment before she walked out, shutting the door quietly.

He stared at the door and wished he could go home.

The door opened and Macy came in again. He started to get up, to yell because she'd had the nerve to come back. But he knew yelling was a bad idea.

She set a bottle of Visine, two aspirin, and a cup of water in front of him. She took a scrap of paper from her pocket, smoothed it out and set it next to the aspirin. Without saying a word she left.

His first instinct was to pick up the things she'd left and throw them across the room. He squashed it. Instead, he took a few slow, deep breaths. He took the aspirin and washed it down with the water. Then he picked up the paper she'd left and read over the list of cars he was supposed to help her photograph.

This was his life— being a slave to his brother— and he'd just have to suck it up. He leaned back in his chair and closed his eyes to wait for the aspirin to kick in.

*** ***

The moment Macy stepped back out of Talan's office and into the space she shared with Keira, the other woman started. "When are you and Zack going out again?"

"Tomorrow."

"Not wasting any time is he." Keira gave her a sly grin. "Where's he taking you?"

She shrugged. "I didn't ask."

"Macy, how are you supposed to know how to dress if you don't know where you're going?"

"I guess when I call to confirm I'll ask him what I should wear."

Her eyes bulging in shock, Keira said, "It's a *date*, not an appointment. You don't," she made air quotes, "call to confirm. And you can't ask a *guy* what you're supposed to wear. How is he supposed to know that? Guys care that you look good, they don't have a *clue* how you get that way."

"How am I supposed to know without asking?"

Keira folded her hands on her desk, reminding Macy of her fourth-grade teacher. "You'd know by the restaurant you're going to."

"Restaurants here have a dress code?"

"Macy. Seriously."

Heat rose to her face. "I didn't mean it like that." She tried to smile, to make it seem like she didn't feel completely ignorant. Having to dress up wasn't a foreign concept; in photography school they'd even had a class on how to dress to shoot a wedding or what was expected if you went to work for a fashion designer in New York. Dinner with Zach wasn't work, though.

Looking exasperated, Keira said, "Look, if he's taking you to Sheffield's you've got to go conservative. Black pants, silk blouse, a simple string of pearls. If you're going to Lane's on Fourth you can show more personality. Jeans, a cute top, heels. If it's Jacques," she leaned forward a bit, "and if I were you I'd hope it is, you've got to wear a cocktail dress. One that shows off your assets without showing too much. You want him to like what he sees, but know just by looking at you that he's got to work for it."

She'd never been to a restaurant that required a cocktail dress. Shit, she'd never been *anywhere* that required a cocktail dress. And she'd never put that much thought into an outfit. If she was going to a concert she wore a concert t-shirt, but not from the band she was going to see. If she was going to a bar she grabbed the top shirt in her drawer.

She remembered, though, Emma steering her towards certain outfits, talking her into saving her favorite t-shirts for another day. And her mom insisting on buying her a dress for her cousin's baby shower. Her grandma calling to say she'd really like it if Macy wore the outfit she'd gotten her for her birthday when they went out to dinner.

Embarrassment burned hot in her face. She'd never realized before that they were quietly telling her she needed to dress appropriately.

She needed help if she was going to avoid looking like a fool again. "If I find out where we're going, will you help me with an outfit?"

"I'll find out where he's taking you. That way you don't seem daft." Relaxing back into her chair, Keira said, "We'll go shopping after work."

Relieved at not having to figure this out by herself, she said, "Thanks, Keira."

"No thanks needed." Pursing her lips and looking her over critically, Keira began a discourse on what she thought Macy would look good in, something about A-Lines and sweetheart bodices, but Macy's mind began to wander. When Gage had handed her the list of cars her heart had sped up. Topping a list of a bunch of things that didn't interest her there'd been something amazing; a 1966 Shelby Mustang. She'd never even seen one in real life. If only she was allowed to drive, she'd take it someplace spectacular. Not that boring commuter lot. But Gage had told her it was either the parking lot or the back of the warehouse, and she hadn't figured out how to get him to branch out.

Keira's office phone rang, interrupting her thoughts. She took the interruption as a chance to escape. If Gage was done with whatever he was doing, she wouldn't have to have Talan drive after all. He was obviously hung over, which she could sympathize with, but it didn't make the idea of being alone in a car with him any more pleasant.

Unfortunately, Gage was nowhere to be found. She wandered over to Paul's office. She loved seeing how he used her pictures and she could tell by the layouts he'd shown her already that Dawson's next catalog was going to be fantastic.

She knocked on the open door and went in. "Hi, Paul."

"Hi, Macy." Indicating the other chair, he asked, "What can I do for you?"

"Nothing. I'm just waiting for Talan to be ready to bring me out to shoot."

"Gage isn't taking you?"

"He's busy."

"They should just let you drive."

She rolled her eyes. "Yeah, no shit." She asked, "What are you working on?"

"Adding the Corvette to the website." He swiveled so she could see his screen.

"Cool." Just then her phone rang. She answered, "Hello?"

"Macy?"

"Yes?"

"It's Talan." He hesitated. "Hey, I'm sorry I snapped at you."

"It's okay." She shrugged, "It happens."

"Thanks, for understanding. Do you want me to help you with the cars?"

"I'll meet you in the foyer." She hung up without waiting for an answer, looked at the Corvette layout, and scanned the information Talan and Keira had put together. "That's a beautiful car."

Paul nodded appreciatively. "It is. And your pictures make it look even better."

"Thanks. Talan's ready. I'll see you later."

Downstairs, she was glad to see that Talan looked better. She followed him through the yard and into one of the warehouses, watched in silence as he got a key from the safe and made his way to the Shelby. Excitement rippled through her as she looked at it, walked around it, made sure it was perfect.

As she sat in the passenger's seat he asked, "Where are we going?"

"What?"

"Where do you want to go?"

"Where *can* I go?"

"Anywhere you want."

After the initial shock of being allowed to choose a place wore off, she closed her eyes and pictured the cherry red car against different backgrounds she'd seen since she'd gotten to Arizona. The shape of the car was so unique, she needed something that wouldn't overshadow it. Not the open desert, with its scruffy looking scrub brush. And not the warehouse, where the texture of the building would be distracting. Something neutral, something… Her eyes popped open; she knew exactly where to take it. "There's an abandoned gas station, if you take Exit 153."

He stared at her quizzically for a long moment, then started the ignition. She tensed. Watching him grind gears in that Willys had hurt. Knowing he was about to abuse a classic Mustang was nearly unbearable.

It was immediately apparent that this ride was going to be different. Talan had no trouble finding first gear. Or any other gear. When he got on the highway her head was pushed back into the seat as he quickly shifted up. When they neared the exit she wished they were going further. It would have been truly amazing to drive this car, but even being a passenger was a thrill.

As he pulled into the gas station she scanned the area for a spot with both good lighting and a good background. She ignored the three garage doors. In a pinch she'd use them, but the white paint flaking off the repeating squares and the single straight row of windows painted black from the inside were too rigid for the graceful lines of the Shelby. There were better options here.

She briefly considered using the windows that fronted the building, making the background a reflection of the car. But as Talan drove slowly past she saw there was no reflection, just a clear view of a jumble of wooden chairs piled in the middle of an otherwise empty room. "Can you pull around to the side, please?" She pointed to the bright side of the building, the spot she'd had in mind in the first place.

The wall was white stucco, not perfect but nearly so. The few cracks that had formed could easily be retouched out, as could the faded blue "Ron's Garage" sign that hung from a rusty hook right below the roofline. A few scraggly weeds had pushed their way through the asphalt at the front of what had once been parking spaces, breaking what would have otherwise been a too-rigid line where the wall met the ground. Best of all, there was no shade.

"Pull parallel to the wall." She barely waited for him to shut the car off and she was climbing out, dragging her camera bag behind her. Not caring where Talan went, as long as he wasn't in her shots, she started to frame the first image. What she saw nearly took her breath away with its perfectness. The light created both highlights and shadows to give the car shape. The flawless red paint popped against the background of white stucco, and that stucco was a perfect match to the rally stripes that graced the car from bumper to bumper.

Bracing her elbows against her sides, she drew a deep breath, held it, and deliberately pushed the shutter release. Exhaling, she quickly adjusted the f-stop and readied herself for the next shot. Pushing the excitement to the corners of her mind, she concentrated on not moving as she bracketed shots, giving herself options of both brighter and darker exposures to choose from later.

She trailed her fingers down the long, smooth hood on the way to the front for her next angle. *God, this car is perfect.* Squatting to do a front three-quarter shot, she focused her camera on the pins holding the hood closed. Even though they broke the line of the hood, she loved that they were there; they meant the car had been built for racing. After a few more shots she slid the pins and opened the hood. She cringed. "That's a damn shame."

"What?"

She glanced at Talan, leaning against a guardrail a few feet away. She'd been so caught up in the car she hadn't realized she'd spoken out loud. Embarrassed, she mumbled, "They should've painted the engine to match the car."

Stating the obvious, he said, "In 1966 all Ford engines were blue."

Speaking louder, she said, "Yeah, but it would have been nice if it matched."

"Engines were color-coded by the manufacturer. If they'd painted it a different color it'd decrease the value of the car."

She turned and narrowed her eyes at him, wondering why he had to harass her with facts. "I don't care. It would look cool if the engine was white to match the stripes."

"If you buy it, you can paint it any color you want."

His teasing annoyed her. She couldn't come up with a retort, so she went back to shooting.

When she was done with the first side she knew she had to ask for him to turn the car. She stalled, taking a few pictures she didn't need as she worked up the courage. "Talan?" She looked to where he was waiting and the request stuck in her throat. He'd let his hair down and the dark blonde waves were highlighted by the sun behind him. At the sound od his name he looked up and the tilt of his head caught the light just right, creating Rembrandt lighting and accentuating his nearly straight nose. Forcing herself to speak, she asked, "Can you turn the car? I need the other side."

"Sure." He sauntered over and opened the door. Before he got in, he looked straight at her.

Their eyes locked and her breath caught. *Oh my god, he's perfect.*

Then he was in the car and she could breathe again. But even after he parked and she started shooting her mind couldn't let go of the moment. She stared at the window of the car, at the reflection of Talan behind her. The way he leaned against the guardrail, the fact that he seemed to be watching her. She told herself it was her imagination. There was no way this guy was interested.

She wasn't paying attention to the car. She stepped back and took a moment to gather herself. This was a 1966 Shelby Mustang and she absolutely had to give it the respect it deserved.

Very intentionally ignoring Talan, she began to frame her next shot.

Once she was done with the exterior she had to choose a new location. Direct sun was great for making the paint shine in all its glossy glory, but it would create a shadow-riddled nightmare on the interior. She glanced up at the sky. The sun was high up and she knew from experience there wouldn't be enough shade on any side of the building to fully cover the car. It was too bad they couldn't bring it into the garage portion of the old gas station. With three big bays it would have been perfect. The next best option was under the awning where the gas pumps had once been.

Nervous, she turned around, wondering if Talan would be looking at her. He wasn't. She spoke hesitantly, "Talan?" He immediately looked up. "Can you park the car there?" She pointed. "So it's completely in the shade?"

He brushed past her on his way to the car, again catching her eye. This time he smiled the tiniest bit.

With the car in position, she began by photographing the interior of the trunk, knowing it was important even though it wasn't exciting. She lay on the ground and did the best she could to get a full view of the undercarriage. It would be easier on a lift, but she didn't have that option.

The full shade provided perfect soft lighting for the black interior, allowing the texture of the leather upholstery to show. Cars from this era always had lines stitched into the seats. They made Macy think of miniblinds.

Finally, she sat behind the wheel. This car wasn't fancy, and that made the few details it did have that much more special. She did close-ups of the simple line of round gages, trimmed in chrome and set into the black dash, and of the cobra on the horn button. She leaned across the passenger's seat to do the emblem, a galloping mustang over vertical red, white and blue bars, on the glove box. Satisfied, she put her camera down on the passenger seat, closed the car door and sank back into the bucket seat.

Sliding her hands over the steering wheel, she flexed her fingers, then wrapped them firmly around the polished wood. If she started the engine this car would beg to go. She'd be happy to comply. She'd take the car out into the desert, following the ribbon of pavement into the hills that reared suddenly from the ground, through passes and over the horizon, to see what lay beyond.

The passenger door opened and she jumped, startled out of her fantasy. She looked guiltily at Talan. He climbed in, shut the door, his expression not showing anything as he handed her the camera she'd set on the passenger seat. "Ready?"

Resigned to giving up the dream, she sighed. "Yeah." She took the camera, but didn't move to get out of the car.

He continued to look at her. "You like this car."

"Yeah." *Duh.*

Checking out the interior, he asked, "What is it about this car?"

"What do you mean?"

"Why does everyone go nuts over it?"

Instead of answering right away, she looked out the windshield. When she'd first started shooting cars she'd been so excited about them, she'd told her friends about every one. They'd either completely not understood why anyone would care, or laughed at her for liking something so obviously not cutting edge. She'd learned to keep her love of the classics to herself. Rather than risk being treated like that again, she said, "I guess, ya know, there's so few of them. Most people will never get to see one in person, never mind drive one."

He pointed out, "There are lots of cars that are more rare. For instance, the Duesenberg SJ. There were only 36 made."

She shook her head. "That doesn't have the personality of this one."

The corner of his mouth curved into a disbelieving smile. "It's a car. It doesn't have a personality."

"All cars have a personality."

"Yeah?"

"Yeah. Even giant, heavy Duesenbergs."

"How does being giant and heavy give a car personality?"

His incredulous tone irritated her. "They're not just giant and heavy. They were designed to be the best, built to say, 'look at me, I'm fancy and expensive.' Because they're all about luxury and affluence. But then, look at cars like this Mustang. They don't care about any of that. They care about being fast. This car is simple. It's compact, aerodynamic. It looks quick." She ran her fingers lightly over the steering wheel. "And it's got such great lines."

"That's a steering wheel. It's a circle."

"I know. But..." She trailed off, thinking she couldn't possibly explain the desire to touch this car.

She turned the camera on, pressed the play button, and scrolled back through images until she found the right one. "Here, let me show you." She held the camera so he could see the screen on the back. "See the way the nose is so long, it just goes on forever in this smooth line until it meets the windshield. But then there's this ridge that starts at the corner above the headlight."

He moved close to see what she was talking about. "Yeah."

"It runs down the side, from the front corner, under the windows," she glanced up, enough to see that he was looking at the camera. She quickly shifted her eyes back to the picture. "That curve draws your eye along the trunk to the rear corner."

"Your images are awesome."

He caught her gaze and held it. This close she noticed how his eyes, so darkly brown, had depth to them, golden lines and ripples that she found utterly fascinating. Her heart started to pound harder. It took everything she had to whisper, "Thank you."

He moved fractionally closer. His voice low, he asked, "So, for you, it's all about how a car looks?"

"Sometimes. But not this one." She swallowed hard. It was nearly impossible to form thoughts with him so close. All she could think was that she wanted to be closer. She noticed the faint scent of something. Not cologne, nothing that strong. But perfectly, utterly male. She breathed it in, her mind spinning with sudden desire. "This car is so fucking hot, I'd love to drive it." She was so shocked that she'd spoken, she jerked back.

His voice losing the intimate quality it had had, he asked, "Why? It's really hard to drive."

The mood broken, already trying to forget what she'd been thinking about her bosses' son, she tried to remember what it was about this car that made it one she wanted to drive. "It's supposed to be hard. It was built to race, not for old men to drive to church in."

"You want to drive a race car?"

"Not so much a race car. A muscle car." She sat back in the seat, put her camera in her lap, and gripped the wheel again. "When you drive a car like this, you know it from the moment you start the engine." Wistfully, she said, "The rumble of power courses through you, you feel it in your chest, in the vibration of the seat, in the steering wheel. It's like nothing else in the world, to have all that power at your fingertips."

He asked, "Do you want to drive back?"

Surprise at the offer was immediately replaced by bitter disappointment, knowing she was passing up the fulfillment of a dream. She shook her head a little. "I can't. I'm..." she hesitated, regretfully admitted, "I'm not allowed."

"Why not?"

Sagging back in the seat, her hands falling to her lap, she answered, "Your father doesn't trust me."

Sarcastically, he said, "That's a shocker." He moved around, pulled the keys out of his pocket, and held them out. "Here."

She was astounded to hear herself refusing the offer. "I can't."

"My father's not here to know."

*Be responsible, Macy.* Remembering the Camaro and what could happen if she wasn't careful, she said, "Talan, we could both lose our jobs."

A smile turned the corner of his mouth again. "You wanna drive this car?"

"Yeah."

"This is your shot."

After another moment of hesitation, she handed him her camera and took the keys. There was a good reason Nate didn't trust her. But there was no ice on the roads, no way she was going to crash another car, and no way in hell she was going to pass up this opportunity. She put the key in the ignition, adjusted the seat and buckled her seatbelt.

She jiggled the stick to make sure the car was in neutral, stepped on the brake and clutch, turned the key, and closed her eyes to let the feel of barely constrained power sink into her. After a moment she opened her eyes. Very aware of Talan next to her, and determined not to look like a fool, she looked down at the shifter, committed the diagram to memory, and moved the stick through the gears. Confident that she knew where each was, she checked her mirrors, then pushed the stick back into neutral, kept her foot on the brake and stepped on the gas just to hear the engine roar. Excitement soared through her, burning away any doubts she'd had.

She shifted into first and tried to creep forward. If she let off the gas the tiniest bit the car protested, threatened to stall. She'd driven cars like this before and she knew there was no creeping forward; it was balls to the wall or nothing at all. Feathering the gas and brake to keep from stalling, she moved toward the road. There were no cars in sight. She let off the brake, stepped on the gas and shot out, tires chirping. She barely slowed to take the highway entrance ramp.

Out in the desert, no one in sight, she let it go.

It was better than she ever could have imagined. The asphalt snaked on ahead, and Macy followed it. The faster she drove the smoother the ride got. She watched the needle on the speedometer soar past 85, hit 95, then 105, as adrenaline screamed through her system.

When she hit a hundred and ten she knew she had to slow down. The rumble of the engine vibrated in every part of her being, satisfying in its intensity. Reluctantly she took her foot off the gas.

At the next exit she got off the highway and pulled into a parking lot. "You have to drive back. So no one knows."

"Okay." After a minute he said, "Macy, we have to swap spots if you want me to drive."

Looking at him from the corner of her eye, she said, "I don't want to."

Grinning, he said, "You don't have to. But if you don't, we're both gonna lose our jobs. And probably our freedom."

She pried her fingers from the wheel and turned the car off. She put two fingers to her lips, kissed them, then touched them to the dashboard. She whispered, "Until we meet again," and got out of the car.

As they passed each other in front of the car Talan said, "You should probably try not to smile like that."

"Like what?"

"Like you just got laid."

She said, "Driving that car was better than any sex I ever had."

"Then you're not having sex with the right people."

Still feeling good, she laughed.

# Chapter 9

"This would look cute on you." Keira held up a silk scoop-neck in a blue and black Aztec print.

Macy shook her head. She didn't bother showing Keira the Led Zeppelin shirt she'd been looking at.

Keira rolled her eyes. "Macy, you have to find something."

Instead of telling her what she really thought, which was that this was stupid and there was nothing wrong with t-shirts, she reminded herself that if she wanted to make friends she was going to have to adjust to her new surroundings.

Holding up yet another shirt, Keira said, "How about this?"

The sky-blue peasant shirt wasn't something she'd normally have chosen. It was flowy and had embroidered flowers in a wide band across the top, but it was the first tolerable thing Keira had suggested. And she was sick of shopping. "Okay. I wear a medium."

Keira shuffled shirts around until she found a medium, which she handed to Macy.

"All set?" she picked up the Led Zeppelin shirt, relieved to finally be able to leave.

Keira asked incredulously, "Aren't you going to try it on?"

"It's a medium, right?" She shrugged, "I don't need to try it on."

As if speaking to a child, she told Macy, "Yes, it's a medium, but that doesn't mean it'll fit right. Plus, you need at least one more."

She almost told her she had another one— the Led Zeppelin shirt— but thought better of it. Keira was taking time out of her life to help, she should be grateful. "Do they have this one in green?"

Keira exclaimed, "Macy! You can't just buy the same shirt in a different color. You need a different shirt. And while we're at it, you need something besides those jeans. Boot cut went out ages ago." Going back to sifting through racks, she said, "Go find something skinny in your size and I'll see what I can do about a couple more shirts. I'll meet you at the dressing room."

Macy wandered away, wondering if this was really worth it. As she passed another table of t-shirts, she ran her fingers over one with the Ford logo on it. She smiled as she thought about Talan letting her drive what she considered to be the most iconic Ford ever built.

She found the Ford shirt in a medium and went to find skinny jeans.

By the time she figured out what kind of jeans she was supposed to get Keira was waiting at the dressing room with a boatload of clothes. "Wait until you see what I found. O-M-G it's going to be perfect for you." She held out a black lace dress. "And it's twenty percent off!"

She was so excited, Macy couldn't tell her she couldn't imagine ever needing to wear something like that. Instead, she added it to the pile of things folded over her arm. Trying to sound happy, she said, "Thank you."

"Go! Try the dress first! I can't wait to see it on you."

Alone in the dressing room, she struggled to get the dress on. It took her three tries— once trying to step into it and realizing it was too narrow for that, then twice over her head because the first time she messed up the crisscross straps. She looked in the mirror and stifled a laugh. All she could think of was when she and Emma had been seventeen and they'd "borrowed" dresses from Emma's mom's closet in an unsuccessful effort to look old enough to get into a bar. She straightened the dress and went out to show Keira.

She clasped her hands and squealed, "Oh. My. God. Macy! You look stunning!" Then she added, "I mean, except for the bra. You'll have to get pasties. Turn around," she made a circular motion with her finger, "I want to see the back."

Wondering what the heck pasties were, she did as she was told and waited. And waited.

Finally, she turned back around to see Keira looking at her phone. She stood, uncomfortable, while the other woman sent a text. When she looked up, Macy smiled nervously. "So, what do you think?"

"Actually, I think maybe for you something in blue, to bring out your eyes. Let's try," she rifled through a pile until she found a navy shirt. "This and the white jeans I gave you before."

There was a change in Keira's voice, a tone that gave Macy the feeling something was wrong. But as Keira handed her the shirt and practically pushed her towards the dressing room, Macy shrugged off the strange feeling and went to change.

*** ***

Normally Talan would have been annoyed at having to stay late at work. But he was still there because a big chunk of his day had been spent with Macy and he considered it a fair trade.

He settled back into his chair, sipped his coffee, opened his music library and began to scan the list of artists. Maybe the Beatles. Macy had a different Beatles shirt for every day of the week, or at least it seemed like it. Or he could go with The Lumineers. Sometimes she sang softly as she edited pictures, probably without realizing it, and "Angela" and "Ophelia" were both regulars in her repertoire. Or he could go with Vance Joy. The day he'd stolen her headphones, unable to resist knowing what had her swaying in her seat, she'd been listening to "Rip Tide."

The crackle of his office phone's intercom interrupted him and his father demanded, "Talan, get the fuck in here."

Apparently he wasn't the only one working late. "Be right there." He stood, stretched, and pulled his hair back in an elastic. The lights flickered on automatically as he opened his door and stepped into the outer office. He glanced at Macy's empty desk and felt a twinge of disappointment that she wasn't there.

He took his time crossing the building. The only thing he could think of that he'd done recently to earn his father's wrath was let Macy drive the Shelby, although he couldn't imagine how anyone would know that. It was irrelevant; he'd known it was a risk and had accepted it. After all, working at Dawson's was already the worst punishment he could think of.

He wondered what his father would do to Macy, though. He didn't believe he'd actually fire her; she was way too good at what she did. But then, his father had done some pretty stupid shit.

The door was open and the old man was pacing. Talan knocked lightly on the door frame. His father turned and glared fiercely at him, his already red face managing to get redder. He growled, "Shut the door," walked behind his desk and sat down.

Talan shut the door and sat in the seat closest to it, furthest from the desk.

His dad narrowed his eyes and said, "If you were anyone else you'd already be gone."

"Okay."

He stood and slammed his hands on the desk. "If I am ever put in a situation like this again—" Leaning forward, a vein throbbing down the center of his forehead, he spoke slowly and very precisely. "People entrust their cars to us because of our reputation. I cannot afford to have that reputation ruined."

That wasn't quite what Talan had been expecting. Maybe this wasn't about the Mustang after all. "Pretty sure that's the whole reason for me being here."

*"No fucking shit! You're supposed to protect us! Not destroy us!"*

He flinched involuntarily. "What is this about?"

"You," he jabbed his finger towards Talan, "were supposed to take that car out, let Macy take pictures, and bring it back. Nothing else."

Smiling was the wrong thing to do, but it was impossible to suppress it as he remembered how Macy had practically glowed with joy when she'd been behind the wheel.

"This is *not* funny. What the fuck do you think would happen if Brent Peters decided to tell all his friends that we took his *1966 Shelby* out for a *joy ride?*"

"They'd probably be jealous they didn't get to drive it."

His eyes bulged and Talan thought he'd finally succeeded in pushing his dad too hard. Then, the red began to recede. He ran his hands over his face, then looked at Talan. "Gage talked Brent off the ledge, gave him some bullshit line about wanting to test limits, get buyers really excited about what the car can do. Brent swallowed it, so now *you're* going to make sure that ad clearly states that the car can do a buck-twenty."

"Do you want it to actually say a buck-twenty?"

Some of the red crept back into his dad's cheeks. "What do you think?"

"I think it should probably say something like 'The car can easily top a hundred and twenty.'"

"Easily?"

Ignoring the incredulous tone, he shrugged. "It didn't feel like it was struggling." He could tell that even from the passenger seat.

Nate's jaw clenched and after a long moment he said, "From this point forward I don't care how rare or fast or *anything* a car is. If Gage asks you to drive Macy you will take her where she needs to go, help her with anything she needs, and bring the car directly back here." His eyes bored into Talan's. "Any questions?"

There was no way in hell he was going to push his luck with something Macy was involved in. "No."

Nate snapped, "Go. I want the write-up on my desk before you leave."

He was more than happy to stay, no matter how long it took him to finish the write-up, as long as his father didn't suspect it had been Macy behind the wheel.

# Chapter 10

Macy stood in front of the closet in her hotel room and slid the hangers from one side to the other, trying to remember what Keira had told her to wear. She mumbled to herself, "Not the blue dress, or this shirt. She said not to show too much skin." She finally settled on a teal drape-neck blouse, super skinny white jeans rolled at the bottoms, and a pair of teal wedge-heeled sandals that she was sure went with the shirt.

*Teal? Or turquoise.* She rolled her eyes. *Ridiculous.*

Satisfied with her outfit, she turned to the pile of makeup Keira had talked her into buying. She picked up a bottle of foundation and read out loud, "Super smooth finish with maximum hiding power." She studied her reflection, the harsh light from the bulbs above the bathroom mirror making her freckles pop, and wondered what she was supposed to be hiding. It didn't matter. Keira had told her to use foundation, so she would.

Next, she eyed the pile of compacts on the counter. The last time she'd used makeup of any sort she'd been about fifteen and even her teenage self had recognized that she'd looked trashy. That wasn't in the cards tonight. She got her phone, searched 'best makeup for blue eyes,' and scanned through images until she found something that she thought looked pretty, with subdued tans and pinks on top and a touch of blue for contrast on the bottom lid. She even had almost the same shade of light pink lipstick the girl in the picture wore.

"Now for the hair." She sighed as she set about straightening her naturally curly hair, per Keira's instructions.

Once she was done, she stood back and stared at this new version of herself. For one second she considered washing everything off and changing into regular clothes. But she'd seen Keira and her friends; this was what Zack would expect. "Wouldn't Emma be proud."

She picked her phone up and ran her finger over the screen. A selfie of her and Emma, faces close together, grinned back. It was weird to be going out without her, weird that she hadn't even talked to Emma about Zack. Actually, she hadn't talked to her at all since she'd left Connecticut.

Usually they'd have texted, made plans, then talked in person. Needing that little bit of familiar, Macy dialed.

Emma answered on the second ring. "Macy! You're finally home?"

"No. I'm in Arizona."

"Oh. When will you be back?"

Of course she'd ask that. "I'm not coming back. The job here is working out really well."

"Yeah, but, I mean…" Emma fell silent.

Macy knew what she was getting at. She hadn't believed Macy was really leaving home any more than Logan had. She forged ahead. "So, what's going on there?"

"Nothing. You missed Logan's party."

She felt a tiny twinge of guilt. She'd never even called him back. "How was it?"

"Not the same without you. I got stuck talking to Sir Lou for half the night, with no one to rescue me."

Hearing even that little bit from home made her smile. "Does he know we call him that?"

"No, he's as oblivious to the rest of the world as always." She began an update of all the things going on with their friends.

After a few minutes Macy stopped really listening. It was all the same stuff that was always going on. She walked over to the window and watched cars on the street that fronted the hotel, wondering if Zack was on his way.

"Hey, Emma, I just realized what time it is. I'm sorry, my date's going to be here in like five minutes. I have to finish getting ready."

"Wait! What? You're going on a date? In Arizona?"

"Yeah, and he's going to be here soon."

"You can't drop a bomb like that and just hang up! Tell me about him!"

She tried to think of something to say. "He's... nice."

"Seriously, Macy? That's the best you can come up with?"

"Ummm..."

"What's his name? How'd you meet him? Is he cute? Did you sleep with him yet?"

"Emma! For crying out loud, this is our first official date. No. I didn't sleep with him yet."

"Is he cute?"

She really had missed Emma's total predictability. "I guess he's cute."

"You *guess* he's cute? Jeez, Mace. What's he look like?"

There was no way in hell she was going to admit she'd been too drunk to actually pay attention. She told Emma the few things she could definitely remember. "He's got short, dark hair and a beard—"

Emma cut in, "He must drive a *really* nice car."

"What?"

"I mean, if it's not the hair, he's gotta have *something* you like."

That was exactly the reason Macy been avoiding talking to anyone from home. They all assumed they knew everything about her. She didn't have some preconceived idea about only dating guys with long hair, and she didn't really care what kind of car they drove. All she wanted was someone who cared about her. "Hey, Emma, I'm sorry, I gotta go. Zack's here." She hung up before Emma had a chance to argue, or catch her in a lie.

She had to calm her suddenly jangly nerves. She closed her eyes and envisioned how the night would go. She'd get outside and Zack would open the car door for her. As she settled into the passenger seat— *wait, what kind of car* does *he drive?*

Macy's eyes snapped open. "Damn it." It didn't actually matter, or at least not the way Emma had said it did. It was just that she wanted her daydream to be as close to reality as possible. Taking a deep breath, she closed her eyes again.

He'd be driving a dark blue Mercedes. He'd open the passenger side door and as she got in he'd tell her how beautiful she looked. Once she was settled, he'd close her door— gently. They'd talk all the way to the restaurant, about work and where he'd gone to school and how many brothers and sisters they each had. He'd take her hand and lead her into a charming—

Her phone rang. Startled, she nearly dropped it as she answered. "Hello?"

"Hi, Macy."

She smiled at the sound of Zack's voice. "Hey."

"I'm here."

"I'll be right down." Nerves fluttered as she checked her reflection once more, worried that her outfit wasn't appropriate. But Keira had picked all the pieces, so it had to be fine.

In the elevator she reminded herself not to talk about cars. She'd had more than one guy pretty much tell her they weren't interested in her obsession, and she doubted Zack would care about the difference between a sports car and a muscle car or why she was so enamored with Mercury Montereys.

Outside, things started almost the way she'd pictured. Zack smiled welcomingly as she crossed the space from the hotel entrance to his car. But in place of her imagined Mercedes was a cobalt blue Camaro. She grinned, "Beautiful car."

"Thanks." He opened her door and she was immediately aware of the scent of cologne. He waited for her to be seated before he shut the door and walked around to his side. He started the engine and hip-hop blared from the speakers. Macy quickly suppressed a grimace. She'd learned way back in middle school to tolerate music she wasn't into.

To her relief, he turned the volume down. "Sorry."

She watched as he jiggled the shifter in neutral, slid it easily into first, and crept to the end of the hotel's driveway. He glanced back and forth once before he shot into the street. She involuntarily gripped the armrest as he shifted up through the gears, moving easily around slower cars and somehow hitting every light on green. Once they were on the highway he settled into driving, his hands loosely resting on the steering wheel.

She noticed that his fingers were much thicker than Talan's, not as graceful. There was none of the nervousness that had radiated off Talan, either.

Uncomfortable to realize she was on a date with Zack and thinking about Talan, she asked, "What year is this?"

"2017."

*Stupid, Macy.* "I meant the car."

"So did I." Zack smiled easily at her.

Feeling even more stupid, she glanced around at the pristine interior. It was very different than what she was used to. But it was still a car, and she knew cars. "Is it a V8?"

"It is. It goes zero to sixty in four seconds. It's top of the line, every upgrade I could get."

She sank back in the bucket seat and watched the lighted trim around the huge LCD panel set into the dashboard change color. She was used to power windows and locks being an upgrade, things like integrated GPS and satellite radio were unheard of in her world. She wasn't sure how she felt about that. Muscle cars weren't supposed to be luxurious. They were supposed to be... muscle.

The song on the radio ended and a new one started. Zack turned it up a little and sang along. After the last chorus he said, "I saw her in concert. Last year. My company has a sky box. Absolutely fantastic way to see a concert." He continued, telling her about the piped in sound and the big screen TV.

She was curious about how it would be to go to a concert in person and watch it on TV inside a glass room. She didn't think she'd like it. But concerts, music in general, was the other thing she knew about. Happy to find something in common, she asked, "Do you go to a lot of concerts?"

"I usually opt for sports, when I have a choice." He glanced at her and smiled. "How about you?"

*Sports? Crap.* She had no interest in sports. Scrounging for at least some connection, she said, "I used to watch NASCAR with my dad."

Zack raised an eyebrow. "Round and rounds? Not really my thing." He started talking about college basketball, which Macy couldn't follow at all. Her only experience with basketball had been high school gym class, and that had mostly been her attempting to stay as far away from the ball as possible.

He pulled into the parking lot at the restaurant and her nerves flared again. Keira had told her the place they were going was casual dining. She'd pictured Chili's. Instead, she followed Zack up a sweeping double staircase into a two-story building of white marble. The building felt like it belonged in Italy or something, not Arizona. "I thought we were going someplace casual."

"This is our first date." He opened the door for her. "I wanted it to be special."

A tuxedo-clad hostess greeted them the moment they stepped into the lobby. "Welcome to Le Petit Chateau."

Zack told her, "Table for two at seven under Zack Pelletier."

"Right this way."

Macy followed them into the dining room, tugging on the hem of her shirt as she tried not to stare at the giant crystal chandeliers or the gold-gilded scroll-work on the walls. She wished she'd worn something different, like maybe that fancy black dress. Zack pulled out her chair and she sat, her stomach churning so badly she was sure she wasn't going to be able to eat.

The hostess, or maybe they called them something different here, had barely left when another woman was there. "I'm Melissa and I'll be taking care of you." She handed them each a leather-bound menu. "Tonight, in addition to the menu, Chef is offering Confit de Canard with a side of sautéed parsnips and an arugula salad dressed with vinaigrette."

"Thank you, Melissa." Zack opened his menu and Melissa left them to decide on their meals.

Macy read over her choices, ignoring the ones in French and looking for something she recognized from the others.

Zack said, "The Scallops Provencal are excellent, as is the Coq Au Vin."

"The scallops sound perfect." She had no f'ing clue what 'Provencal' was, but she knew what scallops were and that was good enough. The second she folded her menu, the waitress was there, smiling.

Handing his menu back, Zack ordered. "I'll have the Filet, and she'll have the Scallops, with the arugula salad in place of the potatoes in both meals, served as a first course. And water to drink, for both of us. No lemon."

Macy was a little irritated that he'd ordered for her, especially the salad in place of potatoes, but the moment he was done he turned his attention to her, took her hand from across the table and held it. She forgot the slight annoyance; there was something about a guy taking her hand that just did it for her. Feeling the need to fill the silence, she asked, "How did you become an—" Heat rose to her cheeks as she realized she couldn't remember. She looked down and admitted, "All I can remember is 'actually,' and I know that's not right."

He said, "Actuary."

Relieved that he hadn't laughed, she looked back up. "How did you become an actuary?"

His hazel eyes considered her. "I've always been very strong in math and…"

Almost immediately she lost him. She stared at him, trying to pretend she was following. Finally, she said, "You like it?"

"I find it very satisfying."

She decided she needed to change the subject. "Are you from Arizona?"

"No, I'm from Virginia, just outside D.C."

"How did you end up here?"

"Once I was ready to enter the workforce I made a conscious decision to choose a location where I'd be able to put down roots and stay. I designed spreadsheets to easily compare…"

She let him talk. It was easier that way.

He didn't stop even when their salads, then their meals, came. Macy was relieved that the scallops she'd ordered weren't anything weird; they were scallops in a lemon butter sauce and they were really good. She ate and tried to listen to what Zack said. After they'd eaten the waitress came back and offered dessert.

"No, thanks. We're all set. Just the check, please." He took the folder the waitress handed him and opened it.

Macy waited to see if he'd give her a total. They hadn't discussed whether this was Dutch. She wasn't sure if she was happy or not when he slid his platinum card into the folder. She knew some guys had different expectations when they paid.

Outside he led her away from the parking lot. She pointed, "Isn't your car that way?"

"It is. But there's this fantastic ice cream place about two blocks from here. You're going to love it." He began telling her in excruciating detail what made it the best.

Ice cream wasn't her favorite, but he'd put thought into this, and she wasn't going to make waves on a first date. And she didn't *dislike* ice cream.

He held her hand as they walked past kitschy little shops selling everything from pottery to jewelry. The stores were all closed this late at night, but they looked at the displays. She stopped and pointed at a big-ass coffee mug, painted in swirls of bright, warm colors. "Oh, I love that." She grinned. "With a mug like that I could tell people I drink one cup a day and not be lying!"

He eyed her curiously. "Drink a lot of coffee, do you?"

They continued down the street. "I do."

"I'll have to remember that."

She imagined that he was going to go home and add that information to a spreadsheet entitled, "Pros and Cons of Dating Macy." She could see the headings above each column; Things Macy Likes, Potential Conflicts, Common Interests. She was already starting to think there wouldn't be too much in that last column.

After ice cream, on the way back to her hotel, she said, "Thank you for the ice cream." Then, quickly she added, "And for dinner. It was really good."

He smiled and she thought he actually was kind of cute. "Glad you liked it." He pulled into the hotel, parked, and turned to her. "There's a place called Crème Glacée where they serve ice cream encased in chocolate globes. At your table they pour heated ganache over it and the chocolate melts and reveals the ice cream inside. I'd love to take you there." He took her hand and looked into her eyes. "Maybe this weekend we can drive up, if you're not doing anything."

She almost said no. But then she thought about an entire weekend alone and said, "I'm not. Doing anything, I mean. I don't even know anyone here."

He leaned closer, his voice dropping. "You know me."

She whispered, "I do." She knew what was going to happen before it did. She could practically see the calculation in his eyes. His lips were firm against hers, his kiss as confident as the rest of him.

After a moment he sat back and looked at her, like he was checking to make sure she was happy. "Until Saturday, then."

# Chapter 11

The first notes of "Heathens" drifted from Talan's computer speakers. Every time he heard Twenty-One Pilots he couldn't help thinking how cool it was that an alternative band from Ohio had recorded a song that eventually became the title track for Suicide Squad. Granted, it was a movie about misfit supervillains turned superheroes, but it starred Will Smith.

He wondered if Macy liked Twenty-One Pilots, but dismissed the thought immediately. That was an entirely different genre than everything else she listened to.

He glanced at the corner of the computer screen. This was about the time Gage and Macy usually got back from shooting. In the moment of silence between songs he could hear Keira's voice and she definitely sounded like she was on the phone, which most likely meant Macy wasn't there. For the first time ever he wished he had an office at the front of the building, with windows that looked out at the parking lot.

He wondered what cars Gage and Macy were doing, if they were cars she'd like. Before his father had shifted his focus to dealer auctions, they'd mostly handled big classics. Now, there were more muscle cars coming through.

Two songs later he glanced at the time again. The down side to playing music was that he couldn't hear Keira, couldn't tell if she was still alone in her office. Looking for an excuse to check, he went out and started rifling through a filing cabinet. She was still alone and still on the phone. Predictably, she completely ignored him and continued her conversation. He read the names on the folders, half listening to her babble about her mother's yippy dog trashing her shoes. He could sympathize. He hated buying shoes.

Keira's tone changed, catching his attention. "Hey, I gotta go. If you have questions about anything else let me know." Barely missing a beat, she said, "Macy! Oh my God! Tell me *everything*."

Talan glanced around, just enough to see Macy drop her camera bag next to her chair. He turned his attention immediately back to the files as she started to tell Keira, "It runs and drives good. In 1954 Cadillacs had baby fins, and the headlights—"

"Macy! Jeez, I don't care about cars. I want to hear about Zack. He said you guys had a great time, and you're going out again this weekend!"

The smile disappeared from Talan's face. *What the fuck?* Macy had gone out with one of Keira's friends?

Macy answered, her voice nervous. "Did he? Say it was good? I wasn't sure, ya know, that my outfit was okay."

*Who gives a shit what you wore?*

"I'd say more than okay. His actual word was *spectacular*." She paused, Talan figured it was for effect, then continued, "What did you end up wearing?"

"The teal shirt and white pants."

"Nice. With the teal heels?"

"Um hm."

"Perfect! We'll have to start working on your outfit for this weekend right away. He's taking you to—"

Talan didn't want to hear more. He closed the drawer, taking a file without looking at it, and went back to his office.

He sat down, tossed the folder he'd brought back on his desk. He'd been so completely wrong about Macy. Her radiant smile in the Shelby, the way she'd whispered when they'd looked at the back of her camera, the pulse he'd seen beating in the hollow of her throat, had all been because of that stupid car. It'd had nothing to do with him. The sting of disappointment was hot and bitter, and he totally deserved it.

With practiced control he pushed thoughts of her away, forced them to occupy the space in the shadowed corners of his mind where a lifetime of other unrealized dreams lived, and dove into work.

*** ***

The convertible Mustang Macy was working on had a completely different feel from the Shelby. This car made her think of cruising to the beach with the top down, singing to the radio. She could feel the sun shining, wind blowing through her hair, practically smell salt water as they drew close to the shore. It was a damn shame Talan hadn't taken her out. Gage never let her do anything other than the commuter lot and this car deserved more.

She'd have preferred that Talan take her anyway, even if it was just behind the warehouse.

She finished the last picture and started burning DVDs. It was ridiculous that they weren't using the Cloud, but she knew classic car guys were notoriously resistant to any technology newer than their car, which meant most everything at Dawson's was decades behind.

Once she had the second DVD done, she labeled it and put it on Keira's desk before she headed out to bring the first copy to Paul. She sat in the chair next to him. "Hey."

He glanced over. "Hey, Mace. What'cha got?"

"The convertible Mustang." She handed him the disc. "What are you working on?"

"That T-Bird from a couple days ago."

She looked at his page layout. "That's not right."

"What's not right?"

"It's not really a Roadster." She pointed at the screen, "The tonneau cover's aftermarket."

"I'm sorry, Macy." He smiled apologetically. "I design catalog pages and handle the website, but I'm not a car guy."

"The tonneau cover is the hardtop on this car."

"And?"

She never minded explaining to people who wanted to learn. "Convertibles were only available with soft tops. If it has a hard top it's a Roadster. But there were only four hundred and fifty-five Roadsters made and they're super expensive, if you can find one. So a lot of people have turned their convertibles into Roadster look-a-likes. If you don't know the differences, and you don't run the VIN, it's easy to be fooled."

"Huh." Paul leaned forward, looking interested. "How'd you know that?"

She smiled a little. "I may not be a guy, but I am into cars."

"What did Talan say about this?"

"I didn't tell him." Suddenly uneasy, she said, "I assumed he'd see it himself."

"I'm sure he did. He probably just didn't update the file yet." Paul tried to shrug it off. "For now, I'll move on to this." He held up the disc Macy had brought.

"I guess I better work on editing the rest of this morning's pictures." She walked slowly back downstairs, thinking she should have said something about the T-bird as soon as she'd noticed there was a problem.

In her office, she saw Keira's desk was empty and Talan's door was open. She stuck her head in his doorway, assured herself that Keira wasn't there. She didn't want to get caught up in another conversation about Zack, especially not in front of Talan. Satisfied that he was alone, she knocked on the door frame. "Talan?"

He raised his eyes to meet hers. "Yeah?"

She wished she'd thought about what to say before she'd knocked. A flash of heat filled her face and she blurted out, "I'm really sorry I didn't tell you about the T-Bird. I should have, as soon as I noticed there was a problem."

His eyebrows drew together. "What T-Bird?"

"The '63."

"What problem?"

"That it's listed as a Roadster." Admitting this was so uncomfortable. All she wanted was to tell him quickly and go back to work.

"It is a Roadster."

Macy shook her head. "No, it's not."

"Yeah, it is."

"No, it's not."

Sounding annoyed, he asked, "How do you know that?"

"Because I ran the VIN when I realized the tonneau cover's aftermarket."

"That entire car's original."

"It's not. The top's got a chip on one corner and the original paint was red. But the car has always been black."

"So?"

"So if the tonneau cover's not original, it's not a real Roadster."

Talan sat forward and threw his pen on the desk. "Maybe they had to replace the top."

"No. That car was a convertible and someone faked it to look like a Roadster." *What the hell? He should know this.*

He snapped at her, "How do you even know what that car is?"

"Because it's my job."

"No, it's not. You're just supposed to take pictures."

"So, you're saying if I know there's a problem I shouldn't tell you?" She crossed her arms and tapped one foot. "I'm supposed to just keep what I know to myself?"

"Yeah, because you don't know anything. You're just the photographer."

Her heart beat harder as anger swelled. She hissed, "I know what I'm talking about, Talan. I decoded the VIN. It's a convertible."

Talan growled back, "No shit it's a convertible. It's a convertible Roadster."

She narrowed her eyes at him. "Those are two different cars, *Talan*. Because it's a *Thunderbird*."

"You can't have a Roadster that isn't a convertible, *Macy*. A Roadster is just a convertible with a hardtop."

"No, it's not. That car also had custom wire wheels, a grab bar, and different emblems." She ticked each thing off on her fingers.

"And the car you photographed has all that."

She could see the vein in his forehead throbbing, knew he was mad, and didn't care. She was mad, too. "I know that. But when Ford assigned VIN numbers to Thunderbirds in 1963 they gave a different code to Roadsters, specifically to differentiate between convertibles. Roadsters have a body code of 89 and convertibles are 85. You should have seen that yourself. Because that is *your* job."

"Get out of my office."

"I'm right, Talan."

"I said, get *out* of my *office*."

She spun on her heel and stalked out. She didn't have to take that. Talan had been right about one thing. She'd been hired to take pictures, not research cars.

\*\*\* \*\*\*

Talan resisted the urge to push everything off his desk. Instead, he picked up a pencil, snapped it in half and in quick succession hurled both pieces as hard as he could across the room. They bounced off the far wall and fell harmlessly to the floor, one rolling under a bookshelf and the other coming to stop in the middle of the room.

There was no way in hell that car wasn't a Roadster. He'd been raised with this shit. He knew what he was talking about.

Macy had no right sticking her nose in his business anyway. Macy, who was dating some fucking guy Keira was friends with. Because, yeah, Macy was so much like Keira and her friends. That was the most ridiculous thought. He couldn't imagine she had anything in common with anyone Keira knew.

But maybe she did. What did he really know about her? Nothing, except she wore cool shirts to work, she took her coffee with cream and sugar, and she was into cars.

Fuck, she was into cars. Maybe she *had* been right. Panic mingled with the anger. He'd been so sure he knew what that car was he hadn't bothered to check it. He *always* checked. Of course the only time he didn't would be the one time he should have.

He turned to his computer and started typing.

*** ***

Macy closed her laptop without bothering to turn it off, smothering the urge to slam it shut only because she knew that if she broke it, she'd regret it. She crammed it in the case with her headphones, grabbed her purse and camera, and stormed out.

Outside, she got in her car, dropped her bags on the passenger side floor, and slammed her door. Her tires squealed as she pulled out of the parking lot and headed for the highway.

The rental car wasn't fun to drive; she'd chosen it because it was cheap to rent and cheap to drive. Even so, driving was good. She flew past the exit for the commuter lot, past the exit for the gas station where she'd photographed the Shelby, and out into the desert.

After a while she began to slow down, the anger slipping away, fear replacing it.

She'd walked out of work.

It wasn't the first time she'd walked out of a job, but it was the first time she'd walked away from one she liked. And it was definitely the first time she'd done it two thousand miles from home.

She started to think she should turn around. Go apologize. But to who? Talan? For what? Pointing out he was wrong? He was wrong. And she'd possibly saved his ass. His, and Gage's and all of Dawson's. People got sued for misrepresenting cars, even if it was unintentional. It wasn't just that one car, either. If word got out and people started to think Dawson's didn't fact-check it would destroy their reputation and most likely ruin their entire business.

Macy knew intimately that making a mistake in this world wasn't something that could be kept quiet.

Righteous indignation replaced the fear. Really, Talan should be apologizing to her.

Maybe she should call Gage and explain what had happened.

Or maybe she should hope that it all just kind of went away.

Paralyzed by uncertainty, she continued to drive. Miles of nothing surrounded her, something she'd never seen before coming to Arizona. The desert wasn't truly flat, as she'd always imagined, or truly empty. The landscape that stretched out before her was covered with low-lying pale green or brown bushes. Here and there cacti broke the monotony. And in the distance— far, far in the distance— there were mountains.

The desolation was undeniable, though. There was not one single building, not even a gas station, anywhere within sight.

There were easily fifty miles behind her when she came to a scenic overlook. She parked in a random spot in the deserted lot, got out and walked to the edge of the asphalt. Sun baked the earth, nothing moved, not even a breath of wind. Sweat began to trickle down her back. If it was this hot now, she couldn't imagine what it would be like in August. That wasn't something that had crossed her mind when she'd agreed to take this job, on a freezing cold day in Connecticut.

She missed Connecticut. Missed living at home, where she ate dinner with her parents every night and her brothers and their girlfriends came over on Sundays. Where her friends were always around, where she'd always had someone to turn to when she had a problem.

Normally she'd have called Logan. Except he expected her to come crawling home again. She didn't want to go home. She just wanted someone to talk to who would listen and not judge her, even when her feelings were conflicted.

It was tempting to call Emma. But then Macy would have to admit how lonely she was, which would lead to Emma reminding Macy that she should have known that would happen and she never should have left Connecticut in the first place.

Tears joined the sweat now running down her face. Nothing was working out the way she'd thought. She hadn't made any real friends. She was dating Zack, even though she didn't really like him, because she was lonely. And Talan had just yelled at her for no reason.

Out of desperation, she called her mom. The phone rang five times, then went to voice mail.

She didn't leave a message.

*** ***

Macy stood in the shower and let the hot water wash the dust off.

Eventually got out, pulled on a t-shirt and a pair of yoga shorts, put her hair in a ponytail, and stood in the middle of her hotel room. Sighing, she thought she had to do something about dinner. Maybe she'd order pizza. She wouldn't have to go anywhere, and she'd have enough left over for lunch the next day.

As she moved to pick up her cell phone it rang. 'Mom' flashed across the screen. She couldn't keep her voice from trembling as she answered. "Mom?"

"Macy? What's wrong?"

The tears came, and between sobs she told her mom how unhappy she was. She missed her family, her friends, her bed in her old room.

Her mom consoled her. "Sweetheart, if you're really that miserable, why don't you come home."

"I can't. I have to work."

"The job with Aunt Holly is still available. I'll call her tomorrow and let her know you're interested. And I heard Emma's looking for a roommate. That would be perfect for the two of you."

"Mom—"

"I don't think we'll be able to get a flight tomorrow." She paused and Macy could hear typing. "They're really expensive on such short notice. If you can wait a couple days…"

She let her mom's voice roll over her, secure in the knowledge that she would make everything all right.

# Chapter 12

Talan ran his finger over the page, down the list of cars. Some things were easier to find online. The quickest way to verify production numbers, though, was still books. He'd been looking numbers up in these books since he'd learned to read. On weekends, during dinner, any time he couldn't find someplace else to be, his dad would send him to check something while he talked to a never-ending stream of clients, buyers, and other dealers.

Vanessa and Sandra came into the outer office to talk to Keira. Talan had started back towards his desk when he heard Vanessa say Macy's name. Ignoring the hurt it evoked, he stopped to listen.

Vanessa told Keira, "You can't see it. She wore some crappy t-shirt again."

Keira said, "I told her specifically to wear the pink cold-shoulder shirt."

Talan had no idea what that was, but he was happy just on principle to hear that Macy hadn't done what Keira had told her.

Sandra asked, "Is it really that bad? I mean, lots of people have tattoos."

"People also pierce their tongues and dye their hair to look like cotton candy." Vanessa's tone was so full of disdain, Talan felt instant sympathy for anyone she didn't approve of.

"It's not even pretty." Keira didn't sound as nasty as Vanessa but

Talan could hear disapproval in her voice, too. "I mean, if you have to ruin your body it should at least be something you can be proud of."

"It's too bad you didn't get a better picture," Vanessa said.

Keira assured her, "I'll get her to wear that shirt tomorrow."

Talan's blood pounded at the idea of Keira trying to trick Macy into wearing a shirt specifically so they could see her tattoo, so they could all talk about her behind her back. He put the book back on the shelf and sauntered through the door. The three women barely glanced at him until he said, "If you want to see Macy's tattoo, why don't you just ask?"

All three snapped around to stare at him. The looks of shock and guilt were priceless. Satisfied, he continued through the office and down the hall to get himself a much-deserved cup of coffee.

By the time he was back, Keira was alone. She didn't look up as he passed through. He settled into his chair, intent on getting work done. His thoughts kept drifting, though, to Macy. He googled 'cold shoulder shirt' and scrolled through pictures. He'd love to see Macy in a shirt like that. Her shoulders would be freckled, like the rest of her. He'd take her hand and pull her in close, kiss the bare skin the shirt would reveal, linger over her exposed shoulder.

Except when he pictured her the cold-shoulder shirt became a Beatles t-shirt. That was better, more Macy. He'd slip his hands up and under the fabric, trace his fingers along her skin and—

"Talan." Gage interrupted his thoughts.

"What?" He jerked his head up, startled back to reality.

Gage shut the door harder than was necessary and came into Talan's office. "What the hell is wrong with you?"

*What's wrong with me?* He was dreaming of getting with Macy. Because even if being with her were possible, even if she'd forgiven him for yelling at her about the T-bird, she was dating some fucking asshole Keira was friends with. That made no goddamn sense. And

Gage was staring at him, obviously pissed off. Exactly not what he wanted to deal with right then. "Do you need something?"

"I need you to not fuck up my life."

"Pretty sure you're capable of doing that on your own."

Gage's eyes narrowed. "*You* can get away with this kind of shit. Macy can't."

Not having to fake puzzlement, he asked, "What shit?"

"The Shelby."

"What about the Shelby?"

"You let Macy drive it."

Not about to change his story, he said, "No, I didn't."

"I'm not an idiot, Talan. There's no way you hit 120 miles an hour in anything."

The insult wasn't nearly as important as his curiosity about how Gage, and their dad, knew how fast Macy had gone. "How'd you know that, anyway?"

"Know that you let Macy drive?"

"Know how fast we went."

The vein in the center of Gage's forehead began to throb. "That car has real-time GPS tracking. A theft-deterrent system that notifies Brent Peters if the speedometer hits a hundred. Lucky for you," his face reddened as he finished, "Brent was more interested in how the car handled than the fact that my dumbass little brother let my fucking photographer drive it!"

"I told you, I was driving."

"Bullshit. You couldn't care less about driving that car." He paced to the wall and came back, slightly calmer. "Here's the deal. Dad thinks you found a car you couldn't resist. He's thrilled, going on and on about how you've finally come around. But if he knew it was Macy, she'd be gone. I need her, so I'm not going to tell Dad who was driving. And you," he pointed at Talan, "are not going to tell Macy I know you let her drive. What you are going to do is never let her drive again. Got it?"

"I got it." He was completely satisfied with his father thinking he'd found a car he couldn't resist. It was much better than the truth; he'd found a girl he couldn't resist. And the relief at not getting her fired was immense.

"Good. Because I've got a meeting this morning and I need you to drive her." Gage pulled a paper from his pocket, set it on the corner of the desk. "I'm sure neither of you will be tempted to push any of these. Macy has no interest in driving big classics."

"I'm busy." Talan pushed the list back.

Gage ignored the movement. "Whatever you're doing can wait."

*** ***

Macy sat on the couch outside Gage's office and played Candy Crush. She felt guilty about playing a game at work, but there was absolutely nothing else for her to do while she waited for someone to take her out to drive. Unless she wanted to talk to Keira, or one of the women from accounting or Buyer Services, and she'd already had her fill of the office girls for one day.

Vanessa and Sandra had been at Celeste's desk in the foyer when she'd come in that morning. They'd made a big deal about wanting to see one of the shirts she'd bought with Keira. It was utterly ridiculous. She wasn't about to wear a fancy shirt to work, where she pretty much always ended up filthy. They'd only left her alone when she'd promised to text a picture of it. Although why they cared was beyond her.

She lined up another row of purple candies and watched them disappear, to be replaced with new candies, her mind not really on the game. She hadn't realized that girl talk was so focused on clothes. It hadn't been like that with her and Emma. They'd talked about a million things; which guys they thought were hot, how unbelievably stupid it was that Brit Lit was a required class, what they wanted to do when they were finally on their own. That had been a big topic of conversation, and it had turned out to be as exciting as Brit Lit. They'd been adults for years and still had never met anyone famous or gone skydiving or been to Spring Break in Cancun. Macy didn't even have her own place; she'd moved from her parents' into a hotel.

Just a few weeks before, she'd thought she was finally going to act on some of those plans. She'd been so excited to go out on her own, to start looking at apartments and really thinking about buying a car.

Now look where she was. On her way back home, where she could slip back into the role of the going nowhere, designated driver, on-call friend. And she wouldn't even have a job she liked.

Her phone beeped and a text previewed over top of her game. Her mom, sending flight options.

Macy shut all the windows on her phone, leaned back against the couch and closed her eyes. Going home meant she wouldn't have to figure out what to eat for dinner every night, and remember to do her laundry, and she wouldn't feel so out of place. *Because you know your place there.*

If she went home she'd have to quit Dawson's. Even in her mind it was hard. She'd be leaving Gage with no photographer, and a whole lot of cars to be photographed, and that didn't feel right. He'd given her a second chance and she felt indebted to him.

Maybe things weren't working out the way she'd thought, but she was shooting cars again. If she walked away it would mean more than just leaving this job. It would be career ending. And this, shooting cars, was her career.

She sat up and began a text to her mom, "Thank you for doing this, but I'm going to stick it out here." *That's terrible.* She deleted it and started again, "Hi Mom, thanks for listening last night. I had such a bad day yesterday. Today I'm feeling much better, and I'm going to make this work."

Not satisfied, she deleted that and typed, "Hi Mom, thanks for listening yesterday and for sending flight options." *Blah.*

"Macy?"

She bolted upright. "What?"

Talan's lips pressed together for a moment as he eyed her. She wondered if the sudden wave of guilt she felt showed on her face. If it did, he didn't mention it. "Let's go."

A million things raced through her mind, foremost among them that she didn't want to be cooped up in a car with him. Blood pounded in her ears as she followed him through the lot and watched him unlock a boat of a Packard. He headed for the commuter lot without asking what she wanted. She stared out the window, fixated on how uncomfortable she was.

He broke the silence. "What's your tattoo of?"

"What?"

"Your tattoo. What's it of?"

She turned in her seat to face him. "How'd you know I have a tattoo?"

"Once Keira knows something, there's no keeping it a secret." He took the exit for the commuter lot.

"It's not a secret." She didn't purposely hide it, but she'd had Logan place it so a t-shirt would cover everything completely. Keira would know, because she'd seen Macy in that stupid black dress. She remembered that Keira'd been texting outside the dressing room. Had she been texting Talan that day about Macy's tattoo? That didn't even make sense. "Why do you want to know?"

"Just making conversation."

"Don't you think that's a pretty personal question, just to be making conversation?"

"No." He parked the car in exactly the spot she always used, shut the ignition off and turned to her.

His gaze made her face feel hot. He was waiting for an answer. There was no real reason not to tell him, other than that she was still pissed about the way he'd treated her. She opened the car door and got out. She was here to do a job, and that's what she was going to do.

"Macy?"

She stopped, considered ignoring him, then turned back.

He stood on the other side of the car and leaned his arms on the roof, toyed with the car keys. "I'm sorry about yesterday." He looked at his hands, at the keys he was nervously playing with. "I didn't check that car." He raised his eyes to meet hers. "I looked at the write-up the owner had given us, matched it to the car, and never went any further."

Usually she was quick to forgive; everyone lost it once in a while. But he'd made that comment, about her being "just the photographer," and that was total bullshit. "Nice, Talan. And you're lecturing me about what my job is?"

His expression tightened. "I'm aware of what my job is."

"Doesn't seem like it."

"This isn't my thing. I never wanted to be here in the first place."

"But you are. And it's your responsibility to research those cars."

"I know that."

Her only response was to raise an eyebrow.

He took a deep breath, let it out slowly, like he was considering whether or not to say more. "Do you know Travis O'Dell?"

"No."

"Up until a couple years ago he was *the* guy to see if you wanted something special. He sold to movie stars, museums, big time shit. My dad knew him from way back. He used to have dinner at our house, they made deals all the time. Then, he was arrested for fraud. He'd been Frankensteining cars. Pulling the engine from a rusted-out car and dropping it into one with a good body and bad motor or taking a car that'd been smashed in the front and pairing it with one that had been smashed in the rear."

Macy shrugged. "That's not a big deal. Wylie did stuff like that all the time."

"But Wylie was upfront about it. Travis labeled his cars as original, numbers matching. He faked paperwork, replaced VIN tags." Talan shook his head. "When Gage took over the classics division, at least half his inventory came from Travis. Gage had no idea if the cars he'd been selling were legit. My first six months here were spent figuring that out. To be safe, we bought back cars, or made trades, did anything our buyers wanted to make sure they were happy and didn't doubt we were doing our best to be honest. So, yeah, I get it, Macy. This is serious shit."

He jiggled the keys, looked around like he was avoiding her purposely, and finally turned his attention back. "I knew as soon as you said Thunderbird that I'd fucked up." His face reddened. "I panicked, and I took it out on you."

He was so obviously upset, she was having a hard time hanging onto her anger. "It's okay."

"No, it's really not." He ran a hand through his hair. "I hate cars. As far as I'm concerned, they get you where you need to go." He shrugged. "I'm not here for the cars."

"Talan—" She didn't really know what to say, so she just stopped.

He dropped his arms, stuck his hands in his pockets. "You were right. That car's faked." He walked away, to wait for her to take pictures.

As she set up her shots, moving to get the best angles and lighting possible under the relentless Arizona sun, she could feel Talan's eyes on her. It wasn't her imagination; every time she glanced in his direction he was watching. She wondered what he was thinking. Probably that she'd gloat about being right.

She didn't want to gloat. It'd never been about that.

She thought about what he'd said, that he'd never wanted to be there in the first place. That's exactly how she'd feel if she went home and took that office job. She glanced his way again, caught his eye and quickly went back to looking through the camera.

It would be nice if they were able to talk again, the way they had the day they'd taken the Shelby out. Maybe she'd ask him why he was there, if it wasn't for the cars. But that seemed really personal. Probably not something she should ask.

Maybe she wanted to get personal with him.

Not really *maybe*.

She set her camera on the front seat, out of the sun, and walked to where he was leaning on the guardrail at the edge of the parking lot. "Do you want to see my tattoo?"

"Only if you want me to see it."

"I can't really show you everything without taking off my shirt." She turned and pulled the back of her shirt up as high as she could.

He moved closer, bending to look at her lower back. She could feel his breath on her skin. She closed her eyes and tried to ignore that she liked it. He stood up and she knew that if she moved back just a tiny bit she'd be against him. Maybe if she did he'd touch her hip, run his fingers over her skin, wrap his arm around her and hold her to him.

*What the hell, Macy!* She was letting her imagination run away with her. She tried to force herself not to think past the moment.

He spoke quietly, his breath soft on her neck. "It's beautiful. May I see the rest?"

She looked over her shoulder. His deep brown eyes held hers. She whispered, "Yes."

*** ***

124

As Talan pushed Macy's shirt higher he was very careful not to touch her more than was necessary. It felt like to do so would violate her trust. She wasn't going around showing this off to just anyone, and despite his cavalier attitude about it earlier he understood wanting privacy. "The Mercury," he deliberately kept his voice soft, "is the first car you photographed."

"Mm hm."

He'd recognize the pointed tail lights of the cherry red convertible anywhere, even wrapped from Macy's side to the small of her back. "The work is amazing. The saturation, the shading, whoever did it is extremely talented. Did they work from your pictures?"

"He did."

Wishing he could trace it with his fingers, he followed the art with his eyes. The view of the car was from the back quarter, looking down so that the dashboard was visible. Stylized sheet music swirled from the car's radio, starting small and becoming wider as it made its way up the right side of Macy's back. Towards her shoulder blade the notes started to change. The flags grew into wings, the stems became legs, and by the top of her shoulder they'd morphed into a line of blackbirds in full flight.

He stepped back, leaned against the guardrail and folded his arms. He knew she was into the Beatles, he didn't need lyrics to guess what she was getting at. "'Blackbird' has always been one of my favorite songs."

Macy pulled her shirt back into place and turned around, one eyebrow arched. "Yeah?"

He smiled self-consciously. "My mom's a huge Beatles fan. Some of my earliest memories are things like her singing 'Ob-La-Di' while she did dishes or cranking 'Hey Jude' in the car."

"'Ob-La-Di' is kind of a messed up song."

"Not nearly as messed up as 'Maxwell's Silver Hammer.'"

"True." She leaned next to him on the guardrail. "It's kind of like 'Pumped Up Kicks'. They're both horrible stories that people love to sing."

She was talking to him. God, he wanted her to continue. "There's a lot of songs people love to sing that are horrible if you listen to the words."

"My friend Emma always gets mad when I try to tell her what songs are about. She tells me to just shut up and sing."

"You can't shut up if you're singing."

He was rewarded with a huge smile. "That's exactly what I said!"

Her reaction was encouraging enough for him to ask, "So what's the story behind your tattoo?"

She shrugged. "No story."

He wasn't buying that. "Every tattoo has a story."

"I'm a car photographer. I like Mercurys."

That much was obvious. It was the song, the birds in flight, that had caught his attention. "Why 'Blackbird'?"

She looked out at the parking lot. He liked the way her nose turned up a little at the end, and the way her curls framed her face. "It's stupid."

He shook his head. "If it means something to you, it's not stupid."

She turned back to him. "Some people say that song's about Alzheimer's."

"Is that what it means to you?"

"No. I don't think that's what Paul McCartney had in mind when he wrote it, either. When I heard that, I dug to see if I could figure out the truth."

He was intrigued. These were things he understood; the need to dig out the truth, a true love for music. No wonder he hadn't been able to stop thinking about her no matter how hard he tried. "And?"

"He's given conflicting stories. I finally decided that this time Emma

126

was right and I should just shut up and sing. Or at least decide on my own what the song meant to me."

"What's it mean to you?"

"To me it's about picking up the pieces, and the moment you first fly."

Softly, so he didn't come across as snippy, he asked, "What's that got to do with the car?"

She fidgeted, then settled against the rail again. The sun shone full on her, catching her eyes, highlighting the lines of sky blue radiating out from the darkness of her pupils. He hoped she never looked away.

"It took me a long time to figure out what I was good at. For a while I was pretty sure I wasn't good at anything." She smiled a bit as she admitted, "I flunked out of college three times before I ended up in photography school, and that was nearly a disaster, too. I went there because I thought it would be fun, running around with a camera taking pictures of whatever caught my attention. But it wasn't anything like that. You have to know how to use a manual camera, position studio lights properly, pose people, make sets, it's really a ton of work. I hated portraiture, I sucked at commercial work, really the only thing I was any good at was retouching. Probably because it doesn't require you to talk to people."

He smiled a little. "You don't seem to have trouble talking to people."

She laughed. "I wish."

"You're talking to me."

She looked at him for a long moment. "Anyway, everyone there was good at something. They did amazing kids pictures or stunning still lifes. I," she pointed to herself, "couldn't even figure out how to balance on-camera flash with natural light."

"That's always been a problem for me, too."

A grin spread over her face. "So, anyway, we had this assignment to photograph a car. Most everyone did pictures of their own cars, but I didn't have one. I thought I was going to have to call my mom and beg her to drive up to Massachusetts so I could photograph hers. I was walking home, thinking about how much I didn't want to call for help, and watching the guy across the street from my apartment washing his car. Ya know, how you kind of just look someplace when you're walking, without thinking about it?"

"Um hm."

"I was halfway up the stairs to my apartment before I realized this guy loved his car. Like *loved*, the way most people love their kids. He probably thought I was nuts, the way I ran over there and begged him to let me photograph it. But it worked out, and we did the pictures, and I was so terrified that I was screwing up. Then, when I sat down to edit them that night, I put the Beatles on, because by then I was really missing my mom and it made me think of her.

"Then the pictures started to open on my screen." She looked at him and he could imagine that the look she was giving him, wonder and pride and pure joy, must have been exactly what she'd felt in that moment. "They were phenomenal. Like, the kind of beautiful the other students were turning in. I could barely believe I'd taken them. It was the first time I'd ever felt that awe.

"The day after I handed in the assignment my commercial photography instructor called me into her office." She paused, messed with the hem of her shirt. "There had been a few times before that I thought I'd done really well on an assignment, only to be told I had it completely wrong, so I figured I'd failed this too." She gave him a half-smile. "I was literally rehearsing how I was going to tell my mom I'd flunked out again when the instructor told me she'd always known I had it in me."

"So you didn't flunk out?"

"Nope. One of the crazy things about photography is that you don't have to be good at everything to succeed. You only need to find a niche."

"And this is yours."

"Yup." She shrugged. "And every time I think about how I ended up doing this, I remember that night, alone in my room with 'Blackbird' playing in the background, and how it just seemed so perfect."

"That's really cool, Macy."

She smiled. It was very sweet, and it made her seem vulnerable. "I should probably finish this car."

He stood to the side until she needed the car moved. He couldn't take his eyes off her. The best thing was, once in a while she glanced at him. And every time she smiled.

*** ***

Macy felt like she was walking on air. The whole morning had been so perfect. As they stepped into her office, Talan glanced at her and a quick smile flickered across his features. Then he was in his office, leaving Macy with Keira. Trying to avoid conversation, she quickly pulled out her headphones. It didn't matter if she had music on or not, as long as Keira thought she couldn't hear her.

A few minutes later the screen on her phone lit up. She glanced at it, saw Zack's name, and her stomach tightened in a very unpleasant way.

There was no way to avoid this. Keira was right there and she'd want to know why Macy hadn't answered. She pushed the headphones off and answered. "Hello?"

"Hey, Macy. It's Zack. I know this is last minute, but I just scored box seats to see YaWon J tonight."

Everything good she'd felt just a second before evaporated. Not only was she not into hip-hop at all, the idea of going out with Zack just didn't excite her.

"Macy?"

"Sorry, I was thinking. I don't know. I have to work tomorrow."

"Don't worry, I've got it all planned out. You get out of work at five, so I'll pick you up at six-thirty which will give you plenty of time to shower and get ready. It's only fifteen minutes away, they've got a full dinner menu so we don't need to stop before, and with preferred parking we won't have to find a parking garage. We can be in our seats by seven. The show starts at seven-thirty, with a half-hour intermission it'll be over by ten. I can have you home by ten-forty-five. Since you normally go to bed at midnight, that shouldn't be a problem."

*He's got it all planned. Of course. Probably on a spreadsheet.* "Zack, I—" *I don't know how to tell you that I'm just not into you.*

"See you at six-thirty." He hung up.

Macy stared at her phone, completely clueless how to get out of this.

"Well?" Keira was looking expectantly at her.

"He has tickets to see YaWon J. Tonight."

Keira clasped her hands together and made a sort of low squealing noise. "Oh. My. God. Macy. What are you going to wear?"

*** ***

Talan tried to ignore what was going on in the outer office. Apparently, Macy was going out with that guy and she didn't have what Keira considered an appropriate outfit. They were discussing in ridiculous detail every piece of clothing she *did* own. They'd gotten Vanessa and Sandra for backup and now they were calling all the women in the office to see if anyone was wearing jewelry that would go with Macy's navy dress because there wasn't enough time for Macy to go buy something. Who the hell bought jewelry to match one outfit, for one date? For that matter, who the hell put that much thought into it?

He stood abruptly, deciding he didn't care about front ends of Ford Fairlanes or portholes on Packards. He walked through Macy and Keira's office without stopping.

He wanted one thing: to be as far from Macy as he could get

# Chapter 13

Macy stood in front of the closet, looking through all the clothes she'd accumulated recently. Keira had been very specific about what she was supposed to wear. *Navy blue dress, ridiculous heels that I'll probably break my ankle in, and the stupid necklace from Tonya.*

She'd always just worn regular clothes when she went to concerts. It was about the music, feeling the energy of the band, being part of the crowd. Not listening to piped-in music inside a glass room, eating watercress sandwiches while holding up a pinky. She giggled at the visual that flashed through her mind.

None of that seemed appropriate for YaWon J anyway. Emma loved hip-hop and when she went to concerts she wore things like super tight leopard print skirts and shirts that could easily be mistaken for bras. The closest thing Macy had to that was the black dress with the crisscross spaghetti straps. The one that showed off her whole back.

She pulled the black dress off the hanger and struggled into it. There were at least three pairs of heels that would match— black to coordinate, red to accent, silver to shine— but Macy chose her purple Converse.

Grinning, she glanced at her reflection. For the first time since she'd met Zack, she was going out without makeup, and without straightening her hair. If Zack didn't like Macy for who she was, he didn't like Macy.

Instead of waiting for him to call from the parking lot, she went down to wait for him. She sat on the bench next to the front door and watched cars go by. She glanced at her phone. *Six-twenty. He's always exactly on time. Ten more minutes.*

Her stomach began to tighten with nerves. A blue car stopped at the light just before the hotel and for a second she thought it had to be Zack.

She jumped up and ran back upstairs.

In her room, she pulled off the black dress and put the navy one on. She yanked her sneakers off without unlacing them and crammed her feet into the ankle-breaking heels. If she was quick she could get her makeup done.

The phone rang just as she finished her mascara. "Hi, Zack."

"I'm here."

Cursing herself for not taking this seriously from the beginning, she headed down to meet him. She put lipstick on in the elevator, but there was nothing she could do about her hair. *Damn it, you had time to do your hair.* As soon as she saw him, she blurted, "I'm sorry, I ran out of time."

He opened her door. "It's fine." He definitely looked at her hair. "You look perfect."

She settled into the seat, but she couldn't relax. There was none of the usual excitement she felt when she was on her way to a concert. This was just nerves.

Once they'd parked the car in one of the spots reserved for Zack's company, she wished she could relax and enjoy the experience. They were escorted through security without being searched and led by an usher up a private staircase to their own door. Inside, the room was divided into two levels. The back, upper part had stools facing a bar, with a perfect view of the giant TV on the wall. The lower level, three steps down, had two black leather couches next to each other from which you could see the stage far below, and a coffee table with a vase of fresh flowers set on it.

Zack led her to the couches and handed her a menu from a side table. "We should order right away."

Macy read the first line on the menu and nearly choked. "Eighteen dollars for French fries?" She scanned down the items. "Thirty-four dollars for a hamburger? They charge an extra four bucks for a slice of cheese?"

He put his hand on her arm and glanced around before quietly telling her, "It's included, order whatever you want."

She set the menu on the coffee table. Even if she was hungry, which she wasn't, there was no way in hell she was going to let anyone pay $56 for a cheeseburger and fries.

The door opened behind them. Zack stood, so Macy did, too. An older man, in a dark blue suit, came in. He had his arm around a woman who looked at least twenty years younger than him. Her black miniskirt was low enough to show off the piercing in her navel.

"Macy, this is my boss, Leon." Zack indicated the man. "And Charla." Macy held out her hand. "It's nice to meet you."

Leon shook her hand, squeezing so hard she had to struggle not to grimace. He smiled warmly as he said, "It's a pleasure to meet you, Macy."

The men sat, one on each couch so the women ended up on the ends. Zack and Leon launched into a conversation about work, which was fine with Macy. She had nothing to say anyway.

A few minutes later a waitress came in. Zack ordered Macy a cheeseburger and French fries without asking her first. She felt her face turn red, both at the indignity of having her meal ordered for her and because that wasn't what she wanted.

Leon ordered for himself and Charla, and told the waitress to put all four meals on his tab. Charla seemed perfectly happy to have the choice made for her, and her meal paid for.

Macy glanced at her, thinking maybe they'd be able to talk. But the other woman was peering intently down at the stage and bouncing slightly in her seat. *Glad one of us is excited for this concert.*

When the music started, Leon and Zack went to the back of the room and sat at the bar to continue their conversation. Charla stood up and danced seductively. Macy sat on the couch and considered playing Candy Crush.

When the waitress came back with their food, she asked, "Do you have Mojitos?"

Zack spoke up, "Macy, are you sure?"

Feeling like a small child who'd been scolded, she said, "I'll have a water."

She sat on the couch and picked at her French fries. Zack and Leon went back to talking. Charla continued dancing, singing every word to every song. *At least she doesn't talk over the music.*

*** ***

Zack pulled up to Macy's hotel at exactly quarter to eleven. He squeezed Macy's knee. "I had a great time tonight."

Guilt gripped her guts. *He's serious.* She dropped her gaze to where his hand touched her leg.

"Hey, are you okay?"

She raised her eyes to meet his. "Yeah. Just tired. Thanks for taking me out."

"I'm happy to." He smiled proudly. "I know you prefer concerts to sporting events."

*Jeez, he doesn't understand me at all. But he's trying so hard.* Still, it was awkward when he kissed her. She purposely kept it short, pulling away and saying, "I better get to bed."

"Call me."

She smiled tightly as she got out of the car. *You need to end this.* She knew he watched until she was through the doors, because she didn't hear the car pull away.

She would end it. She just had to find a way to do it without hurting Zack. Because as much as he was an overbearing prick, he wasn't actually an asshole.

# Chapter 14

It was way too early on a Saturday for the phone to be ringing. Talan rolled over and squinted at his sister's name on the screen before answering, "Hey, Liss."

"Hi, Uncle Talan!"

Recognizing his niece's voice, he said, "Hi, Sonja."

"Are you coming to Grandma's today?"

He sat up, rubbed a hand over his eyes and tried to think what holiday it was that he was supposed to go to his mom's. Failing, he asked, "Am I supposed to?"

"We're going. So, if you were going too maybe I could show you how much I've been practicing."

"Yeah, I'll be there. What time?" He hadn't intended to go to his mom's, but he didn't have anything else planned, and Sonja sounded so excited.

"My mom said we're leaving in five minutes."

He glanced at the clock. *Nine-thirty on Saturday? Seriously?* "I'm, um, just have to take a shower and I'll be there."

"Okay. I'll see you then."

He pulled the covers over his head. After a minute, he gave in and got up. If he was going to teach Sonja how to play the piano, he better figure out how.

He started coffee brewing, then sat at the island and searched the internet for basic lesson plans for beginner pianists.

*** ***

Talan couldn't suppress a smile as he opened his mom's front door. In the back room, Sonja was already playing "Hot Cross Buns" repeatedly.

He sat next to her. "You *have* been practicing."

She grinned. "Every day after school."

"I stopped by the music store on my way over. If you really want to learn, we have to do this right." He handed her a book. "And you should have your own book."

She read the title, in white across the top of the orange cover. "Book one, for piano." Earnestly, she said, "I really want to learn."

He gently took the book back. "The first thing you do, every time you sit down, is make sure you're in the right position. In the center of the bench, with your back nice and straight. Do you remember where to place your hands?"

She put her hands over the keys.

"Good. Do you remember the names of the keys?"

They went over the basics; how to read music, how the notes on the paper went with the piano keys, what a whole note was. Then they worked on songs, starting at the first one in the book.

When Sonja started to fidget, he assigned her pieces to practice for the following weekend. He wrote the date in the corner of each page, remembering how his teacher had done it all those years ago. "You need to practice every day, for at least half an hour."

"Is that how long you used to practice for?"

"I practiced a bit longer than that."

"How much longer?"

It didn't seem quite right to tell her the truth; hours on end, every single day. Instead, he said, "Grandma couldn't keep me away from the piano."

"I'll practice, I promise." Her gaze shifted to the windows, and her siblings in the pool. "Does practice with you count for today?"

"Yes, definitely." He smiled, glad she wasn't as single-minded as he'd been.

She gave him a huge hug. "Thank you for the book, and for teaching me."

He hugged her back, "No problem."

Alone, he turned back to the piano.

Playing had been a lifeline for him. When his father had tried to sign him up for a second year of football, something Talan was neither interested in or suited to, his mother had stepped in and said they couldn't risk him injuring his fingers. Later, when he'd wanted to avoid going on trips, being trapped in the truck with his dad and Gage while they drove trailers full of cars all over the country, he'd started volunteering to play for the local community theater, for school plays, for anything that would give him an excuse not to go. And when his parents fought, he'd sat at the piano and played.

He stared at the ivory keys, hearing his father in his memory. How he'd yelled about dinner not being on the table, or about how much Talan's mom had spent at the grocery store, or that she didn't appreciate how hard he worked. Talan had tried to drown out their voices, played louder and faster.

No matter how hard he tried, it hadn't been loud enough to drown out his father yelling about Talan. That Talan should be spending his time on more worthwhile things. How much his lessons cost. That he needed *peace and quiet* and could Talan *just stop that fucking noise!*

Talan would teach Sonja to play piano, but he'd never play for himself again.

# Chapter 15

Macy followed Talan silently. Although he still brought her coffee all the time, they hadn't had a conversation since the day she'd shown him her tattoo.

She'd have liked to talk to him, but it was impossible since she shared an office with Keira. All Keira ever wanted to talk about was Zack. And what outfit Macy was going to wear out to dinner. Both were topics she tried to avoid, especially when Talan was in the room.

Talan led her to a baby blue Chevy Step Side. As soon as she saw the pickup truck she broke the silence and asked, "Talan? Can we take this out to Route 32?"

He didn't answer; he just got in the driver's seat and closed his door. But once she was settled, he headed for Route 32.

In the days between deciding to take this job and actually starting there, she'd researched locations. This one had been a surprise. She'd had no idea there was commercial agriculture in Arizona, much less that they had citrus groves. After she'd found out she wasn't going to be allowed to take cars where she wanted, she'd filed all her research in the back of her brain and waited for a chance to use it.

After miles of driving in silence the citrus grove came into view, rows and rows of trees on both sides of the road. She asked, "Can you stop? Just up here."

He started to pull to the side. She clarified, "No, just stop. I want it to look like you're driving down the street."

He looked at her, hard, and spoke for the first time in days. "I can't stop in the middle of the road."

"Why not?"

"Because blocking traffic is illegal."

She made a big show of looking around before she said, "There's no one around. So just stop, duck down, and I'll take the pictures I need. You don't even need to shut off the ignition."

"If someone comes I'm leaving your ass here to deal with it."

She rolled her eyes, but once the truck was stopped in the middle of the road she worked as fast as possible, framing her shots, adjusting settings, and shooting.

A pickup truck, faded red and in desperate need of a new muffler, passed them and her stomach tied into knots. She finished the front three-quarter shots and moved to do side shots. She didn't check the back of her camera to make sure she got what she wanted, she just bracketed exposures so she'd have both lighter and darker versions to work with. She could tweak the exposures in Photoshop if they were a little off.

After she'd done the rear three-quarter angle she ran back and got in the truck.

Talan sat up. "Ready?"

"We need front and back shots. It looks like there's a road up there." She sat on the edge of the seat, not buckled, as he turned onto a dirt road. It was perfect, except for the sign declaring this as private property. There was no way she was going to pass up the chance to do this truck on a dirt road between rows of citrus trees, though. "Just stop right here. I'll be quick."

He looked skeptical. "Macy, this is private property."

"I'll be quick." Before he had a chance to argue she jumped out of the truck. She ran to the front, did five shots, ran to the back and did five more, then ran and climbed back in the cab.

Talan sat up and immediately put the truck in gear, pulled a U-turn and headed back the way they'd come. The red truck with the loud muffler turned onto the street and stopped, blocking the way.

Macy's heart hammered as Talan came to a stop. The driver of the truck wore a cowboy hat and Macy was sure there was a shotgun mounted behind his head. She whispered, "Talan, I'm sorry."

The red truck began moving towards them. Straight towards them. She buckled her seat belt.

Talan also began moving, but he steered as far as possible towards the right side of the road. At the last second, the other truck moved to the left.

Once they were back on the public street, she slumped into the seat. "We have to do the other side. Can you just pull over here?"

She wasn't really all that excited about this anymore, but she couldn't go back to Dawson's until she had all the pictures she needed.

*** ***

There was a police car at Dawson's when Talan pulled into the parking lot. It seemed ridiculous that it could be because he and Macy had been trespassing, but the coincidence was too much for it to be something else.

After the face-off with the guy in the red pickup, Talan hadn't been in any mood to help Macy take more pictures. He'd let her finish the exterior pictures but told her she could do the interior and engine after they got back. He grabbed the license plate off the truck, put the keys in the key cabinet, and left her to do what she needed.

He hadn't made it two steps into the building before Celeste stopped him. "Your father wants you."

"Thanks." As he walked down the hall, he tried to imagine what he'd feel like if his father fired him. Relieved. Happy? Definitely free.

Maybe he'd just quit and save his old man the trouble.

The same thought he always had when he considered quitting surfaced; *Gage needs me.* The issue with the T-bird had proven that. Dawson's needed someone conscientious to make sure their cars were legit. Although if Macy hadn't said anything he'd never have caught it, so apparently 'conscientious' didn't describe him anyway. He really did deserve to be fired.

He raised his hand to knock and his father's door opened.

"Get in here." His father held the door open until Talan was through, and then shut it. "Talan, you remember Officer Nebolt?"

He didn't. He nodded to the cop, who stood with his fists on his hips in front of the desk.

"Talan Dawson?"

"Yes."

"Were you driving an older, blue pickup truck this afternoon? Dealer plate DA496?"

He still had the plate in his hand. He held it up. "Yes, sir."

"Are you aware that you were on private property?"

He thought fast. "I am. We were just turning around and we were already on the street before we saw the sign."

Officer Nebolt jotted something in a note pad. "What were you doing there?"

"Taking pictures of the truck we were driving."

He answered a bunch of other questions, only leaving out that Macy had taken pictures on the private road. As soon as he could, he'd tell her to delete those.

Officer Nebolt slipped the pad into his breast pocket. "In the future, stay off private property."

"Yes, sir. I will."

Talan tried to follow the cop out but his father stopped him. "Sit."

He dropped into a chair, noticing that his dad's face was already pink.

"First the Shelby, now this? What the fuck is the matter with you?"

"It wasn't a big deal. We stopped on the side of the road to take pictures."

"Because you're a Dawson's employee, I'm responsible for anything that happens when you're driving a vehicle with a dealer's plate on it. The only reason we weren't issued a citation today is that I sold Don Nebolt a car a couple years ago."

"Dad, seriously, we were just turning around."

"The DOT is very strict with dealership licenses. I can't have you out there, with a dealer plate, messing around."

"I was not messing around. I just did what you said. I took Macy where she wanted to go."

His skin darkening to nearly maroon, Nate stood up. "If you're not going to take this seriously, leave."

Unsure what he really wanted, Talan stood, looked at his dad for another moment, then walked out.

*** ***

Now that Macy was back at her desk listening to Parsonsfield while she edited the truck pictures, she was happy they'd gone that morning. The pictures were exactly what she'd wanted.

Talan tapped her shoulder, making her jump. "We're wanted in the conference room. Right now."

She glanced at Keira, who shrugged. Talan stalked out. Macy made her way slowly down the hall. She'd obviously been wrong about no one knowing what had happened that morning and she wasn't in a rush to face whatever punishment was about to be doled out.

The moment she stepped into the conference room she saw Paul.

She took the empty seat next to him, leaving Nate and Gage at one end of the long table and Talan alone between empty chairs across from her.

Everyone seemed to be avoiding looking at each other as they waited in silence for the meeting to start. Macy examined the framed posters advertising past car shows that decorated the white walls. The names were familiar, iconic in the car world; Auburn, Hershey, Pebble Beach. She wondered if maybe someday one of her images would make it on a poster like that.

She expected Nate to speak. Instead Gage stood up, paced a few times, then stopped at the head of the table. "I'm sure you all know Bernadette Barker was here, and that Rick's collection has been cleared for sale." He looked for a moment at each of the people seated around the table before continuing. "Bernadette would like us to handle the entire collection."

Macy had no idea what Gage was talking about but from the looks on everyone else's faces she assumed this was big. She leaned over to Paul and whispered, "Who's Bernadette Barker, and Rick?"

He whispered back, "He was this huge collector, he died a while ago. She's his wife."

"There's a catch, though," Gage continued. "She wants all the cars sold at the next auction."

Paul immediately spoke up. "We can't do that."

Gage held up a hand. "I know, the catalog's already submitted. I called the printer and they haven't started it yet. We're going to pull it, stop work on everything else and get this done."

"It's impossible." Paul looked at Macy for a second, then back to Gage. "We have to get all those cars here, research them, photograph them, and put the layouts together. That catalog is supposed to be shipped out to our bidders in three weeks. It'll take at least that long to get everything together for this new collection. Then the catalog will have to go back to the printer. We won't get it in time to ship and if there's no catalog there's no auction." He leaned back in his chair and crossed his arms. "Forget it."

"We'll adjust the timing. As long as the catalog gets out a week or two prior it'll be fine."

Nate agreed. "Paul's right. That collection's gotta be fifty cars. It'd be three, four days at least until we can get the first load here. And I have other obligations, I can only spare one truck. We can move six cars at a time, and it's a day to drive there and back. There's no way we can work that."

Gage was adamant. "I'm not going to lose this. We'll hire transporters, move them quicker."

Nate stated flatly, "It can't be done."

Macy listened to Gage, Paul, and Nate argue. As they went back and forth she formed an idea. When she'd thought it through, she interrupted, "Excuse me."

Everyone fell silent as they turned to her. "I know how to make this work." She was very uncomfortable with everyone looking at her. She gripped her hands together in her lap to keep them from shaking. "Leave the catalog the way it is. Let it go to print, and ship it the way you'd planned. Then, do this as a completely separate thing, shipped later."

Gage shook his head. "Bernadette wants the cars in the next auction."

"I didn't mean to have a separate auction." She swallowed. Working hard to keep her voice steady, she said, "This is something really special, right? So make it stand out. Give it its own book, rather than a few pages in the catalog. Add in some history of the family, a tribute to Rick, play it up."

Paul was nodding. "Yeah, that's good. That would buy some time."

Seizing on the approval, Macy added, "You can sell that to Bernadette, that she's getting an entire book for her cars. And I bet the owners will keep the book with the car, like they do when their car is in a magazine. So Dawson's name will continue to be associated with those cars."

Nate wasn't convinced. "We still have to get all those cars here, research and photograph them. That still doesn't give us enough time."

Macy tried not to squirm. "What if we didn't have to get them here?"

Gage said, "I sold her on your pictures."

"What if we go to the cars? Gage can inspect them while I shoot, and we'll email everything to Paul and Talan at the end of every day. That would save all those days of transporting."

Skeptical looks started to become smiles. Heads were nodding. Except Gage. "I can't go."

Nate gave him a look Macy thought would've frozen her blood had it been directed at her.

Gage didn't back down. "Dad, I swore to Annie that I wouldn't take any trips." He looked truly upset. Not at all the salesman Macy was used to seeing. "If I go, she can take Isabelle away from me." He paced, then turned back to his father. "Send Macy alone."

"Someone needs to verify the cars."

Talan spoke for the first time. "Macy can do it. She knows as much about cars as I do." Turning to her, he said, "More, probably."

"Absolutely not." Nate shook his head, his face red.

Gage looked desperate. "Why not?"

Nate's expression was hard. He growled, "Because I said so."

"I've been working on this for two years." Gage clenched his fists, anger seeping into his tightly controlled voice. "Two fucking years. If we pull this off it would do more for this company than all the paid advertising in the world."

"She's not going alone and that's all there is to it. There will be a Dawson there, or there won't be anyone there. This is our name on the line."

"Bernadette *chose* Dawson's. We *have* to make this work." Then suddenly, Gage's expression became speculative. "Why don't you go?"

Flatly, Nate said, "I have responsibilities, too."

Paul suggested, "What about Talan? He's a Dawson, and then he can inspect the cars himself."

Talan looked startled. "No. Hell no."

Gage looked at his brother as if for the first time. "Yeah. Yeah, that works."

Nate looked at Talan, then at Macy, his nostrils flaring. Bluntly, he said, "You think I'm fucking crazy? You think I'm going to send *Talan* and *Macy, together*, to the biggest deal this place has ever seen? Over my dead body."

"Why not?" Gage looked from Nate to Macy to Talan and back to Nate. "It's perfect."

Macy could almost see Nate thinking. After a really long silence Nate stood and pointed at Gage. "You, come."

They shut the door, muffling their voices. No one around the table spoke. Macy stared at her hands. She really wanted to look at Talan.

The door opened. Nate snapped, "Macy, in my office. Talan, go talk to Gage about how this is going to work."

*** ***

Macy sat on her bed and thought about what she was going to say to Zack. The entire day had been emotionally exhausting and she really wasn't up to dealing with another issue, but she also couldn't put it off. First thing the next morning, she and Talan were leaving to photograph and catalog Rick Barker's car collection.

That she was being sent on location with Talan would have been stressful enough on its own. That her entire career hung in the balance was just so much worse.

She'd been naïve enough to think Nate hadn't known about her driving the Shelby, or about the debacle she and Talan had had with the pickup truck that morning. When Nate had called her into his office, both those misconceptions had been blown. He'd been very clear that he didn't trust her, and he definitely didn't trust her with Talan.

It hurt to know he had good reason.

This was her last chance. If there were any issues at all, even the slightest hint that she or Talan had put so much as a toe out of line, she was done.

This was a chance, though, to prove she was reliable. And, in some ways, the events of the day had given her a perfect way to end her less than desirable relationship with Zack.

She dialed.

He sounded so happy when he answered the phone, she felt awful. "Hey, Zack."

"Macy, this is a nice surprise."

"Um, not really. This big thing just came up at work and I have to go out of town for, I'm not sure really. At least two weeks. I'm so sorry, I have to cancel our plans for this weekend. And, actually for...." This was it. She was going to just do it. "I'm sorry. I really appreciate everything. The dinners, and the concert, and you're a really nice guy. This just isn't going to work. For me. I'm just not... right... for you." Guilt surged through her. He really had tried to make her happy.

There was a long pause before he said, "Thanks for letting me know. Take care, Macy." The line went dead.

Relief washed over her, knowing she'd never have to see Zack again.

# Chapter 16

Bags of camera gear were neatly packed and waiting on a luggage cart, along with one small suitcase of Macy's clothes. It was a tiny portion of what she now owned. Every time she'd gone out with Zack she'd had to have a new outfit and she'd accumulated a disgustingly large wardrobe.

She thought she should just dump all those clothes in a donation bin.

Her phone beeped, interrupting her thoughts. She opened the text to see just one word, "Here."

She took one last look around her room and sighed. This was going to be...interesting.

She pulled the cart outside to where Talan was leaning against the side of an older, blue, crew-cab pickup truck. Macy couldn't help noticing that he looked comfortable in jeans and a t-shirt, his hair down, hands stuck casually in his pockets. "Do'ya think you could have packed a few more things?"

She retorted, "If you'd like, I can leave my clothes here and go naked for the next two weeks."

"You don't need a new outfit for every day. You can do laundry."

She gave him a dirty look. "I think I liked you better when you weren't speaking to me."

"Fine." He climbed into the truck, leaving her to muscle her bags into the back seat herself.

Metallica blasted from the radio the moment he turned the key. She ignored it and settled into the seat as he pulled away from the hotel. She sang along in her head, refusing to give in to the desire to sing out loud. If Talan knew she liked his music choice he'd probably change it out of spite.

Miles rolled by and she watched out of the corner of her eye as he relaxed into driving. After a while he switched to the radio, putting on the same alternative rock station she listened to. A few songs later he began to sing.

He had the most amazing voice. And he knew all the words, even the parts that most people mumbled through. She listened to him, more than to the music.

The song ended and a commercial started. Remembering the day they'd talked about the Beatles, she ventured, "I've never understood that song."

He didn't look at her, he just kept driving, his long fingers gripping the steering wheel.

She went on, trying to make conversation. "I mean, why would you put your finger in someone's mouth?"

"Have you ever had your fingers sucked?"

"No. Of course not."

Without taking his eyes off the road, he asked, "Then how do you know you wouldn't love it?"

Utterly speechless, she turned back to the window. *None of the guys I've been with would ever have done anything like sucking my finger. Because that's so weird.* Except, thinking about it was making her uncomfortable, in the same way Talan's glances sometimes did. *He has such long fingers.* She began to imagine his fingers sliding over her lips.

The day they'd driven the Shelby, he'd made a comment about her not having sex with the right people. *Maybe he's right.* She fidgeted in her seat, very conscious of him close enough to touch. The image of Zack, always putting his hand on her knee when he wasn't shifting, flashed through her mind.

Talan's hands were both firmly on the steering wheel. *Of course they are, because he isn't interested. If he was, he'd have said something already. Or done something. That day in the Shelby, he could have kissed me. But he didn't, because I'm misreading this.*

When her phone rang she hit ignore without even looking at who it was. She was not in any condition to hold an actual conversation.

Talan snapped the radio off. "You can answer it."

She looked straight at him, eyes narrowing defiantly. "I don't want to."

"Why not?"

"I just don't."

"Who is it?"

"Does it matter?"

"No."

"Then why do you care?"

He smirked. "I don't."

The phone started ringing again. She refused to touch it, either to make it stop ringing or to answer it. His fingers tightened on the wheel. She smiled, *glad it's annoying you, Talan.*

"You really should get it. It could be important."

"Does it bother you?"

"Yes." He looked at her for a second, then back at the road. "It's disrespectful to whoever is on the other end."

She crossed her arms and looked straight ahead.

After a few minutes he said, "You should at least see who it was. They called twice, they obviously wanted to talk to you."

She didn't have to look to know it was probably Emma. She always called twice. "Probably not, actually."

"What if it was work?"

Macy snorted. "If they didn't get me, they'd call you. They know we're together."

"What if it was your boyfriend?"

"What if?" *That* was none of his business.

He turned the radio back up. Two seconds later, he turned it back down. "What if there was an emergency?"

"Jesus Christ, Talan! If it's so goddamn important to you!" She pulled out her phone and looked at the call log, just to make him stop. It had been her mom, both times. Not exactly who she wanted to talk to. She was about to shove her phone back in her purse when it rang, the screen displaying Emma's name. She answered, "Hi, Emma."

"Hey, Mace. What's going on?"

"Not much. How are you?"

"Fine. Hey, are you coming home?"

"No." She glanced at Talan, who seemed to be trying to pretend he wasn't listening. "I'm on my way to shoot a collection of cars. Why?"

"It's just that your mom called me, asking if I had space for a roommate."

"Oh geez. I'm sorry, Emma."

"I didn't think you were coming home. But your mom said you're not happy at work and you're living in a hotel?"

She didn't want Talan to hear her say she wasn't happy at work, but she had to answer. "That's half true. I do live in a hotel."

"But you like your new job? And being in Arizona?"

"I do."

"That's what I thought. I mean, last time I talked to you, you were about to go on a date." Her tone changed from confused to speculative. "How'd that go?"

Another thing she didn't want to say out loud at that moment. "It didn't work out."

"You don't sound upset."

Macy smiled, "I'm not. How are things with you and that guy from the bar?"

"That didn't work out, either."

"Oh, Emma, I'm sorry."

"I'm not. I'm seeing Sir Lou."

Shocked, Macy blurted, "What?"

"Turns out he's a really nice guy." Her voice becoming soft, she added, "He treats me like I'm special. Actually listens when I talk. I'm just sorry I never gave him a chance before."

"I'm really happy for you."

"Thanks. So, if your mom calls again what should I say?"

Macy sighed. "I'll call her and straighten this out. But if she does call, just don't answer."

After she hung up, Talan asked, "Was that so hard?"

She sagged back into the seat. "No. I guess not. Except now I have to call my mom."

"Call whoever you need to."

That was not a conversation she was going to have with Talan in hearing distance. "I will, in a bit."

"Family can be tough."

"Yeah."

They lapsed into silence. She stared at the miles of nothing and thought about what she was going to say to her mom. Really it was pretty simple; stay out of my life. But if she said that, that way, it would hurt her mom. And her mom loved her and wanted to help her. *Except I don't want help. I want to be my own person.* She'd spent too many years allowing her mom to direct her. She was done.

Talan broke into her thoughts, "Why do you live in a hotel?"

She felt her face get hot and knew she was blushing. "What's it matter where I live?"

"It doesn't. I was just curious."

She played with her phone, twirling it between her fingers. She had to work with him for the next couple weeks, just the two of them. If things stayed this way, it was going to be horrible. She answered, "I, um, can't…I don't…"

"Forget it." He turned the radio back on.

She turned it back off and muttered, "It was supposed to be temporary, just until I found an apartment. But, it just kind of…" She didn't quite know how to explain that the idea of being in an apartment on her own was overwhelming. "It's a big deal, to rent a place. To buy furniture, and dishes, and remember to buy toilet paper…" She felt so stupid. And so childish. *No wonder my mother thinks I need help. I do.* She admitted, "Staying in a hotel just seems… easier."

"It must be pretty cool. You don't have to clean, or change your own sheets. And you always have fresh towels."

"You never run out of hot water in the shower."

He smiled at her, his brown eyes twinkling mischievously. "You can leave empty pizza boxes on the floor and someone else will pick them up."

"They have an automatic pancake maker at my hotel."

"That's pretty cool."

It surprised her that he didn't make fun of her. And it felt good, that he accepted her decision without question. Maybe the next two weeks weren't going to be that bad after all.

*** ***

Talan was relieved to get out of the truck at their hotel. *Motel. Definitely does* not *qualify as a hotel.* He stretched his cramped muscles, headed into the office at the front of the property, and gave the guy behind the desk his name.

"Mr. Dawson, I have Room 13 reserved for you." The guy's bored expression, pasty complexion, and lackluster brown hair made him seem like the perfect overnight hotel clerk.

He handed the guy a credit card. "You can put Macy LaPorte's room on this card, too."

"Don't have a Macy LaPorte registered. Just Mr. Talan Dawson, one room, two adults."

He stared in disbelief. "We're supposed to have two rooms, each with one adult."

Not sounding like he cared in the least, he said, "There's two beds."

"We need separate rooms."

The clerk shrugged. "Sorry, can't help. Reservation's for one room, two adults. That's what you get."

"We're on business. We can't share a room."

The guy snorted. "No need to explain yourself to me."

He would have loved to share a room with Macy, if his life was completely different. If being that close to her, having to hide that he wanted her, wasn't going to drive him out of his fucking mind. He looked back to see that now, when he didn't want her to use her phone, she'd decided to check texts or something. For Christ sake. "We need two rooms."

The guy shifted his uncaring eyes from Talan to Macy, then back. "You can always try another hotel."

"I have a reservation here. I've been driving for hours and I want to sleep. In my own room. *Alone.*"

"You can go home any time you want. There's a one-night penalty for not canceling the reservation 48 hours in advance."

Frustrated at his inability to get anywhere, he said, "We didn't even have these reservations 48 hours ago."

Macy stepped up next to him. "It's fine. We can share a room."

Talan pulled her away from the desk. "We booked two rooms."

Keeping her voice low, she said, "Did you see any other hotel anywhere near here?"

He tried to remember the last thing they'd passed. Nothing came to mind.

She reassured him, "I'm a big girl, I can share."

He stalked back to the counter. "When can we get a second room?"

The clerk looked at his computer screen for way too long. "You're staying two weeks?" Talan grunted in agreement. The clerk kept his eyes on the screen. "Three weeks from tomorrow."

Talan's fingers flexed on the counter.

Macy spoke up. "We'll take the room you have reserved for us."

Once the clerk checked them in, Talan moved the truck to the parking space in front of the room they'd been given. He mumbled as he got out, "This place is a dump."

Macy looked around. "I kind of like it. It reminds me of this place in New Hampshire my mom and dad took us on vacation when I was a kid."

Once upon a time the design had probably been cute; one long building made to look like ten individual cottages, each with their own peaked roof and bright red door. Now, even the semi-dark parking lot lighting didn't hide that the white siding needed to be power washed and there was moss growing on the roof. Across the parking lot was an identical line of ten units. He supposed if this was the only hotel around they were lucky to get one room.

They'd been given a single key, an actual key rather than a key card, and he took his time getting out of the truck and unlocking the room. As soon as he had it open Macy went in. He expected her to use the bathroom straight off, that's what all the girls he knew did. Instead, she turned on all the lights, pulled the corner of the sheets off a bed and began inspecting the mattress.

Curiously, he asked, "What are you doing?"

"Checking for bed bugs."

He stood in the middle of the room, astounded. "Are you serious?"

She continued her inspection on the second bed. "Yes."

"Whatever." He turned toward the door.

"Where are you going?"

He stopped. "To get my shit."

"You should wait and make sure it's safe first." She flipped the desk chair over and looked at the bottom.

He watched, unable to believe she was actually inspecting for bed bugs.

After she put all the furniture back, she started for the door. "All clear."

He followed. "You're nuts."

"You wouldn't be saying that if I'd found something." As she pulled her bags out of the truck, she continued, "It's a good thing this room is okay. According to all three major travel sites most everything around here are vacation cottages, rented by the week. There isn't another available hotel room for almost fifty miles."

He stopped, a bag half out of the truck. "Are you serious?"

"Yeah."

"How'd you know that?"

She slung her laptop strap over her shoulder. "I checked while you were arguing with the clerk."

He stared at her back as she walked into the room. "Huh."

Back inside, she asked, "Which bed do you want?"

"One in a different hotel." He eyed the brown floral bedspreads with disgust.

"It's not that bad. Just a little dated."

"A little?" He pointed to the orange and brown tweed couch. "I think my grandparents had that couch. It was a hand-me-down. In 1975."

"So, don't sit on it. At least the carpet's newer."

Talan snorted. "True. Berber was in style in the '90s."

"Do you shower at night or in the morning?" She started putting her bags in order.

Ignoring her question, he moved to put his bags in the closet. "Did you check in here for bugs?"

"It's safe. I checked the sheets, too. They're clean." She finished organizing her things. "Sometimes I have to shower after work, but I always shower in the morning. If you do, too, we'll have to figure that into what time to set the alarm for." She headed to the bathroom, carrying a change of clothes.

He sat on the bed closer to the closet and turned the TV on. This was insane. And she was acting like this was all perfectly fine— them, sharing a room.

For her it probably was. He knew damn well she wasn't interested in him. She was dating *Zack*, there was no reason for her to be all uncomfortable and weird the way he was around her. He'd spent the whole ride up there trying not to see how beautiful she was, the way the sun shone on her hair, the freckles that covered every inch of her skin. He'd have loved nothing more than to take her hand, just to hold it, to feel her next to him.

When she came out of the bathroom she walked around to the other bed and pulled the bedspread off, letting it fall on the floor. Then she went back to her suitcase and pulled out a package of bleach wipes, picked up the TV remote from the nightstand between the beds and wiped it off.

Wishing she hadn't braided her hair, he watched her with curiosity. "What are you doing?"

"You should never touch the remote in a hotel room." She set it back down and dropped the bleach wipe in the trash.

"Why not?"

She wrinkled her nose. "People do stuff in these rooms, then they watch TV." She looked over at him and cocked an eyebrow. "They sit on the bedspreads, too. Naked."

He jumped up and glared at her as he pulled the bedspread off, then stalked to the bathroom to wash his hands. She was doing this just to fuck with him. And it was working. *Why do you even like her? She's a fucking pain in the ass.* But she wasn't. Not really. Not when he stopped trying so hard to keep her away. Not when they talked, for real.

*Because she's someone you get.* He wondered if she'd get him, if he were to tell her the things he thought about. *Maybe. But you can't find out. Because if you do, you'll lose her completely.* The image of the Mercury on her side flashed through his mind. This job meant something to her, he wasn't going to put that in jeopardy. *Better to stay away. As much as you can, anyway.*

He brushed his teeth and went back out to the room. She was curled up in her bed, facing the windows. He tried not to look at her, but he couldn't help himself. On the drive up, he'd noticed the most amazing thing. *She waits until the commercials between the songs to talk.* He'd never met a girl who didn't talk over the music. If he hadn't already been into her, that'd have done it.

As soon as he'd shut the lights off it hit him; he was sharing a room with Macy. He couldn't get into bed. *God damn whoever screwed this up.* He turned the lights back on and dragged his suitcase out, began pushing things aside looking for something useful, swearing under his breath the whole time.

It'd been years since he'd worn anything to bed, hadn't even thought about it when he'd been packing, and the thought of sleeping in jeans was horrible.

He jammed everything back in his suitcase, pushed it back into the closet and turned the lights back off. He yanked his shirt off, set it on top of his suitcase, and crawled into bed with his jeans on. Once he was under the covers, he shimmied his pants off and put them on the floor next to the bed, just in case he had to get up in the middle of the night.

And he'd harassed Macy about bringing too many clothes.

Being careful to keep the blanket in place, he moved to turn the TV off. He almost couldn't do it. "Thanks. I'll never be able to touch a remote again."

Without turning over, sounding suspiciously like she was smiling, she said, "No problem."

# Chapter 17

Macy pretended to still be asleep as she lay in bed listening to Talan moving around. It was weird to be sharing a room with someone; she hadn't done that since her first attempt at college. She waited until she heard the bathroom door close before she sat up and looked at his bed, the sheets rumpled and the god-awful ugly bedspread on the floor where he'd dropped it the night before.

She tried to steady her nerves. Last night had been bad enough, being alone with him. She'd been so nervous, she'd babbled about the most stupid crap.

Having to be with him all day, in front of really important clients, was going to be ten times worse. They'd have to pretend they got along. Nate had told her blatantly that if she screwed this up she was fired, and that had included a specific warning about not doing anything stupid with Talan. She'd assured him it wouldn't be a problem.

Except, it was a problem.

She didn't mean to get in trouble, and she couldn't explain why it happened with Talan. It just did.

It would have been better if Gage had come instead. Sometimes he was annoyed that he had to help her, but at least he was predictable.

Talan came out of the bathroom fully dressed, hair wet from the shower, in khakis and a dark blue polo shirt. She thought the jeans and t-shirt from the day before looked more his style.

As she got clean clothes from her suitcase, she briefly thought it would have been nice if she had one of the dressy shirts she'd bought with Keira. She chose a Weezer t-shirt and went into the bathroom.

Instead of a typical hotel setup, where the sink was outside, this was a traditional bathroom. The white pedestal sink sat next to the toilet. The harvest gold tub, with its plain white shower curtain, took up the far wall. She undressed, folding her pajamas and carefully putting them on the chrome towel rack above the toilet. Under normal circumstances, she'd have dropped her clothes on the floor and let housekeeping put them in a pile. But she didn't want to do laundry here.

She picked her toothbrush up from the glass shelf mounted over the sink and squirted toothpaste on it, stuck it in her mouth and pushed the shower curtain back. She stared, surprised at what she saw. There was a toothbrush balanced on the edge of the tub.

Being careful not to bump Talan's toothbrush, she got in the shower. She let the water wash the sleep away as she brushed, and smiled a little as she set her toothbrush next to Talan's. It was goofy, but she felt a sudden kinship to him, knowing he also brushed his teeth in the shower.

She washed, dried, and got dressed in the bathroom. She took a deep breath, let it out slowly, and left the cramped room.

She put her pajamas on top of her suitcase and picked up her purse and two of the camera bags, ignoring Talan as she went out to the truck. He followed, just as silently. As he backed out of the parking space she said, "Can you stop at the office, please?"

He eyed her. "Is that your official 'first day of work' shirt?"

She glanced down, thinking there must be something wrong with her outfit. "What do you mean?"

He gave her a funny little smile and put the truck in drive. He parked in the space marked 'Check-In Parking Only' and they went inside.

The same guy was still at the front desk. Macy smiled as best as she could as she asked, "Where's your coffee?"

The guy gave her an amused look. "Down the street at the gas station."

She gave him a murderous stare, spun on her heel and stalked out. She slammed the door getting back in the truck, crossed her arms over her chest and waited.

When Talan got in, she said, "This place is a shit-hole."

A smile tugged at the corners of his mouth. "So it's okay that it was decorated when Kennedy was in the White House, but it's not okay that they don't serve coffee in the lobby?"

"Yes. Drive. Before I kill you."

He stopped fighting the smile.

*** ***

Dust motes danced in sunlight streaming through the barn windows and the smell of old wood competed with the smell of old motor oil. Macy stared, open-mouthed, at the chaos in front of her. There were cars everywhere, mounds of what could only loosely be called cars, and piles of fenders, stacks of tires, and shelves packed with headlights and radios and a million other parts.

Next to her, Talan mumbled, "Holy shit." He stepped forward, knocking over a stack of hub caps. The clatter broke the still morning air, rang in their ears for long minutes after.

She tried to get her mind around what she saw, and to somehow begin to plan what to do. There weren't just a lot of cars. There were more cars than she'd ever seen in one place outside of Dawson's.

Talan pulled out his phone and called Gage. She listened to his side of the conversation as he tried in vain to describe what they were seeing.

"No, Gage, I'm not fucking with you. It's a fucking mess. They don't have paperwork. The cars aren't ready. Every one's got an inch of dust on it. Roger Barker doesn't give a shit. He handed us a box of keys and told us to go at it. A box of keys, Gage. Not marked."

Half-listening, Macy began counting the cars. There were fifty-seven, if she counted everything that had four wheels on a chassis. Although if she narrowed it to cars that also had seats and at least something resembling a body, it went down to fifty-three.

Fifty-three cars, all of which looked like they were going to need to be pushed if she wanted them moved. If she did seven or eight a day, that'd be a week solid. That was do-able, if nothing went wrong and she shot from sun up to sundown. Not so do-able if they actually had to push every car. It was a damn good thing they had two weeks.

"Here. You talk to him." Talan held the phone out to her.

"Hi, Gage." She watched Talan slowly thread his way across the room, being very careful not to knock anything else over.

Gage stated, "Bernadette told me the cars were ready."

As she scanned the room, she told him, "If you want them barn-fresh, they are. If you want every one washed and gleaming, we're going to need a couple guys. And a couple more weeks."

Neither the distance or the sketchy cell connection dimmed Gage's anger. "This is not what we signed up for. We don't have time for this shit."

There was something about these cars, something she could almost taste. If she could concentrate for one minute… "Gage, we'll call you back." She hung up on him and looked closer at the cars directly in front of her. "Talan?"

His voice drifted across the space. "Yeah?"

"Look at these cars."

"I am."

Getting excited as she became more and more sure, she said, "No, I mean look at them. This is an Auburn Boattail Speedster. And that's a 1953 Corvette. That," she pointed at an orange car with a huge, rectangular air foil, "is a 1970 Superbird. Those were only made for one year. There's like two-thousand total."

After a moment, Talan added, "That's a 1932 Cord L-29. And that's a Packard Darrin."

"Super rare, right? And, Talan, do they look like they've been messed with?"

Macy waited patiently while Talan inspected the car closest to him; a Pierce Arrow Dual Cowl Phaeton. When he was done, he said, "I'll have to check the numbers and verify the specs, but from what I can see there's no welds, no bondo, and everything looks period correct and in the right condition to be original. At least on this car."

Elated that he saw the same thing she did, she said, "Call Gage back. Tell him at first glance at least some of these cars are unmolested. And rare. Tell him they're rare."

"He knows they're rare." He made his way back to her and took his phone. "But I'll tell him anyway."

"Can you call him from outside? I'm going to document this entire room before we move a thing." Glancing at the stack of hub caps he'd had knocked over, she added, "I'll avoid that spot."

*** ***

Macy put her hands on the rear bumper of a Studebaker and glanced at Talan.

He stood with the driver's side door open, one hand on the steering wheel and one hand on the door frame, waiting for her to be in position. "Ready?"

"Yup."

"One, two, three."

They pushed. The car began to roll, very slowly, and Talan steered it through the doors. The front wheels dropped from the concrete floor of the barn onto the packed dirt of the driveway and gravity lent a hand to pull the car forward. As soon as the rear bumper was far enough from the barn that they'd be able to close the doors behind it, she stopped pushing. "That's good. Just straighten the wheels, please."

Talan let the car go a few more feet while he muscled the steering wheel, then pulled the emergency brake. "I'm not turning it." He went back into the barn before she had a chance to tell him she didn't expect him to. She'd known, as soon as Gage had forbidden them to start the cars, that they weren't going to be moving these any more than they had to. She'd make do with the weathered grey of the barn and the trees on the other side of the driveway as backgrounds, avoiding the back side of the Barker's sprawling ranch as much as possible.

It had been ages since she'd been alone with a car. It was nice, not to have her every move watched. She walked slowly around the Studebaker, taking in the unique upside-down teardrop shape of the headlights, the odd circle around a bullet-shaped protrusion in the center of the nose, and considered how best to show that a car could be rounded everywhere but still look boxy. Sure of what she was doing, she started shooting.

*** ***

By the end of the day Macy wanted one thing— a shower.

Talan was on the phone with Gage when they pulled into the motel, meaning she got the bathroom first.

Happy to be washed and in clean clothes, she sat on the bed with her headphones on and her laptop in front of her. She ignored Talan when he walked through the room, instead concentrating on the pictures she'd taken.

The shots she'd gotten of the barn before they'd moved anything

167

were a huge bonus, but they'd taken time. By the end of the day she'd only managed three cars. It wasn't a great start, but considering what they had to work with those three had been better than she'd expected.

In the time she'd been at Dawson's she'd gotten to know the kind of images Paul usually used. She chose what she thought he'd like and started moving them to a new folder. She looked up to see Talan staring at her. Pulling her headphones off, she asked, "What?"

"Are you done yet? I'm starving." He stalked to the door and flung it open.

She jumped up, panicking because she wasn't dressed to go anywhere. "Talan, wait!" She grabbed her shoes and purse and ran after him. He was already in the truck, the engine running.

She slammed the door to the room, checked the knob to make sure it was locked, limped barefoot to the truck and yanked the passenger door open. "Talan, I'm not dressed!" She indicated her yoga shorts.

"Who do you think you're going to see?"

She gave him a dirty look. "Can I at least put my shoes on?"

"In the truck, if you're coming with me."

She climbed in. He jammed the truck in reverse and backed up so fast she had to brace herself against the dashboard to avoid falling off the seat, and just as quickly pulled forward, spraying gravel everywhere. She opted to buckle first, then stuck her feet in her sneakers, swearing under her breath at not having socks.

She finally sat back. "Where are we going?"

"Wherever the fuck we can find." He didn't look at her.

She rolled her eyes. He was so impossible. She pulled her phone out and searched restaurants. "There's a diner not far from here."

"Whatever. Where?"

She gave him directions.

They saw the glow of the red neon "Diner" sign long before they reached the rounded chrome building. Forgetting for a moment who she was with, she exclaimed, "Oh, this is so cool! It's like a real diner!"

Ignoring her enthusiasm, Talan went inside. He didn't hold the door for her.

After the waitress came and they placed their orders, they had nothing to do but stare at each other. She was acutely aware of the silence, and of the fact that he was so close. He drummed his fingers on the table rhythmically, his hands mere inches from hers.

The memory of the first day they'd met flashed through her mind; his smile, the awkward way he'd talked about the Hemi 'Cuda, how it'd felt when they'd touched.

She tried to sneak a peek at him and, of course, he chose that moment to look straight at her. She stammered, "Thanks for helping today."

Losing his usual angry tone, he shrugged it off. "No problem. That's what I'm here for."

"It's too bad we can't drive the cars."

"I'm sure Gage wouldn't mind if you wanted to drop the gas tanks and clean them all, then put new gas in every one."

Her face burned. She'd been around long enough to know about old gas. She'd been trying to make conversation, not an actual suggestion. Wishing she could explain, but afraid to make it worse, she didn't say anything.

He cleared his throat. "So, how are things going with that guy?"

Completely thrown, she asked, "What guy?"

"The one Keira set you up with. Zack."

She could lie, say it was going great. Instead, she said, "That didn't work out, actually."

"Oh." He pulled out his phone and stared at the screen.

Silence was fine after all. Better than having to discuss Zack, anyway.

With nothing else to do, she looked around. This place was older than their motel, straight out of the '50s, with white laminate table tops, red vinyl seats, and black and white tile everywhere. She could almost see the girls in poodle skirts popping gum at the counter, guys in leather jackets with cigarettes dangling from their lips at the jukebox. Back then, there'd have been Cadillacs with huge fins sitting in the parking lot, instead of sedans and minivans. There was a Cadillac in the Barker's barn; the diner would have made a great background, if there'd been a way to get it there.

Their food came and they ate without speaking. Talan paid and they left.

Back in the truck, she said, "I can pay for my own meals."

"My father was very specific. He's paying all your expenses." He turned the radio up, ensuring they didn't talk.

They were halfway back to their motel when Macy's phone rang. She'd have ignored it but Talan turned the radio off. Things were tense enough between them, she didn't want to antagonize him intentionally.

Surprised to see her mom's name on her screen, she answered, "Mom? Is everything okay?"

Her mom sounded worried when she said, "Yes, why?"

"Isn't it like eleven o'clock there?"

"It is, which is why I'm calling. I haven't heard from you in a couple days and I was worried."

"Sorry about that. We landed this huge client and the pictures need to be done right away so I'm really busy."

"Too busy to call home and let me know you're alive?"

"Sorry."

"You never got back to me on what flight you wanted, so I talked to Aunt Holly and Emma. I'm going to book your flight for next Friday. Aunt Holly said you can start work as soon as you want, and Emma's moving in on the first, which is the following Monday, so that'll give you a few days to pack what you've got here."

Macy hated that her mother was engineering her life. She only had herself to blame, though, since she'd known what was going to happen when she'd told her mom how unhappy she was.

Her mother continued, "Dad and I talked and we agree that you can take all your furniture. And I saved the dishes from the last time I replaced mine. Emma said she doesn't have a set yet."

"Mom, stop, please." Macy wished she could continue to avoid this, and double wished she didn't have to do this with Talan right there. "I'm okay after all."

"You weren't the other night."

"I was having a rough day. But it was just a day, it wasn't the end of the world."

There was silence on the other end.

"Mom?"

"Well, I guess it's a good thing I didn't buy a plane ticket."

Macy wasn't sure if her mom was angry or hurt. Or maybe something else. "I'm sorry. I'll call Emma and straighten everything out."

"If you wouldn't mind, I'll call Aunt Holly. She went out on a limb for you, and I'd prefer this come from me."

Guilt blossomed in Macy's stomach. After she hung up she stared out the window, watched as they passed a seemingly never-ending line of trees. She shouldn't feel guilty. She hadn't asked her mom to call her aunt or Emma. Hadn't actually asked her mom to fly her home, either. It had been her mom's idea to do those things. And still, Macy felt responsible, felt that she was disappointing her mother.

At the motel, Talan went straight to their room. Macy followed slowly, but she couldn't face the thought of being alone with him. She sat on the ground next to the door and looked out across the parking lot as the last rays of sunlight touched the tops of the tree-covered mountains surrounding their motel.

It was very pretty there. Sort of like what she was used to seeing at home. Not that it was like home, but it was a whole lot closer than Arizona.

When she'd left Connecticut she'd told herself things were going to be perfect. She'd make all new friends, meet a guy who really got her, have the perfect job. She'd be so busy going out and having a great time she wouldn't miss home at all.

Tears obscured her vision. She hadn't made new friends, or found a guy who got her. The few times she'd gone out had been horrible, her job wasn't what she'd expected and she missed home all the time.

The door opened and Talan stepped outside. She put her head down, not wanting him to see her crying. He barely paused on his way past her. She didn't care. Her heart hurt too much to bother with Talan.

*** ***

Talan glanced at Macy. He'd gone outside to make sure she was okay, but seeing her huddled next to the door, her head down, he wasn't comfortable interrupting her.

Since he'd gone outside, he was committed to doing something. Otherwise it would be obvious he'd been checking on Macy and he didn't want her to think that's what he was doing even though it was true.

He wandered into the motel's office. He smiled and nodded at the girl behind the desk. She was nothing like Macy. Her eyes were bored and her smile lacked any spark. He glanced around, paying more attention than he had the previous times he'd been at the desk. He hadn't had any real purpose for coming into the office, and now he had to make it look like he'd had some idea of what he was doing.

The only things in the room, besides the clerk and the counter, were a rack of tourism brochures and a vending machine. He fished his wallet from his back pocket and checked the contents, verified that he had plenty of cash. He stood in front of the machine for a moment before deciding on peanut butter cups. It was, at least, a valid excuse for being there.

As soon as he stepped back outside he saw Macy, still on the ground next to the red door of their room. It was seriously rude not to get her something, too. He went back in and bought a second package of peanut butter cups.

He'd barely turned around when he realized that might be a mistake. He'd had a thing for this girl since the first time he'd seen her, but he actually knew very little about her. It was entirely possible that she was allergic to peanuts.

*Third time's the charm.* Standing in front of the machine once more, he scanned the rows of candy bars and bags of chips. Now that he was thinking about it, it was more complicated than just the possibility of an allergy. Maybe she liked plain chocolate. Or dark chocolate. Or maybe she didn't like chocolate at all. She could be a salty/sweet person. Or a no-frills nougat only person.

By the time he left he had a dozen candy bars plus chips, cheese curls, and pretzels.

He made his way slowly back across the parking lot, trying the whole time to come up with a plan. He wanted to talk to her, he just had to figure out how.

No matter how slowly he walked, he was there way too quickly. He stood for a moment, looking down at her, then he sat. He cleared his throat. "Macy?" She didn't answer. "I brought dessert." Mortified at saying something so lame, he added, "If you want to call it that."

She turned her head, checked out the pile of snacks in his arms. "What the hell did you do, rob a convenience store?"

He nearly snapped back, but he deserved the attitude she was giving him. Instead, he said simply, "I didn't know what you liked."

There was a long pause, then she looked up at him. Her eyes were red-rimmed, the blue of her irises even more striking than usual.

Sounding defeated, she said, "Talan, you don't have to try to be nice."

He tried to figure out how to fix this, took a deep breath, and said, "Macy, I'm sorry. I never wanted…" He stopped; that wasn't right. He tried again, "I'd really like it if we could…" He almost said 'be friends' but that wasn't true. Frustrated at not being able to say what he wanted, he blurted out, "I wish we could start over."

She scrutinized him for a moment, then suddenly held out her hand. "Hi. I'm Macy."

Relieved, he smiled and shook her hand. "Talan." On impulse, he picked up a package of peanut butter cups and held them out.

A hint of a smile touched her lips as she took the candy.

# Chapter 18

Macy tried to concentrate on the car in front of her. It was long and sleek, maroon and black, a chauffeur driven masterpiece. She thought of Flappers in super short, beaded dresses. She couldn't quite lose herself in the vision, though. Her thoughts kept drifting to the night before, when Talan had shown up with an armload of vending machine snacks.

It'd been so sweet. And so genuine. She snuck a peek at him, his face serious with concentration. He pushed a strand of hair back; she wished he'd left it down.

Turning back to the car she was supposed to be shooting, she tried to refocus. She really shouldn't even be thinking of Talan. Aside from the fact that they worked together, and that probably made thoughts of him bad on principle, she'd just come to the end of a relationship. She knew you weren't supposed to jump right into another one, even if the first one had been bullshit from the start.

Except she'd known Talan first. And she'd liked him. It wasn't something she'd had to work at, or talk herself into. It was something that just was. Even when they'd had issues, she'd been drawn to him. Fighting the urge to glance at him again, she remembered the feel of his fingers on her back as he'd pushed her shirt up to look at her tattoo. She'd wanted so badly for him to do more.

She shook her head, trying to clear it. They were on a schedule and she had to get going. Hoping to put herself in the right frame of mind for this car, she opened her music library and chose a compilation she'd labeled Roaring '20s. Piano erupted from her phone, much louder than she'd meant it to be. Fumbling, she quickly turned it down, then looked at Talan across the yard. He was staring at her. Smiling apologetically, she mouthed, "Sorry."

With saxophones and trumpets to set the tone, envisioning women kicking long legs in intricate dances and men dressed in Zoot suits, she went back to shooting.

"That's an interesting choice of music."

She jumped at Talan's voice and stammered, "Oh, yeah, well, ya know, it's for the car."

Raising his eyebrows, he asked, "You play music for the cars?"

Apparently, sarcastic Talan was back. Feeling foolish, she said, "Every car has a soundtrack."

"You've got the right idea, but not quite the right era." Glancing at the car, he added, "The car is actually a '40."

Embarrassed for her mistake, she stopped the music. "I didn't know. It just reminded me of Flappers."

"That's not surprising. There isn't all that much difference between a car from the late 20's and this." Giving half his attention to his phone, he said, "This car was built for a big band leader. If you want to play music for it, you can play music written and recorded by the original owner." He tapped the screen a couple times and music started; a man's voice, very deep and full, was backed by tubas and light drums.

She listened for a minute, giving the music a chance, then wrinkled her nose. "I don't really like it."

"Try this." He touched the phone's screen and the song changed. The same deep voice began a much more upbeat song full of trilling flutes and airy violin.

She burst out laughing. "That's terrible."

He tapped stop, a smile lighting his eyes. "Yeah, it is. A lot of the music from that era was really good, though."

"Usually when I do cars from the '40s I listen to The Andrews Sisters and Glenn Miller."

"Good choices." He asked, "What do you listen to when you're not shooting cars?"

Completely serious, she said, "Metallica."

He narrowed his eyes at her.

It gave her a ridiculous amount of satisfaction to say, "I saw them at Giant's Stadium in 2013. They were amazing." She loved his incredulous expression. Trying to sound flippant, she said, "I guess you'll have to find some other way to annoy me."

"What makes you think I try to annoy you?"

"Seriously?" She leveled her gaze at him. "I know you crank music on purpose."

"Maybe I like it loud."

She crossed her arms and tapped her foot.

He gave her a real smile. "Okay, maybe I was trying to annoy you."

The smile was utterly disarming. She asked, "So, besides the Beatles, what do you listen to when you're not trying to aggravate me?"

He casually leaned against the car next to her and put his hands in his pockets. "Mostly I like modern alternative. The Lumineers, X Ambassadors, Imagine Dragons, that kind of stuff."

She could easily picture him listening to modern alternative. She said, "I saw Imagine Dragons last year. They were fantastic."

"I saw them at—" He was interrupted by his phone ringing. He answered, his voice instantly taking on the not-so-pleasant tone she was used to hearing from him. "What?" He walked away.

She figured it was Gage because she could hear him saying that they were doing the best they could, he couldn't help that it was taking too long. She went back to photographing the car she was working on, but she kind of paid attention to Talan, too. He paced while he talked. After he hung up he stalked into the barn.

Seeing him go from casually smiling to rigid with anger made her want to scream. She liked that other Talan so much. She just didn't understand why he was so impossible.

She queued up a playlist and cranked the volume. She didn't care that Metallica didn't match the car, it matched her mood.

When she was done with the band leader's car, she had to get Talan. She'd have preferred not to, but she couldn't move cars alone.

He was standing next to a Model T, a clipboard in his hand, making notes. She stood in the doorway for a minute, watching him. He pushed his hair back, a motion that seemed to be as much a part of him as his brown eyes. "Talan?"

"Yeah?" He didn't turn around.

"I'm sorry to bother you. I need the next car."

"Which one do you want?"

Not feeling all that agreeable herself, she sarcastically answered, "One that runs."

"It doesn't matter if they run or not. If I start one Gage'll fucking kill me. Barn-finds, original unmolested condition and all that." He opened the Model T's door and got in.

She walked over to the car and got in the passenger's side. Ignoring the puff of dust as she sat down, she slammed the door.

He sat in the driver's seat with his hands on the steering wheel and stared straight ahead. She waited, her arms folded across her chest, wondering why the hell they were in the car since they couldn't drive it.

Not looking at her, he said, "I don't mean to snap at you all the time."

"It's okay."

"No, it's not." He leaned back in the seat and turned to her.

She thought he was going to say more. Wanted him to say more, to

178

tell her what was going on.

Instead, he got out of the car and dropped his clipboard on the seat. He left the door open so he could push and steer at the same time. "Ready?"

Leaving her camera on the passenger's seat, she got out to help.

When they had the car in position he went on to the next car on his list. She thought about asking what year this car was, but decided it didn't matter. She wasn't going to play music from then anyway; she wanted something mellow. She picked a genre-specific list instead of an era, and let the familiar notes of "Blackbird" settle her.

Talan turned towards the sound. Their eyes met across cars for a second before he turned away. Almost immediately she heard him singing.

When the second song started and Eddie Vedder's voice filled the air she couldn't help herself. She turned the volume up and sang, too.

*** ***

Talan headed for the diner. Based on Macy's reaction the night before he figured it was a safe bet. They placed their orders and settled back to wait. Trying really hard to keep the uneasy peace between them, he asked, "What'd you think of today's cars?"

"I'd like them a hell of a lot better if we could drive them."

"Yeah, right?"

She tipped her head a little, looking at him quizzically. "You know an awful lot about cars, for someone who hates them."

He shifted his gaze, watched a family in the parking lot getting into their crossover, the kids smiling, the parents talking; it looked perfect. They pulled away and he turned back to Macy. "I don't have a lot of choice. In my family it's all cars, all the time."

"That must be hard, when it's not your thing."

He drummed his fingers on the table, thought about that and if he wanted to respond.

Before he could figure it out, she asked, "If you weren't working for Gage, what would you be doing?"

That wasn't really something he could answer. He told her the absolute truth. "I have no idea."

She nodded, almost imperceptibly. "How do you go from Metallica to Imagine Dragons?"

"I could ask you the same thing."

"I just like a lot of different kinds of music, depending on my mood. So I don't limit myself. I'll listen to just about anything, from pop and country to doo-wop and bluegrass." She smiled, "Except I strongly dislike hip hop."

"There are some very talented artists working in hip hop."

"You like songs that glorify violence and are degrading to women?"

"No, actually I don't. But I appreciate diversity, and that a lot of those artists are overcoming some pretty adverse circumstances and finding a voice."

"Yeah? Like DopeD Up, whose adverse circumstances include a mother who is a world-renowned viral diseases specialist and a father who's a lawyer? He had it real rough, using his trust fund to buy an apartment building in a slum so he could say his address was in the 'hood."

"That's valid. But not all rappers have those advantages. And in every genre there are artists who had those kinds of advantages, and artists who didn't. All I'm saying is, it takes hard work and dedication to write songs that work, and to get them out there. None of that is easy, no matter what kind of advantages you have. I have a lot of respect for anyone who can do that. I mean, do you have any idea how hard it is to break into music?"

She was grinning hugely.

"Why are you smiling like that?"

"It's nice, to see you passionate about something." She folded her arms on the table and leaned forward. "So, how does one go about breaking into music?"

He narrowed his eyes at her. "Are you teasing me?"

"No. Not at all."

Still not totally sure she was interested, he started slowly. "Well, you need a band. And original music. The band and the music both have to be good."

"By good, you mean it has to be what people want."

"Yes. There's plenty of really amazing bands out there who are playing what they love, but they're not hitting it big because their music isn't 'right' right now."

She nodded. "Yeah, and there's plenty that suck but for some reason people want to listen to them."

"Macy, it's not about your personal taste."

"I know. It's about sing-ability. Like 'Ob-La-Di.'"

"Exactly. The Beatles are actually a really good example of how to make it big. They weren't a hit right away, either. They played to basically empty rooms when they first started, but they worked hard and built a following, and it was the right music at the right time. And they changed with the times, so they stayed relevant."

"Things are really different today than they were back when the Beatles made it big. Now, anyone can make a video and post it on YouTube. So, doesn't that make it easier?"

"Not really. You still have to find a way to gain followers. And without a label backing you, that's really hard. You can't get on the radio as an indie artist, and believe it or not that's still where most people hear new music."

"What about Pandora. And Spotify?"

"You still need followers to put you on their playlists. And getting followers isn't as easy as it sounds."

"Huh."

"And streaming music is actually making it harder for bands to make a living, because no one buys music anymore. So, the only way to make money is to play concerts. And even then, everyone else gets paid before the band, so they still don't make all that much. The only thing they really do well with is merchandise." He glanced at her shirt. "All your t-shirts? They're what's really supporting the bands you love."

"In that case, I'm really glad I've bought a shirt at every concert I've ever been to."

Curiously, he asked, "How many shirts do you have?"

"No idea." Grinning, she said, "All I can tell you is, they don't fit in my drawers anymore."

He looked back at the shirt she was wearing. "I've never heard of Parsonsfield."

"Oh! You should definitely check them out. They're a lot like the Lumineers. Or, maybe more like Mumford and Sons. Here," she pulled her phone out and typed for a minute before handing it to him. "They have the coolest videos."

He watched as the camera followed a trail of masking tape, inscribed with the lyrics of the folk-inspired song, as it snaked through a house. He'd definitely add them to his list of who to watch for. When the video ended, he asked, "Do you like jam bands?"

"No idea."

He ran a quick search, found what he wanted and handed her back her phone. "So, this is Creamery Station. I like this because they lean towards folk, too." He grinned. "And, incidentally, they're from Connecticut."

While she waited for the video to buffer she asked, "How'd you find them?"

"I had a roommate in college who's from Vermont, and these guys have a serious following there."

She propped the phone against the napkin dispenser as the video started.

Talan pointed at the screen, to marbled swirls of colors lighting the band and the background. "See the background? They have a person in the sound booth doing this thing with oil and colored water, and they're projecting that live."

"That's freaking cool." When the video ended, she said, "I love the harmonica. I'd go see them."

"You'd look good in a tie-dye."

She raised her eyebrows.

He elaborated. "They're a jam band. Their shirts are tie-dyes."

"Do you have one?"

"Not yet, although I'll buy one if I have the chance." He smiled as he typed another name. "I do have one for these guys, though."

Talan watched Macy's face, intent on the screen, and thought about other bands he could share with her. And wondered if, just maybe, she might want to go to that festival he'd bought tickets for.

# Chapter 19

Being up at eight in the morning went against every bone in Talan's body. Having to do it on a Saturday was straight up inhumane. Still, as soon as Macy was ready they climbed into the truck, drove to the gas station for coffee, and headed to the Barker's.

The only upside was that he got to watch Macy as she worked. It'd have been pretty much impossible not to pay attention to her. She was playing something that reminded him of the soundtrack from a 70's porno, and it was downright fascinating. Perfect for the orange Superbird she was working on. The oddball car had flopped when it was new but had gained popularity, and value, in the last few years. *Must be that giant air foil on the back.* The most obvious feature of the car, the air foil stood about a foot higher than the roof. This one still had the original Road Runner decal on it, too. And the giant Plymouth logo in white on the rear quarter. Driving that thing would be like screaming, "I belong in a 70's porno!"

*Hence, the music.* Struggling not to laugh out loud, he forced his eyes back to the clipboard in his lap, determined to list the options for the Cadillac he was working on. *Macy's gonna love this car. Tail fins, giant chrome bumpers, useless trim everywhere.* He could actually picture her running her fingers down the high-gloss, powder blue paint, with that dreamy expression she got when she really liked a car, her eyes catching the light as she looked at him.

"Talan?"

He jumped. "Yeah?"

"Do you have a minute to help me?"

She was standing next to the car, staring at him. Every time his eyes met hers, his mind stopped working and all he could think about was how badly he wanted to take her hand, pull her close, and kiss her. Even in the crappy light of the diner the night before, her fascinating eyes had demanded his attention.

"Talan?"

"Sorry. Yeah. Be right there."

She smiled and went back to the Superbird.

*Get your shit together. And do not act on whatever you're thinking.* He left his clipboard in the Cadillac and helped Macy push the Superbird back into the barn.

They'd just put their hands on the back bumper of a Corvette when his phone rang. He stood, "Hang on." He glanced at the name and his heart sank. He answered, "Hello?"

"Hi, Uncle Talan!"

"Hi, Sonja. What's up?"

"Are you coming today?"

He moved away from Macy. "I'm sorry, I'm working. Your mom didn't tell you?"

"Can you come later? When you get done with work?"

"Sonja, I can't. Uncle Gage sent me on a trip. I won't be able to see you for probably two weeks." It annoyed the piss out of him that Felicity hadn't told Sonja. "Is your mom there?"

"Yeah, hold on."

He could hear her yelling, away from the phone, for Felicity. When his sister came on the line, he said, "Liss, what the hell? You didn't tell her I wasn't coming today?"

"I did." She sounded exasperated. "She must have misunderstood, thought you were just at work. I'm sorry, I'll explain it to her."

He hung up, stuck his phone back in his pocket, and went back to the Corvette. "Ready?"

Instead of smiling, as he'd sort of expected, Macy looked at her feet. "Whenever you are."

The moment they had the car in position, she started shooting. No walking around it first, no music. Wondering what was up, he leaned on the car.

She stopped shooting. "Gage'll be really mad if you scratch the paint."

"Gage'll be mad no matter what I do. He's a total asshole."

Something flickered across her features, leaving her eyes unusually stormy. "Can you move, please? The quicker we get this done, the quicker we can go back to our lives."

Just a few minutes before she'd been sneaking peeks at him, smiling when they talked. He looked at her, wondering what was up. She folded her arms, awkwardly because she was holding her camera in one hand, and tapped her foot.

Completely confused, having no idea how to fix things because he didn't know what had gone wrong, he went back into the barn.

*** ***

Macy dropped into the driver's seat of the Corvette and fought back tears. Yeah, Talan was cool. And sometimes he was nice to her. But if she really thought about it, he'd never done anything to indicate he was *into* her. She'd just given meaning to a bunch of random moments, because she wanted so badly for them to *have* meaning.

*Hey, Sonja. What's up?* Then he'd walked away, to have a private conversation.

The night before at the diner, the whole thing with the candy bars, that he brought her coffee every day. Those things were just him being polite. Making the best of a situation neither of them had any control over. *It's high school all over again. Stupid Macy, thinking someone likes you for who you are.*

She wiped the single tear that had escaped down her cheek, took a deep breath and looked around the interior of the car. Might as well get to work. She began shooting.

Finished with the Corvette, she went to find Talan. He had music playing. Piano. Just piano, not a band. She followed the sound and found him sitting in a convertible Chevy Bel Air, watching a video.

The music stopped and he said, "Slow down. It's not a race."

A child's voice spoke back, "It's fun to play it fast."

Even from behind, she could tell he smiled. "I know. And before you know it you'll be playing fast songs. But this song is meant to be played slowly. And for now, while you're learning the basics, you have to show me that you can play the music the way it was written."

Sounding resigned, the girl said, "Okay." The song started again.

Macy stood back, not wanting to interrupt.

When the song ended, Talan said, "Much better. I want you to practice that one again for next week, and I want you to concentrate on the tempo. That's how fast you play, remember?"

"I remember. Can I try the next one?"

"Turn the page and let me see it."

Macy moved, trying to see what was on the screen. Her movement caught Talan's attention. He glanced at her and, to her surprise, waved her over.

The voice from the phone said, "Uncle Talan? Can you see it?"

He directed his attention to the screen. "Yeah. Just hold the phone still."

*Uncle Talan? So...Gage has kids?* That idea was super weird. As quietly as she could, she settled into the passenger seat of the Chevy.

Talan's face was serious as he studied the screen. After a minute, he said, "Sonja?"

Macy's heart leaped, *Sonja is his niece, not his girlfriend!*

There was a blur of motion on the screen, then a girl's face. "Can I try it?"

Talan nodded. "This piece combines things you've already learned. Go ahead."

Macy sat with Talan and watched as he gave his niece a virtual piano lesson. While Sonja played, Talan closed his eyes. Every once in a while he'd ask her to stop and he'd make a verbal correction. And he gave her a lot of encouragement.

After a while he let her play through the entire new song. Then he said, "That was an excellent first go. You can keep practicing that one, but I also want you to go back to the one before and concentrate on the tempo. I can't write in your book, but it's only those two pieces."

"'Kay."

"If you get stuck, call me. I'm working, but you're not interrupting."

"Okay."

"Can you get your mom?"

Sonja yelled for her mom, who came into view a moment later. "Hey, Talan." She smiled, "This made her day. Thank you."

"No problem. I'm glad she thought of it." He continued, explaining his plan.

Logically, the woman could have been Gage's wife, but Macy was pretty sure it was Talan's sister. Despite that she had brown hair, there was an undeniable resemblance. She had the same dark eyes, the same thin face, and the same straight nose, although hers was lacking the lump at the bridge that Talan's had.

Next to Macy, Talan said, "If she needs help, have her call me."

They hung up and Talan turned to Macy. "Thanks for being patient." He smiled a little, looking somewhat embarrassed. "My niece has been working so hard, when she called and said she had a way to do her lesson today I couldn't say no."

"I'm glad you didn't." There were so many questions racing through her mind. Questions about his family, and that he played piano, and if he liked her.

"Me, too." He smiled, "I've never taught anyone to play before. It's surprisingly satisfying."

"You're very good at it."

He shrugged. "I'm not sure I'd go that far."

"I would." She gave him a half-smile. "Maybe if you'd been my teacher, I'd have stuck with it."

"You played piano?"

"For a bit. And violin, and clarinet. But I sucked."

"Actually, you blew."

She laughed. "Nice, Talan." More seriously, she asked, "What about you?"

"I don't suck. Or blow."

"Ha ha. I meant, well, obviously you play piano."

"I did, growing up. Then I switched to guitar."

"Electric or acoustic?" *Stupid question.* She tried to cover how dumb she felt. "I know nothing about guitars, by the way."

The way he was looking at her, smiling just a little, was so nice. "Both, depending on my mood and what I'm playing."

"I wish I could play guitar." *Stop talking!* She didn't though. "Or anything, really. I always thought it'd be so cool to be in a band."

"It can be cool, if you're in the right band." He held her gaze. "If you really want to learn, I could teach you the play the guitar. Or any other instrument, actually."

"What else do you play?"

He shrugged. "I can play pretty much anything. The flute, saxophone, drums," he grinned, "the tuba."

189

Memories of conversations they'd had flashed through her mind and suddenly she was too hot. She'd been talking music with an actual musician. *God, he must think I'm so stupid.* But he hadn't laughed at her. And he was leaning a little towards her, giving her all his attention. She'd already said more than enough stuff for him to taunt her with, adding another wouldn't make much difference. "It would be pretty cool to learn guitar."

"I'd like, very much, to teach you." With no hint of teasing, he said, "Electric, acoustic, bass, whatever you want, Macy."

They sat looking at each other for a long moment. She had the strongest feeling that he was going to kiss her. *Oh my God, please do.*

He cleared his throat. "We should probably do the next car."

Disappointment settled in her. "We probably should."

# Chapter 20

The bench seat of Talan's truck, upholstered in white vinyl, was possibly the most comfortable thing Macy had ever sat on. She slumped against the door, exhausted. Normally, photographing six cars would be a full day of shooting. Under the current circumstances that full day also meant she and Talan had pushed six cars out of the garage, then back in because they couldn't leave them outside.

Talan parked in front of their room. "Macy, take the first shower."

"I can wait." He'd helped all day, had made sure she was set before he continued with his own job, and she wanted to show her appreciation.

"It's fine, I have to call Gage anyway."

She felt guilty for going first. Although standing under the water felt utterly amazing, she didn't stay in too long. Once she was dressed in yoga shorts and a t-shirt, she pulled the bedspread off her bed, dropping it on the floor, and settled down to start editing while Talan showered.

The bathroom door opened with a rush of steam. He came out, his hair wet, wearing just jeans. She tried not to look. Or at least not to be obvious about it. Keeping her head down, she lifted her eyes to peek at him. Immediately she wished she hadn't. She was going to have a hell of a hard time not thinking about what she'd seen; his lightly muscled shoulders, the curly dark blonde hair that spread across his chest and down his abs, the way his jeans sat on his thin hips, and the dragon tattoo that curled up his back, over his shoulder to his chest.

He yanked the bedspread off his bed and collapsed on the blanket underneath. "Think there's any chance of getting a pizza delivered?"

"I don't know." It was nearly impossible to keep her eyes on his face. "I mean, the people who live around here have to eat, don't they?"

He sat up and reached for the phone between the beds. Right before his hand touched it, he pulled it back. "This place is a shit-hole." He stood up, wiping his hand on his jeans like he'd touched something gross. "I'll go see if they can give me a name in the office." He stuck shoes on, grabbed a shirt and left.

Macy fell back on the bed, squeezed her eyes shut tight, and thought about what had just happened. Her pulse raced; she was seriously turned on. Talan'd kept his eyes on her from the moment he'd come out of the shower until he'd almost touched the phone. Like he'd been—

She sat up abruptly. That thought was bad. *He likes the same music I do. And he's so sweet, like when he brought all those candy bars, and always making sure I'm all set with each car. And he's hot as hell. But he's also prickly as hell. When he comes back, he's probably going to snap that there are no pizza places that deliver and if I want dinner I better get my ass in the truck. Because you're seeing what you want. Because you like him. And if he really liked you, he'd have kissed you in that car today. Damn it.*

Crushing on a guy who had no interest in her had been her specialty, pretty much her whole life. *Stop thinking about him.* She sat on the bed and started at the door.

The door opened and Macy jumped.

"We're in luck." Talan perched on the edge of the tweed couch and unfolded a paper menu. "What kind of pizza do you like?"

Her heart beat so hard she could feel it in her chest. "Whatever."

He gave her a smart-ass grin. "Anchovies, pineapple and mush-rooms?"

She tried hard not to react, but she knew she made a disgusted face. "If that's what you want."

A small smile touched his lips. "Macy, what kind of pizza do you like?"

"Bacon, onion and tomato."

"Really?"

Wishing she'd said something normal, instead of the truth, she said, "Plain cheese."

"I like chicken, garlic and bacon. I also like Hawaiian." He brought the menu to her. "I've never had bacon, onion and tomato but it sounds really good."

She didn't take the menu. Instead, she said, "Bacon, onion and tomato. If you really want to know."

He nodded. "I really want to know."

Once he'd ordered, he sat on his bed with his laptop. She thought about putting her headphones on, but hearing his keys clicking, knowing he was just a few feet away, was nice. After a minute The Lumineers started singing about fame and fortune. Surprised, she glanced at Talan and wondered if he'd chosen The Lumineers on his own, or if he knew she liked them. He was staring intently at his clipboard. He had such a beautiful profile, the slight lump on the bridge of his nose making it just enough not perfect to be interesting.

He turned, caught her staring. And smiled.

Heat rushed through her. She jerked her eyes away, back to her screen. *Oh my god. Ohmygod. Oh. My. God.*

*** ***

Talan knew it was a bad idea. It didn't matter. He set his clipboard down and moved to sit next to Macy. She didn't look at him. *Keep it professional.* He nearly laughed at that thought, since they were sitting inches apart, on a motel bed. It was enough, though, to make him think past the desire coursing through him. "How are the pictures?"

"Not bad, considering the constraints we're working with." She turned her computer towards him.

He didn't look at her screen, though. Instead, he looked into her eyes.

*** ***

Macy could barely breathe. Slowly, so slowly, Talan raised his hand and touched her cheek. She inhaled, closed her eyes to concentrate on the sparks his fingertips sent into her. *Please let him want me.*

She opened her eyes. He moved forward. His lips touched hers and every thought in her head disappeared, replaced by the feel of the kiss. He slid his hand back, tangled his fingers in her hair, as he gently parted her lips with his tongue. She leaned into him, slid her tongue to meet his, and for long moments felt nothing else.

Feeling a bit dizzy, she stared into his eyes as he brought his other hand up to rest on her shoulder. Time slowed, nothing mattered but him. He sunk both hands into her hair, kissed her again.

She reached for him, gently pulling at his shirt, traced over his hip, the bare skin of his side smooth and warm under her fingertips.

He wrapped his arms around her, pressed his lips to her forehead and whispered, "Macy, I've wanted to do that since the first time I saw you."

Her heart hammered in her chest. "You have?"

The smile he gave her, sweet and a little crooked, was so cute. "You are the most beautiful woman I've ever seen. That day, your first day at work, I saw you standing next to that Hemi 'Cuda, in a Weezer t-shirt and purple Converse, I could barely put two words together. All I could think about was getting to know you."

*He remembers what I was wearing?* "I didn't think you liked me."

"I like you, Macy." He kissed her again, a soft brush of his lips over hers. Concern creased his brow. "I'm sorry you thought I didn't."

"I thought I was misreading you." She felt too warm as she added, "Because a lot of times you were... prickly."

"I'm sorry about that, too." He ran his thumb over her cheek. "You work for my dad and that makes this complicated, and I didn't want to risk putting you in that situation. Which is why I was trying to keep my distance." He shook his head. "But I can't. Every time I talk to you, I just like you more and more."

"Even that day in the citrus grove?"

"Well," his grin made her tingle inside, "maybe not that day." The grin fading, he said, "Macy, this is complicated. Are you okay with that?"

She didn't care. He liked her, that was all that mattered. "What we do in our private lives is private."

He kept his eyes locked on hers. "Keira has had no problem making your private life very public."

Heat filled her face. "That wasn't me. Keira knew Zack, she talked to him all the time."

He brushed his fingers over her cheek. "I know. I'm just saying, once Keira knows something, everyone will know."

"Then we'll have to make sure Keira doesn't know anything." Nerves screaming, she touched his hair, ran her fingers through it until they rested on his neck, then she kissed him.

He wrapped his arms around her, held her close, and returned the kiss.

*** ***

Talan handed Macy a plate of pizza and settled on the bed facing her. There were plenty of ways this thing between them could go horribly wrong. His dad could find out, and Macy would be fired. Keira could find out, make their lives hell, which would also basically ensure his dad found out, and *then* Macy would be fired. The relationship could not work out and they'd be stuck working together.

It was too late to turn back, though. *And I don't want to.* If she was willing to accept the risk, so was he.

And the risk was worth the smile she gave him as she said, "This is really good pizza."

"Glad you like it." He smiled in return, "Since it's the only pizza place in this area."

"That's totally crazy. I'm from a small town. Small, like, we only have one gas station. But there's seven pizza places."

His eyebrows shot up. "Seven?"

"Yup. And if you ask anyone, probably in all of Connecticut, they'll be happy to tell you what their favorite place is and give you a detailed explanation of exactly why. Which kind of crust they like, what kind of sauce, how they like their toppings. I never knew that was odd until I went to college and my roommate didn't understand why I wouldn't order from the national chain restaurant everyone else used." She grinned, "I couldn't make her understand that I wanted real pizza."

Curious, he asked, "So what, exactly, is real pizza?"

"There's more than one 'real' pizza. It can be New York style, or Neapolitan." She counted on her fingers. "Sicilian, which is really thick. Or New Haven, which is like paper thin and cooked in a brick oven so it's black on the edges. It just has to be handmade, and good quality, and not from a chain restaurant."

He loved how she could just spiel all that off. Intrigued, he asked, "What kind do you like?"

"It depends. New Haven style pizza is amazing, but you have to go into New Haven or Hartford to get it. If I was ordering at home, I like New York pizza because it has a thin, chewy crust. No matter what, the sauce should be basically like stewed tomatoes that have been put through a blender, so there's no chunks. But I don't like it to be pasty.

And not with a lot of spices, just basic plain tomato. Sometimes I like fresh mozzarella, especially on New Haven pizza. On New York style the cheese can be shredded, but it has to be good quality so it's not too greasy. And I like the toppings sliced thin so they don't get soggy. And there shouldn't be too many toppings, because then it overwhelms the pizza." Her cheeks tinted pink. "You're giving me the same look my roommate did."

He grinned. "Sorry. It is a pretty intense list."

She looked down and softly said, "Well, you asked."

Sometimes she spoke so confidently. Then there were times, like just now, when she was nervous. He didn't want her to be nervous with him. He gently lifted her chin and leaned forward. Stopping almost close enough to kiss her, he said, "I did ask. And when we get home, we'll order from whichever place in town makes the kind of pizza you like."

Sadly, she said, "I haven't found one yet."

He had to fight a grin. "Then we'll order from every place we can find until we find one you like." Then he kissed her. "And if we can't find one you like, we'll learn how to make it at home."

Sounding dejected, she said, "You can't make pizza at home. You need a brick oven."

Being careful not to crush their plates, he pulled her to him, specifically to hide that he couldn't stop grinning. "Macy, you're beautiful when you talk about pizza."

"That's weird."

He laughed. "I don't care. It's true."

*** ***

Macy carefully folded her clothes and set them next to her suitcase. They were filthy and needed to be washed, and normally she'd have left them in a heap on the floor, but she didn't want Talan to think she was a slob. Very aware of him moving around the room behind her, she messed with re-folding clothes so she could have another minute before she had to face him.

He asked, "Do you want to watch TV?"

"Sure." She turned to see him sitting on his bed, towards one side. Nerves fluttered in her stomach. It didn't matter that this was what she'd wanted all along, actually going to sit with him, on his bed, was scary. She sat next to him anyway.

"What do you want to watch?"

She hated that question. It almost always resulted in jeers. "Whatever you want is fine."

He narrowed his eyes at her for a moment before turning the TV on. She watched in silence as he channel surfed, even when he went past her favorite show— a sitcom about scientists. He stopped on a reality show about a lawyer's office. "How about this?"

She'd never watched any reality shows, but Emma did. She said, "My best friend from home loves this show."

"You don't?"

She raised an eyebrow at him. "Do you?"

He laughed. "No idea. I've never seen it."

She almost told him to go back to the scientist sitcom. But he'd teased her about the pizza, and she wasn't ready to open herself up to the possibility of more embarrassment. All she had to do was go along with whatever he wanted, just like she had with Zack. "This is fine."

After a few minutes, though, she couldn't sit quietly. The show was too annoying. "The office manager is seriously calling a meeting about how to answer the door?"

Pointing at the screen, he said, "It's obviously an issue. That delivery guy was stuck out there for hours."

She turned and stared at him, stunned that he thought the manager's behavior was okay.

He looked at her with a puzzled expression. "What?"

"The office manager was one of the people standing there, in plain sight of the door, listening to the delivery guy knocking. Why didn't she let him in?" She'd promised herself she was going to stay quiet, but the storyline made her so mad. "Plus, I mean, that girl the manager laid into about this didn't do anything wrong. She said if he'd rang the doorbell she'd have gotten it. But how was she supposed to know that's what the banging sound was? She couldn't see the door from her desk. And when you have a doorbell, you don't expect people to knock."

Talan was grinning. "Mace, it's fake."

She crossed her arms, feeling stupid for getting upset over a fake reality show. And feeling a bit mad about Talan teasing her. "I know. I just feel bad for her. I mean, it's obvious that the office manager is on some sort of power trip."

He wrapped his arms around her and kissed the top of her head. She let him pull her to him as he leaned back against the pillows, but she didn't relax. *Why's he hugging me, and kissing my head which is so sweet, if he's going to tease me? I'm just not saying anything. Period.*

"That girl? The one who keeps talking about her shoes? She reminds me of Keira."

Despite her renewed resolve not to say anything, Macy snickered. "Totally."

"That one? Who likes telling everyone what they're doing wrong? That's Vanessa." He ran his fingers over her arm. "And that one, who tells it like it is, is you."

"Me?" The girl on the show totally had her shit together. Macy felt more like the girl who got yelled at for not opening the door, always doing something wrong. "What have I ever done that's even remotely like that?"

Talan said, "When you first came to Dawson's, you didn't let Gage tell you where to take pictures. And you didn't back down about the Thunderbird. And even though we're working in crappy conditions here, you make sure the pictures of each car are perfect."

Feeling defensive, she said, "Well, I mean, Gage hired me to take good pictures. And the Thunderbird, I just didn't want Dawson's to get in trouble."

"I like that about you. That you don't back down." He pulled her closer, so her head rested on his shoulder, and whispered, "I like everything about you, Macy."

Her insides suddenly felt all mushy. *See, he's not being mean. He's just teasing you, like Logan does.* She knew Logan didn't mean it when he kidded her, it was just his way. And since she'd known him her whole life, they'd shared a lot of things they could kid each other about. Except Logan had never held her like this. And he'd never kissed her forehead.

She inhaled, let the scent of Talan fill her. She'd noticed, when she'd been close enough before, that he smelled very slightly of something that reminded her of wood, but more spicy, kind of. He began to trace random patterns on her back. She closed her eyes and concentrated on the feel of being with him.

It was so nice, to be there, to have him holding her against him. The TV droned on in the background but she ignored it, instead listening to Talan's heart beating softly. Her own heart beat harder as she slid her arm over him, found the bottom of his shirt and pushed it up so she could touch his skin. He inhaled sharply.

His skin was soft and smooth over his hip, then as she moved her hand across his abs there was the tickle of hair. She liked that sliding her hand over his hair made her hand feel tingly.

Fear warred with desire inside her as she considered doing more; unbuttoning his jeans or sliding her hand up his side. If she did more, he'd want more and eventually she'd have sex with him. *Once we have sex this'll be over. Damn it. I really like him.*

She wished she hadn't let her mind go there. *Just enjoy this. Worry about that when you have to.*

It was impossible to stop thinking about it, though. She didn't like sex, and it always became an issue. Not that she'd been with that many guys, but as soon as she'd told any of them, they'd been determined to prove her wrong. And she wasn't wrong.

And worse, as Talan had pointed out himself, doing this led to the possibility of someone at work finding out that they'd had sex. She'd had to rehash every date she and Zack had gone on with the entire office, and they'd never even gotten serious. She couldn't imagine what it would be like to have to discuss someone she was actually sleeping with.

Talan's hand slid down her back. He pushed her shirt up just enough to run his fingers over the bare skin of her lower back. Tingles of pleasure, like little sparks, spread through her.

She tensed, tightened her legs together. *Not ready. How am I gonna tell him no?*

He pulled her shirt down and moved his hand up to her mid-back. For a second she worried that he'd noticed her reaction, and that he was going to be upset. But then he brought his other hand to her arm and caressed her skin. And he didn't move to do anything more. She began to relax, to enjoy being held. *Maybe this time will be different.*

The voices on the TV started to fade. The only thing that mattered was Talan next to her. She tightened her arm. In response he kissed her forehead and mumbled, "Macy." At least, she was pretty sure he did. Maybe it was a dream.

She smiled. If this was a dream, it was perfect and she didn't want it to end.

# Chapter 21

Talan hit snooze on his phone, then slid an arm around Macy and pulled her close. "Morning."

She whispered, "Morning," as she slipped her arm over him.

He traced his fingers over her arm, pictured her freckled skin. *Wonder if she's got freckles everywhere.* What he really wanted was to find out. To kiss her, starting at her lips and working his way down her neck to her shoulders, across her chest, and eventually down her side and across her stomach, then down, until he reached her center. Just thinking about it had him turned on.

But he didn't do any of that, because he remembered the way she'd tensed the night before. He hadn't intended to do more than touch her side, but there was no way she could have known that. So he'd pulled back the moment she'd shifted and her previously relaxed breathing had, for a moment, paused. *What happened to you, Macy, to make you react that way?*

He had no trouble imagining ten different things it could have been. All of them made his blood boil. Whatever it was, he wouldn't push her to do anything she didn't want to do.

She was totally relaxed now, though, with her arm draped over him, her fingers at the waist of his jeans, and her head comfortably resting on his chest. He liked having her close, was totally happy just to be with her. "I thought I'd skip showering, since we're going to be filthy by the end of the day anyway."

"Okay."

"That buys us a few minutes, too."

She stiffened. Damn it. He wasn't looking for sex right then, but she must have thought he was. Wanting to stay as far away from that as possible, he asked, "Why do you brush your teeth in the shower?"

She lifted her head and gave him a completely puzzled look. "What?"

He wished she'd put her head back down. He touched the side of her face, ran his thumb over her skin. "I noticed your toothbrush in the shower and I just wondered. I do it because I used to live in a house with a whole bunch of people and there was always a line for the bathroom, so it seemed like it saved time. But then, I had this girlfriend who thought it was the weirdest thing she'd ever seen. And I've never met anyone else who did it."

Her eyebrows drew together. "Because..." She looked down, answered softly, "My hair's insane, and I used to get toothpaste in it sometimes and the kids would tease me. So, I learned in middle school that if I took a shower in the morning, and brushed my teeth in the shower, I didn't have to worry about it."

"Middle school kids are the worst." He moved, gently pushed her to lay down and propped himself up on his elbow so he could see her. Careful not to be forceful, he kissed her. "If I'd been in school with you, I'd have decked anyone who messed with you."

She smiled a little. "You don't really look like the fighting type."

"You'd be surprised. See this lump?" He pointed to the bridge of his nose. "Gage broke my nose, because I punched him in the face."

Her eyes widened. "You and Gage had an actual fistfight?"

"Yeah."

"Oh my God! Why?"

He shrugged it off, not wanting to get into his family issues. "We were teenagers, and brothers do shit like that."

"My brothers didn't." Her expression softened a bit. "Well, actually, maybe they did. I don't think either of them ever broke a bone, but they did break the coffee table." She snickered. "Then they panicked that our parents were gonna be mad, so they said Alex, my oldest brother, tripped over the dog and fell on the table."

"Yeah, I think all kids do shit like that." He lay next to her, took her hand and laced their fingers together. "My mom knew about my nose, because she broke up the fight. But there was plenty she didn't know about." He laughed, "A couple years ago at Thanksgiving, me, Gage and Felicity got into this whole conversation about all the shit we broke. My mom was pissed, because she never realized most of it. And Gage was pissed because he got in trouble for putting a hole in the kitchen wall but really Felicity was riding a skateboard in the house and she fell, but she never told anyone."

"Felicity's your sister?"

"Um hm."

"It's just the three of you?"

"It is."

"Is that Sonja's mom? The one you were talking to yesterday?"

"Yup."

"She looks like you, just with dark hair."

"Everyone says that. Then they all say Gage looks exactly like our father." It was nice, to just have this conversation and not worry about keeping anything from her.

"How many kids does Felicity have?"

"Four. And Gage has one."

She smiled, "I can't picture Gage as a dad."

"I couldn't, either." He added, "He's actually a really good one, though."

"Is he married?"

"No. He and Isabelle's mom broke up before she even knew she was pregnant."

She studied him for a moment before saying, "You and Gage never talk about your family."

He brushed her hair back, just because he wanted to touch her. "We don't bring home into work."

"When I first came out here, I went out for drinks with Keira, Vanessa and Sandra."

"I'm sorry."

Grinning at that, she continued, "I'm not. It was an experience, and I was lonely. The point is, they were asking me about what Gage does on the weekends. I thought it was so weird, that they didn't know anything about him."

"It's not. A few years ago Gage got a little too friendly with the receptionist. Not Celeste, the one before her. It got messy. Like, office supplies thrown through windows messy. She was fired and my father made it very clear that personal relationships and work were the be kept separate."

Very softly, she said, "Talan, if this doesn't work out, I won't make it messy for you."

He hated the fear in her voice. He lay back down and pulled her to him. "I've waited months for the chance to tell you how much I want to be with you. That, what you just said, is literally the furthest thing from my mind." He kissed her deeply.

She held him, even after the kiss ended. "You kiss with your eyes open."

"So do you."

"If you closed your eyes, you wouldn't know that."

He grinned. "I could say the same to you." More seriously, he told her, "I don't want to miss anything, Macy. And that includes seeing you when I kiss you."

Her cheeks went a bit pink. "I don't know what to say to you sometimes."

"Whatever you want."

"Sometimes I say such stupid things, though."

He'd said his fair share of stupid shit. He said, "Like trying to sell the new photographer a 'Hemi Cuda on her first day of work?"

She smiled enough to wrinkle her nose. It was downright adorable. "That was so cute. I love that you did that. And, just saying, if I had enough money to buy it and a place to keep it, I'd totally have bought that car."

"Yeah?"

"Yeah. The Hemi 'Cuda, the Shelby, that Superbird."

"You *like* that car?"

"The Superbird? Yeah! It's freaking awesome. I'd totally drive one. In blue." She batted her eyes, in a goofy overtly 'look at me' kind of way. "So it would match my eyes."

"Jeez, Macy. Now for all eternity I'm gonna picture you in that Superbird, with 70's porn music playing in the background."

The smile disappeared. "You're teasing me."

*She's right.* "Yes, I am." He let go of her hand and brushed the side of her face. "Because I don't know what to say to you, either. Because when I'm with you..." He had no idea how to put what he was feeling into words. "I don't know. I just say stupid shit when you're near me."

"I don't think you do."

He snorted. "No? What about the day I told you that you hadn't been having sex with the right people?" The moment it was out of his mouth he mentally kicked himself. *See that, stupid shit.*

She didn't tense up, though. To his surprise, she tipped her chin down, looked up at him and smiled. "Maybe you were right." Her entire face went bright red. "I certainly wasn't kissing the right people."

He could have taken her right then. Instead, he slowly moved his hand to her face, caressed her cheek, and touched his lips to hers. Her eyelids fluttered, then closed. He, too, closed his eyes, wanting to be completely immersed in the feel of having her in his arms.

Intent on not doing anything to scare her, he opened his eyes and pulled back. Her eyes opened slowly. He said, "You closed your eyes."

"Um hm."

"So did I." He kissed her forehead. "Macy."

"Hmm?"

Feeling ridiculous, he said. "Nothing. Sorry."

She sat up. "What?"

Grinning like a fool, he said, "Nothing. I just like the sound of your name."

She raised her eyebrows.

He pulled her back down. "And I like being able to say it to you."

"That's ridiculous."

"Yeah, well, I'm pretty sure we've established that being with you makes me say ridiculous things."

She smiled against him, but she didn't argue more. Instead, she snuggled closer.

*** ***

Macy stood with her hands on the bumper of a Cadillac and waited for Talan.

He glanced back and asked, "Ready?"

Ignoring that his gaze made her feel all mushy, she nodded. "Ready."

"On three. One, two, three." They pushed.

Slowly the car began to roll. Her shoulders burned with the effort but still they pushed. Finally, they cleared the barn doors. Talan grabbed the wheel and turned the car, trying to make it to a spot a few feet away where it would be in full sun.

She said, "That's good."

He reached in and turned the wheel once again while the car was still rolling to straighten the tires for her.

She sat on the bumper with her hands braced on her knees. When Talan joined her, she asked, "When's someone coming to take the cars we've done?"

"Tomorrow."

"I was hoping they'd be here this afternoon. I so don't want to put all these cars back into that freakin' barn."

Sitting next to her, he glanced around at the cars they'd pushed around the yard. "We're making pretty decent progress at least."

"I guess."

"What do you have in mind for a soundtrack for this?" He indicated the car they were sitting on.

Wishing she hadn't started playing music in front of him, she said, "I never told anyone that before."

"It's so cool. I'm glad you told me."

He was so sweet, about everything. She smiled a little. "So, um, for a '59 Cadillac Biarritz? Elvis."

"What about Chuck Berry?"

Immediately she felt stupid. "Is that more appropriate?"

He shrugged. "Not really more appropriate, but in the late '50s there was a lot of great music. Bobby Darin, The Big Bopper, that kind of stuff." He did a quick search on his phone and tapped play. "Do you know Ritchie Valens?"

"Yeah. My grandfather loves the '50s." Very upbeat drums and guitar began. She tapped her foot in time.

Talan stood, set his phone on the trunk of the car, and held out his hand. "Would you like to dance?"

"I can't dance to this." She took his hand anyway.

He pulled her up. "Sure you can." He put one hand on her back and held her other hand. "Put your hand on my shoulder and let me lead."

She tried to imitate him, but everything was too fast. She couldn't figure out what he was doing and she kept misstepping. "Sorry. I'm a terrible dancer."

"Hold on." He stopped moving, paused the music, and said, "This is basically three steps with a tap between each. Forward, tap, back, tap, side, tap." He led her slowly.

Feeling completely uncoordinated, she said, "My dance teacher told me I should try football."

"And my piano teacher tried to keep me from playing guitar. Do what you want, and never let anyone tell you not to."

She concentrated on mirroring him. Forward, tap, back, tap, side, tap.

"That's it." He smiled as moved her through the steps a few more times. "I think you've got it." He restarted the music from the beginning. "Ready?"

She snorted. "I can't be held responsible for what happens to your feet."

He held her firmly in position. "Follow me, you'll be fine." He began to lead her again.

She kind of got it, except where she concentrated on just moving her feet where she was supposed to, he had actual rhythm.

When the song ended, he said, "See? No football players." He pulled her closer and kissed her. "Just me and my beautiful Macy."

The next song started, much slower than the last one. And Talan, still holding her, began swaying. She had no choice but to follow. As he moved her around the yard he sang softly about hungering for her touch. She stopped thinking about where she was putting her feet.

When the music stopped, he still held her. "No football players at all."

Her heart hammered in her chest, so hard she could hear it.

Then, he let her go. "Let me know when you're ready for the next car."

*What the holy hell?* Feeling shaky, she watched him walk to the barn. Just as she was about to turn away, he looked back. Their eyes met and he gave her a half-smile before he disappeared inside.

*** ***

Macy sat on her bed and worked on the day's pictures. She sang along to whatever Pandora played on her modern alternative station and tried not to think about the fact that Talan would be back soon.

It was a lost cause. Every song reminded her of him, or was a song she wanted to talk to him about.

That was the coolest thing about Talan. He was the first person she'd known who she could talk music with. She and Emma had very different opinions on what was good and Emma was not open-minded at all. Logan listened to the same stuff she did, but he wasn't into music the way she was. He'd never understood her obsession any more than he understood why she loved cars.

Not that *Talan* loved cars. But he seemed to at least respect that she did. When they talked cars he didn't get all *'Mace, please, it's a car'* the way Emma had. Or doubt that she knew what she was talking about, like Logan, just because she was a girl. She did know what she was talking about, and not just with classics. Her dad had taught her how to change her own oil and do brakes, and she had a basic understanding of how transmissions and alternators worked, among other things.

She'd never needed to know any of those things, since she'd never owned a car, but she thought it was cool to know.

The song about sucking on fingers started. *Has Talan sucked on someone's fingers? Or had his sucked? So weird.* Even though she thought it was weird, she was suddenly very curious. And turned on. She glanced at the time on her screen, calculated how long he'd been gone.

It seemed like hours.

*Go back to work. He'll be here soon.* She tried to focus on editing, and got through three pictures before her cell rang. Not looking at the caller ID, she tapped the mute button on her computer and answered the phone. "Macy LaPorte."

"Hi, Macy."

Gage's voice was a letdown. She'd been hoping for his brother. "Hi, Gage."

"What are you doing?"

"Editing today's pictures."

"Talan's not answering his phone."

Propping her phone between her shoulder and ear so she could go back to working, she said, "He's probably driving."

"Where the fuck is he?"

Ignoring the f-bomb, she said, "Getting dinner. There's nothing around here. It's ridiculous, the only thing for miles is a diner and the only thing we can get delivered is pizza."

Changing the subject abruptly, he asked, "How many cars did you do today?"

"Six."

"You've got to do more than that. We need this done."

The impatience in his voice put her on edge. "Yeah, Gage, I know. But it takes a long time. It's just me and Talan, and we have to push every car by hand. They're old and heavy, and it's not easy."

"Paul wants more variety with the backgrounds."

"So do I, but we don't have much choice. If we could tow the cars, or push them with the truck—"

"No."

Irritated with his flat out refusal to listen to a perfectly good idea, she snapped, "Then you can either come up here yourself and push the cars around, or you can deal with what me and Talan can do."

"I can't come up there."

"We can't work any faster." The door opened and she watched Talan as he carried bags in and set them on the table.

"Have Talan call me." Gage hung up.

She dropped the phone next to her. "Gage can be a real asshole sometimes."

Coming to the side of the bed, Talan said, "You have no idea." He held his hand out. She took it and he pulled her up, against him. "I missed you."

The aggravation Gage had stirred up melted away. It was weird to be missed by someone, in a really good way. She didn't want Talan to know that she'd watched the clock the whole time he'd been gone, trying to calculate how long it'd be until he was back, so she said, "You were only gone for a few minutes."

He clasped his hands behind her back. "It was still too long."

She put her hands on his face, ran a finger across his lips.

His phone rang. "Of course." He moved away, swiped his finger across the screen. "What?"

*Probably a good thing.* She sat back on the bed and listened to him talk to Gage.

"I just walked in the door. She hasn't had time to tell me anything." There was a pause, then, "No shit. Everyone figures out you're an asshole at some point." Unexpectedly, he winked at her. His tone stayed nasty, though, as he talked to Gage. "What the fuck ever." He hung up, dropped the phone on the table. "He said I must be rubbing off on you."

"Why?"

He asked, "You told him off?"

"Not really. I just said unless he comes up here and helps us, we can't do more cars than we already are." She glanced at the bags on the table. "You found a grocery store?"

"I did." He smiled, "Wait until you see. They had rotisserie chicken and all the trimmings."

"Awesome." She joined him at the table as he began pulling containers from the bags. "Creamed spinach?"

"I love creamed spinach." Singing the new Blink 182 song under his breath, he scooped green stuff out of a container and plopped some on each of two paper plates.

They'd talked about what he'd get if he found a decent store, and chicken had been on the list, but he'd thought of everything, from mashed potatoes to a can opener for the cranberry sauce. It made her very self-conscious. She knew if she'd been in charge of getting dinner they'd probably be eating pre-made salad. Or maybe yogurt. Just yogurt. She'd been telling herself it was because she lived in a hotel, but she knew that wasn't true. The only time before coming to Arizona that she'd actually had to feed herself was when she'd been in photography school, and while her roommate had cooked things like beef stew or spaghetti and meatballs, she had pretty much lived on cold cereal and granola bars.

Once Talan had everything served, he set a candle in the middle of the table and lit it. He sat across from her and tried to be serious, but couldn't hide a grin. "Welcome to Chez Hotel From Hell."

She picked up the bottle of water he'd put out for her and raised it to toast. "Here's to shitty motels in the middle of nowhere."

He raised his own bottle and they tapped them together. "Cheers."

She tried the spinach first. After forcing herself to swallow, she wrinkled her nose and told him, "This is disgusting."

"Maybe it's an acquired taste." He tried a bite and immediately spit it out. "Or maybe it tastes like shit." He gulped water. "My mom makes it way better."

Raising an eyebrow, she said, "I'm not sure anyone could make it worse."

"When we get home, I'll get my mom's recipe and make it for you."

That was the third time he'd mentioned doing something with her when they got home. As they ate, she wondered if he'd really teach her to play guitar. And if he'd really make creamed spinach for her. She'd try it, even though she didn't think she'd like it. *That's the sweetest thing, that he's going to cook for me. No guy has ever done that.*

"What are you smiling at?"

She hadn't realized she was. "Nothing."

He gave her a look that seemed to say he didn't believe her, but he didn't push it. Instead, he said, "When do you think we're going to be done here?"

"Ooohhh, not you too. I'm working as fast as I can."

He gave her a crooked smile. "I'm just curious because this band I like is playing next Saturday and I was thinking that we could go, if you want to."

It was weird, and nice, to realize he was thinking about being with her away from work. And she knew she was going to do everything in her power to make that happen. "We've got twenty-three cars left and five days? I think we can probably manage that."

"Cool." He tapped the screen on his phone, moved his chair to sit next to her, and said, "Here, see if you like them."

She took the phone and propped it against her water bottle so they could watch videos together.

# Chapter 22

Macy stood in the bathroom, staring at her reflection. She hadn't used anything in her hair after her shower. Instead of perfect curls, her hair frizzed out of control. *Why did I do that? So stupid.* If she re-wet it she could possibly add anti-frizz serum. Sometimes it ended up looking greasy if she did that, though. Plus, she was literally going to bed. It felt ridiculous to "do" her hair.

Talan saw her every day— sweaty, filthy, sometimes in a bad mood. She didn't have to hide from him, pretend she was something she wasn't, like she had with Zack. Talan had already seen her, all through dinner and while they sat together and worked on getting the info for the days' cars sent to Dawson's.

Still, she wanted to look nice. She decided to put her hair up. While she worked to tame the curls, twisting them into a loose braid, she thought about what was going to happen when she left the bathroom. The night before she'd slept in Talan's bed, but it hadn't been on purpose. They'd been watching TV and she'd fallen asleep there. She didn't know if he'd want to share his bed again or if it had been a one-time thing.

With her hair under control, she turned to the door. *Here goes nothing.* She left the bathroom.

Talan sat on his bed, fully dressed and very obviously to one side. Their eyes met and he smiled, just a little. Relief coursed through her.

Except as she made her way to the bed, it was replaced with nerves. Sleeping with a guy usually meant *sleeping* with a guy. And she wasn't completely sure she was ready.

As she sat next to him, he reached for her hand and held it. "Do you want to watch TV?"

She shrugged. "If you want to."

"Do you want to see if the office manager fires that girl?"

She snorted. "That show's terrible."

"How about the sit-com about the scientists, instead?"

She narrowed her eyes a little, wondering if he knew she liked that show or if it was a coincidence. "Do you like that show?"

"I don't really watch TV. But you have that shirt, with the catchphrase on it. In scientific notation."

There was a flutter in her stomach. This wasn't the first time he'd mentioned one of her shirts. "Do you always pay attention to my shirts?"

"Macy, I pay attention to *you*."

She didn't know how to respond to that. It was weird, in a really nice way, to have someone paying attention to what she did.

Instead of turning the TV on, he reached for her, touched her hair, ran his hand down the braid. He pulled the elastic from the bottom. Then, he pulled her to him and kissed her.

She melted into the kiss, and the feel of his hand as he pulled her braid out and the way he sank his fingers into her curls. He ran his thumb over her cheek, slid his hand to the back of her neck and kissed her again.

She touched his side, slipping her hand under his shirt, running it up his back.

He pulled his shirt off and dropped it on the floor. She loved the way he looked. The way his muscles rippled, his tattoo, the way he had hair across his chest and in a line all the way down to where it disappeared into his jeans.

He took her face in his hands and kissed her. She kept her eyes locked on his, ran her hands over his shoulders, his arms, his chest, wanting to touch every part of him. She toyed with the button of his jeans. If she undid it, she could touch him. If she touched him, she could make him feel good. And she really wanted to make him feel good.

The button popped apart under her fingers. She started on his zipper, touched his bare skin, making him inhale sharply. She gently took him in her hand, began to slide up and down, squeezed a little harder as he moved against her. Wetness dripped from his tip. She ran her thumb over it, spreading it on his head.

He was perfect. Exactly, perfectly perfect. And she was touching him.

"Do you have any idea how good that feels?"

She shook her head.

He kissed her neck, along her collar bone, across her chest. His hand trailed down her side to her waist. Her heart beat so hard, she was sure Talan could actually hear it as he kissed her.

He began to push her shirt up. His fingers grazed her skin, sending shivers through her. His voice low, he asked, "Is this okay?"

She nodded.

He took her shirt off and dropped it on the floor, on top of his.

*We're going to have sex.* Nerves tightened in her stomach. *What if I'm loud? Or I make faces? I wish he'd turned the lights off.*

*** ***

Talan lay back on the bed, bringing Macy with him, gently making her lay on her back.

He knew where he wanted to end up, but he was going to take his time getting there. Especially because he could feel how tense she was. He began by kissing her lips, letting his hand slide down her side, over the smooth skin of her hip. He touched gently, fascinated with the shape of her. He whispered, "You have freckles everywhere." He took her arm and began to kiss the inside of her wrist. "Someday I'm going to count them all."

"Do you have any idea how many I have?"

Her tone was incredulous, but his reply was very serious. "No. That's why I need to count them." He turned her arm over, knowing there were a lot more freckles on the top of her arm than on the inside. "Starting here. One, two, three." He traced his fingers over her arm. "Five, seven, hundred... thousand." Up her arm, to where her pulse beat on the inside of her elbow. He accidentally brushed her breast.

Her eyes closed and she ran her hands over his shoulders.

He moved to kiss her chest. "Eleven... thousand... million." He brushed his lips over the soft swell of her breast. "There's no freckles here."

Her breathing was quick, shallow. "No?"

"No." He pulled her breast into his mouth. Her fingers dug into his shoulders.

*** ***

Macy struggled to concentrate. She needed to give Talan what he wanted. It was just that it was so hard to think. Every pull of her breast into his mouth was mirrored by throbbing pleasure between her legs. And what she really wanted was for him to touch her there.

Moving, trying to make that spot touch *something, anything*, she ran her hands down his sides to his hips. "This can't be comfortable." She tugged at his jeans.

"It's not." He struggled, got his pants off and let them fall to the floor, on top of her shirt. Next to him, she took her shorts off, too, then lay back. He ran his hand down her leg, slowly moving towards her center. She concentrated on breathing, on not freaking out. If this was what he wanted to do, she'd let him.

A jolt of ecstasy shot through her and, against her will, a moan escaped from her lips. She tried to tell him he wasn't supposed to touch her there, but she couldn't get the words out. She spread her legs, wanting more.

Instead of more, he pulled his hand away and moved to be above her. *Thank God, he's going to take me.* He reached between them and touched her.

*** ***

Talan rubbed the head of his cock against Macy, sliding it between her lips. She was so wet, he nearly slipped into her. It'd be so easy. He wasn't looking for fast and easy, though. He'd wanted her for so long, he was going to draw this out, to enjoy her. To learn what made her feel good.

He rubbed around the tempting softness of her opening, but had to pull back as she arched up. Very slowly he slid up between her lips. He knew he'd hit just the right spot when she gasped, her body shuddering beneath him.

"Talan, now."

Her breathy tone, the sudden burst of heat and wet, were too much. "Do I need," he was already sliding back down to enter her, "a condom?"

Her body trembled as she reached for his ass, tried to pull him down. "I have an IUD."

"This is safe?"

"Yes, are you?"

"Yes." He let the tip rest just inside her. Closing his eyes to concentrate, he waited for the right moment. Then he felt it— she tightened.

She whispered, "Please."

He pushed into her. He exhaled hard, groaning against her neck.

Then he was pulling back, the feel of her soft friction exquisite around him. Almost to the point of withdrawal, he stopped. She clenched and he pushed. The slippery hotness squeezed him and a spike of need twisted his gut. Again he pulled back, and immediately sank back into her, straining to touch deeper.

He could feel his tip touch all the way in. It was too late to stop. He thrust, hard and fast, as deep as he could, his cum exploding inside her, throb, again and again until he couldn't give more.

Spent, he wrapped his arms around her and whispered, "Give me a minute." That had been way too quick, she hadn't been anywhere near ready. Wishing it'd been different, that he hadn't needed her so badly, he took a moment to recover.

Once he was able, he asked softly, "What do you need?"

*** ***

Macy breathed in his scent, his weight on her a comfortable closeness. "Nothing."

"I didn't mean for it to be so fast."

She liked it fast. She didn't say anything.

His words tinged with worry, he asked, "Did I hurt you?"

"No."

He kissed her shoulder. "Am I squishing you?"

"No, you're fine."

He moved off her anyway, lay beside her with his arm over her.

She rolled over, keeping his arm where it was, and snuggled her back against him. It felt so right, to be there with him. She loved the way he trailed his fingers over her waist, to her hip, just barely touching her. She closed her eyes and let her mind drift. The memory of how it'd felt to have him inside taunted her. She could practically feel him entering her, his head pushing deep, his entire length filling her, wave after wave of pleasure surging through her, radiating from the pressure of him. When he'd finished and pulled out she'd felt... empty.

She still felt it. It was absurd, but she wished he was still in her. So much so that it was uncomfortable. She moved, tried to alleviate the annoyance. He pulled her closer, kissed the back of her neck, sending tingles through her. She moved again. This time, when she settled back down she could feel him pressing against her back, wet from what he'd left in her.

He slid his fingers slowly from her hip across her stomach, then down lower, making her suddenly uncomfortable. Her breath caught in her throat as he touched just above her hair. Panic curled in her stomach; she knew where he was going. His fingers drifted, touched, sent a burst of heat into her. Trying hard not to sound panicked, she whispered, "Stop, please."

Softly, he asked, "What's wrong?"

"Nothing."

"Do you want more?"

She shook her head. "Just hold me."

His hand stilled. "Is this okay?"

"Um hm." Closing her eyes, she let herself enjoy the way he held her, the warmth of him behind her, the way she could feel his slow, steady breathing. The way her pulse beat under his fingertip. The finger he'd stopped moving but hadn't pulled away. That finger, gently resting between her lips, was enormously distracting.

She pushed her hips back, trying to move so that spot would stop pulsing. Except he was hard again, and when she moved back he slid between her legs. Need shot through her. He began moving his finger again, gently circling. She wanted to tell him that he wasn't supposed to touch her like that, that it was masturbation, but it felt good and she didn't really *want* him to stop.

His head slid between her lips and his finger continued its slow, tortuous circles. Her insides began to tighten. She wanted the pressure of him in her, the way he had been just a short time ago. Refusing to admit what she wanted, she whispered, "You can take more, if you need it."

"This is for you."

Her intention was to reiterate that she didn't need anything, but when she opened her mouth to say so, he slid his finger down towards her opening. The pleasure it sent into her turned her protest to a moan as he rubbed just inside her. She shuddered against him. She wanted more, wanted his entire finger in her. She pushed back against him, but instead of touching more, he withdrew completely.

He ran his hand up her thigh, barely skimming the soft skin before pulling her leg and bringing it over his. He rubbed himself against her again, pressing his tip into her opening. She moved, tried to take all of him in, but he wouldn't let her.

The hand he'd used to pull her leg slipped back over her and his fingers started circling again, sending pleasant ripples into her. She felt herself beginning to clench. She needed him in her, to feel his hardness as she tightened. The tightening subsided and she sank back against him. But before she could catch her breath, it started again.

She knew what was happening; he was going to make her come. Desperate, praying that if he was in her he wouldn't notice what she was doing, she begged, "Talan, take me."

He moved, touched his tip to her, rested almost inside her. She focused on the feel. Her body heaving with need, she pushed herself onto him. Determined not to make a fool out of herself, she clamped her mouth shut, but as he entered her she moaned in relief anyway. She barely noticed; all she felt was how huge he was.

Arching against him, every muscle in her body contracted, then released, over and over, as she tried to find a way to get him deeper. She ground her teeth as she clenched around him, strained as he pushed into her, making her come harder and harder.

She stopped breathing, tightened uncontrollably once more, then lay limp, her insides still pulsing. Gasping for breath, she buried her face in the pillows, so glad he couldn't see her. She couldn't believe she'd let him touch her like that. Having him know that she liked it, that it would make her get off, was mortifying. She wished she could crawl away, but he had his arm around her, holding her tight to him.

When her breathing finally evened out, her body stopped quaking, he spoke. "Macy?"

Wishing she could pretend she was sleeping, she barely made a sound. "Hm?"

"Are you ok?"

"Um hm."

He ran a finger over her shoulder. "Can you look at me?"

With no reason not to, other than shame, she rolled over and looked at him.

He kissed her gently. "Are you sure everything's okay?"

He was so sweet, she didn't want him to feel bad. After all, it was her that was the problem. Forcing a smile, she told him, "Yeah. Everything's perfect." Then, to make sure the conversation ended there, she curled up against him with her face tucked under the covers.

# Chapter 23

The first thing Talan was aware of was the warmth of Macy's bare breast pressing against his arm. It was a relief to find that she'd stayed in his bed. After they'd made love she'd shut him out, burying her face under the covers, and he'd been afraid he'd wake up alone.

He rolled over and traced his fingers over the curve of her hip. She opened her eyes and smiled sleepily in the dim morning light. He ran his hand over her hair, pushing it back from her face. "You're beautiful."

She mumbled against his chest, "It's raining."

He listened to the soft tapping on the window. "Here we call it a monsoon."

"I don't work in the rain. And definitely not in a monsoon."

He pulled back enough so he could see her. Raising an eyebrow, he asked, "Afraid it'll ruin your hair?"

"Afraid it'll ruin my camera, actually. And I doubt Gage would like it if Rick Barker's cars got monsooned on."

Chastised, he said, "I was thinking about how my sister always freaks out about her hair when it rains."

"Yeah, my friend Emma's like that, too."

He pulled her back against him and closed his eyes as he took in the scent of her, the feel of her in his arms. She slipped her bare arm over him, a move that made his blood pound. He spoke softly, "If you can't take pictures, I guess that means we have the day off."

"Um hm."

He held her a bit tighter. "So we can stay here all day?"

"If that's what you want to do."

Trailing his hand down her back, he said, "Me and you, staying in bed all day? That's *exactly* what I want. The real question, though, is what do you want?"

*** ***

Macy wished she could tell Talan she wanted to stay there, too. It felt so good just to be with him, to be held. It was scary to let herself feel that way, though, and impossible to admit out loud. She closed her eyes and concentrated on his fingers on her shoulder. She mumbled, "Your fingers are scratchy."

His hand stilled. "I'm sorry. They're calloused."

She moved to her elbow, so she could see him. "From what?"

"Guitar."

"Like the Beatles." She added, "That was blisters, though."

"And it was actually Ringo."

Surprised, she said, "I never knew that."

"I don't think most people do. Probably because I doubt very many people think about it."

"I never did before. And I definitely didn't think you could get blisters from playing drums."

"I'd think you can get them from anything that rubs the same area of skin for a long time."

"Yeah, I can see that." She ran her fingers over him, tracing the dragon on his chest, the guitar clutched in its talons. "You must play a lot."

"I guess that depends on what you mean by a lot."

"Enough to want a guitar tattooed on you. And to have callouses from it."

"I do play that much, yes." He touched her cheek, brushed her hair back behind her ear.

She took his hand, brought it to her lips and kissed his palm. As soon as she did it, she wondered what had possessed her to do such a thing. He probably thought she was nuts.

He folded his fingers over her kiss.

She ran her fingers over his arm, admired the fine black lines of the dragon's wing, the shading that gave depth to the two-dimensional drawing. "How many sittings did this take?" She knew she was only looking at the front of the animal. It flew over his shoulder, one wing spreading down his arm and the other across his back, its tail curling down to his waist. Something that big, and that detailed, wasn't easy.

"Three." His hand wandered to her hip. "How about yours?"

"I did all the black one day and the colors once that had healed."

"I've heard the coloring is the worst."

Shrugging, she said, "It was worth it."

"Do you ever think about getting another?"

"Not really. I haven't had anything else happen that I'd want to commemorate like that." She shifted her gaze to his face. "What about you?"

"I haven't ruled out the possibility."

"What do you think you'd get?"

He touched the blackbirds on her shoulder. "That's one reason why I haven't gotten another. There's nothing that I really want. Yet."

She lay down, her head on his shoulder. "Do we have to call someone and let them know we can't shoot today?"

"I guess we should tell Gage." He rolled over, disturbing her from her spot, picked up his phone and typed a text.

His profile, lit by the light of his phone, was so beautiful, with his perfect lips, his not-quite-perfect nose. She wished she had her camera in bed, she'd love a picture of him like that. She could get up and get it, but she was naked and just the thought of walking across the room in front of him made her want to pull the blankets tighter around her.

When he'd finished typing and set the phone back down, she said, "He's gonna be pissed that there's a delay."

"I don't care." His voice dropping, he said, "I've got much more important things to think about." His eyes drifted to her shoulders. He pressed his lips against her skin and sucked gently before moving to her collar bone, then her neck. Finally, he moved away and looked into her eyes. "I've wondered, since the day I met you, what your skin tastes like."

She didn't know what to say to that.

He continued, "I thought you'd be salty, like the sea."

She tried so hard to ignore the sudden curiosity. But she had to know. She licked her own arm. Satisfied, she said, "I'm not salty."

A smile crept over his face. "No, you're not."

She looked at his arm. Before she changed her mind, she grabbed it and licked. He laughed, making her grin as she said, "You're not salty, either."

He snorted. "I am salty, just ask my father."

"Yeah, actually, you can be."

He touched her cheek. "I don't mean to be, especially not with you." He trailed his fingers down her neck. "Seeing you every day is about the only thing I look forward to."

Her stomach did this funny little flip-thing. "Glad I can be of service."

His fingers wandered lower, down her side, sending shivers through her. She ran her hand over his chest and stomach, liking the tickly way his hair felt. As she touched lower, he shuddered under her hand, his breath caught, and his fingers tightened on her waist.

That was exactly what she wanted. For him to feel good, for him to be satisfied. Because if she could satisfy him, he'd hold her. And she needed him to hold her.

*** ***

Talan paid very close attention to how Macy reacted as he moved his hand slowly over her body. Something he'd done the night before had been wrong, and he needed to figure out what so he didn't do it again.

Starting at her shoulder he traced small circles over her skin, down her arm, to the inside of her elbow, all the way to her wrist.

He shifted his eyes, noticed her nipples were hard. He kissed the fullness of her breast, pulled it into his mouth while he caressed the other, pressing his fingers into her soft skin. She moaned, pushed her hips up towards him. He felt her heat against his stomach. Keeping his mouth on her breast, he slid his hand down her side, across her hip. He moved off her so he'd have more room to touch her. *So far, so good.*

He glanced down at his hand, watched his fingers tangle in her hair briefly before slipping between her lips.

Her body went rigid. He quickly withdrew his fingers, jerked his gaze back to her face, saw the way she'd tightened her mouth, squeezed her eyes tight shut. *Shit.* "Macy?"

"Hm?" Even her response sounded strained.

*Damn it.* "Macy, I'm sorry."

Her expression became more puzzled than rigid and she opened her eyes. "For what?"

Carefully, he pulled the blankets up to her shoulder, then ran his fingertips over her cheek. "For whatever I did that wasn't good."

"Everything you did was good."

"Macy," he paused, thought about how she never wanted to give her opinion. "I need you to be honest with me. If I hurt you, or I did something that made you uncomfortable, or I did something you didn't like, I need to know, because I don't want to do it again."

She whispered, "You didn't hurt me, I swear."

"But I did do something wrong."

"I'm sorry."

It was his responsibility to make sure she was taken care of, no matter what that meant, and the first time they'd made love he'd gone and screwed it up. He thought about the night before, looking for cues he'd missed. Everything had been right. Her tone when she'd told him she was ready, that she was wet, her reactions. *But she didn't enjoy it. And I missed it.*

He hadn't missed it, though. Not completely. After he'd satisfied her, she'd been different. Guilt filled him. "Macy, I am so sorry." He took her hand and held it. There was no excuse for this. None at all. "I rushed you, and misread you. I wanted to please you and I didn't, and I am the biggest jerk ever."

"You're not. You didn't. Everything you did was good. It's that there's something wrong with me. I'm sorry, I should have told you. I just," her voice dropped. "I wanted you to like me, and now you won't."

"Why would you think, even for one second, that there's anything about you that would make me not like you?"

She squirmed. "Because that's what's always happened before."

"This isn't before."

"Talan, that's what every guy I've ever been with said. It's what you said, the day we took the Shelby. That I'm just not having sex with the right person. But I had sex with you last night. And I still didn't...." Her face turned a deep shade of pink.

"If I didn't make you feel good, that's not a problem with you, Macy. It's a problem with me."

"No, Talan, you don't get it."

"Then help me get it."

She whispered, "It's embarrassing. That you touched me. And made me..." Her face was deep red and she refused to look at him as she finished, "I mean, that's like, touching yourself."

All of a sudden it all made sense. He cupped her face in his hands and kissed her gently. Pressing his forehead against hers, he said, "Th—" and his phone rang. He closed his eyes, knowing without looking that it was Gage. No one else could possibly have such perfectly bad timing. "I'm so sorry. I have to answer that." Letting her go, he grabbed the phone.

*** ***

It was the hugest relief that Talan's phone rang. Macy slipped out of bed and headed to the bathroom, grabbing a shirt off the floor as she went.

Alone, with the door firmly closed, she pulled the shirt over her head. *Of course.* She'd grabbed Talan's shirt. She held the fabric to her face and inhaled his scent. She liked him. Really, *really* liked him. She loved talking to him. About music, and cars, and whatever else came up. And the way he held her, *god*, she couldn't get enough.

Now he'd never see her the same way again.

That was the worst part. Knowing that when he looked at her, he'd *know*.

It was impossible to forget the last guy she'd been with telling her it'd been great as he pulled his jeans on and grabbed his shoes on the way to the door. He'd paused just long enough to say he'd call her. She knew that was code for 'don't call me'.

When she opened the door, Talan was pacing. They were sharing a room, there was no way to avoid him. She steeled herself for whatever torture he'd devised while she'd been in the bathroom. But instead of saying anything about her confession he came to her, took her hands and smiled. "That's my favorite shirt."

Ears burning, she glanced down at the Tootsie Pop owl on the shirt. *Why couldn't I have grabbed my own shirt?* "Sorry."

"It looks good on you." He kissed her.

Surprised, she kissed him back.

He let go of her hands and wrapped his arms around her, and for a long moment did nothing more than hold her. She couldn't help it, she relaxed into his arms. He pulled the hem of the shirt she was wearing and spoke softly, "Although it'd look better on the floor."

She wasn't sure how to respond to that. It turned out that she didn't have to. He let go of her and said, "Gage wants to talk to you."

As Talan went into the bathroom, she called Gage. "I can't take pictures today. It's a monsoon." She went to the window and pushed the curtains aside to see rain lashing the glass.

Gage sounded annoyed. "If it stops early enough maybe you can get a couple cars in today."

"It doesn't look like it's going to stop. But if it does, we'll go."

She hadn't seen a drop of rain since leaving Connecticut. She was still at the window, watching, when Talan came out of the bathroom. He came up behind her and slipped his arms around her waist. "That would definitely ruin my sister's hair."

"And my camera."

"Your hair is so long when it's wet."

Quietly, she asked, "Do you notice everything?"

He pushed her hair from her shoulder and kissed her neck. His breath was hot against her skin as he said, "I notice everything about you."

She closed her eyes and leaned back into him. How the hell could anyone say such perfect things? How the hell was she supposed to not fall for him?

"Mace?"

"Mmmm?"

"Get back in bed. I'm going to get us coffee."

She turned in his arms and looked up at him. Her heart felt like it had exploded. She could barely hold herself together. She couldn't let him see that. Instead, she'd go for smart-ass. A slow smile spread over her face. "Talan Dawson, I think I love you."

He grinned. "Macy LaPorte, I always knew the way to your heart was through a coffee cup."

As he closed the motel room door, she whispered to herself, "You don't need the coffee, Talan."

*** ***

The coffee was hot and bitter, even with cream and sugar. Macy didn't care— it was coffee. She held the cup in both hands, sitting in bed with the blankets pooling around her waist, and sipped.

Talan sat next to her, his hand resting on her thigh. "The guy at the gas station asked where you were."

"Oh yeah?"

"Yeah. He figured I'd finally got sick of you and sent you back to live with your people."

"My people?"

"The ogres." His expression was completely serious as he said, "I told him there's no need. You're exactly like Fiona. Except instead of turning into a princess when the sun rises, you become tolerable after you've had your coffee."

She couldn't help it, she laughed. "I should be offended."

"But you're not."

"No."

"You can have this back anytime you want." He took the cup from her hands. "I know better than to stand between you and caffeine."

"Then why are you?"

"Because nothing can stand between me and you, right this second." He set the cup on the nightstand and pulled her to him. "I missed you."

"You were only gone for a minute."

"It felt like an hour." He moved them both to lay down.

She held him, listening to the rain beat on the window, feeling like she was suffocating. Air wasn't the answer, though. He was. Holding him tighter, she kissed him hard, slid her tongue against his lips, and when he opened for her, she tasted him desperately. "Tal—"

"Shhh." He squeezed tighter, kissed her. He pushed at her shirt, his shirt that she was still wearing, kissing her stomach, her breasts, her neck.

She arched against him, desperate need exploding inside her. She yanked at his jeans.

He stood and pulled his clothes off. She watched, appreciating the way he looked naked. She expected him to take her right then. Instead, he lay next to her and traced his finger over her arm.

"Macy, if I do something you don't like, anything at all, tell me to stop." He held her gaze. "I will, I swear to you. Because the last thing in the world I want is to hurt you or make you uncomfortable."

Her heart beat harder at his words. Even if it was a lie, it was a sweet one. "You can do whatever you want."

He shook his head a little. "This isn't about what I want. It's about us, together." He leaned down and kissed her softly. Speaking against her lips, he added, "And if there's anything you want me to do, no matter what it is, ask."

"Great idea. 'Hey, can you stop making love to me and just let me masturbate?'" She snorted. "*That'll* ruin the mood."

"If you say it like that, yeah, it will."

The aggravation she'd kept hidden for years bubbled to the surface. "How the hell am I supposed to say it?"

He ignored her tone. Continuing to kiss her, he began to move his hand slowly down her side. "You start by kissing me." Moving to kiss her neck, he spoke, his breath tickling her ear. "Then you touch my side." His fingers trailed slowly down her waist, across her hip. "Until you get here."

His touch sent sparks of need deep into her. She reached for him. He didn't let her touch him, though. His voice deep with need of his own, he said, "Then you say 'Talan, touch me, please. Because it feels so good when you do.'"

His fingers were pressing into her skin, just inches from where she wanted them.

"Talan, I know how weird I am. You don't have to pretend to like this." Blood rushed to her face and she blurted out, "And you don't have to do that again. What you did last night. I mean, you can just take me, so you're…" she finished meekly, "satisfied."

He studied her, his eyes drifting away from her eyes to her lips. He kissed her gently, pulling her lip a bit before resting his forehead against hers. "You're not weird." He smiled a little, "Well, you are weird. But not the way you're thinking. Wanting to feel good is very normal, and making you feel good makes me feel good, so, yeah, I do want to do that again. And again, and again, as many times as we can."

"Yeah, but, I mean, it's not normal. It's not the way it's supposed to be." She stared at him, wondering why he didn't understand.

"There's not any particular way it's supposed to be."

"Yes, there is." She couldn't believe she had to explain this to him. "We're supposed to have sex, and we're supposed to be facing each other, and it's supposed to feel good, and we're supposed to," she squirmed a little, uncomfortable saying it out loud, "get off. Together." Sure he would understand now, she waited for him to agree.

"Macy, it's hardly ever that simple, there's tons of positions, and almost no one gets off together. Almost always you have to take turns, like we did last night."

"Yeah, I'm sure." She didn't mean to be obstinate, but she knew she was right.

His response was much calmer than hers, his tone kind and patient. "I'm sure, too. Only about thirty percent of women can reach orgasm with penile penetration alone. Of the remaining seventy percent, about ten percent will never have an orgasm and the rest need stimulation other than penetration. That means you're in the majority, and not weird at all."

Still feeling belligerent, she said, "You sound like an encyclopedia."

"I should. I researched it thoroughly."

She couldn't imagine actually researching sex. "Why?"

"Because I was young and inexperienced, and I wanted to make sure that if I ever managed to get a girl in bed I'd know what I was doing."

"It's kind of self-explanatory, isn't it?"

"No, actually, it's not. Because it's not about sticking your dick in her hole." He caressed her bare hip. "It's about being together, and understanding what each of us needs."

The shame she always felt when she thought about what she liked filled her and she shifted her eyes from his.

He trailed his finger over the contour of her waist, up her side to her breast. She shivered at his touch. He smiled knowingly and continued to move up to her shoulder, then down her arm.

When he finally got to her hand, he said, "Men and women are made differently. I'm sensitive all over." He took her index finger and traced from her fingertip to the base, and back up. "But I'm most sensitive at the tip." He moved his finger around the tip of hers. "So, when I'm inside you," he wrapped his hand around her entire finger and slowly moved it up and down, "You touch every part of me, but especially the tip.

"Sex feels amazing to me. Inside you is hot and wet and slippery, and there's friction because you're tight. And when you come, you get tighter." He squeezed her finger. "And that feels even better. It's like you're pulling me in, until you get so tight I have to work to stay inside you."

She could practically feel him in her.

He continued, "Women are sensitive inside. But," he moved their hands, made her curl her thumb, ring finger and pinky down. "You're more sensitive on the outside. Specifically, your clit." He rubbed in a circular motion in the V where her index and middle fingers met. "Some women's clits are at their opening. When they have intercourse the guy's penis touches it and they orgasm."

This whole thing was making her extremely uncomfortable, in part because it was such an odd thing to be talking about but also because hearing about it was turning her on. She whispered, "The way you talk about this, it makes it seem so normal."

"Because it is. Every woman has a clit, and it's the most sensitive part of them. It's basic human anatomy. But most women can't orgasm just from intercourse, because their clit is further from their opening." He stopped circling the V and slid his fingertip up a little towards the back of her hand. "Some are just a little further up. And some, like you, are very high. Because that spot isn't stimulated during intercourse, they need something more than penetration to reach orgasm."

Her voice sounded breathy, even to her. "How do you know I'm like that?"

"Because I paid attention when I touched you."

It was devastating to have it explained in such understandable terms why she'd never liked sex. "You're saying I can't get off during sex."

"No. I'm saying you need more." He let go of her hand, brushed her hair back and kissed her softly. "And I'm saying that it's really important that you tell me what works for you, and that you don't pretend something's good when it's not."

"You really don't think I'm a freak?"

"No. Not even close."

"Talan," she swallowed hard, trying to keep her voice steady. "Will you touch me now?"

He slid his hand down her body, held her gaze as he began to circle his finger around her clit.

Closing her eyes, she concentrated on the feel of his fingers sliding over her, spreading wetness from her opening to her clit, making her insides clench and throb. In moments she felt the orgasm building. "I need you in me."

To her disappointment, he moved to his back, pulled her to straddle him. It never felt all that good when a guy wanted her that way. She'd do it, though, because this was what he wanted.

She started to lay down on him, but he stopped her. "Put your hands on my shoulders and keep yourself up." She did, although she thought it was weird to be kind of kneeling over him, on all fours.

He reached between them, took himself in his hand and began to slide his head between her lips, up to her clit. He circled it, pressing against her. She closed her eyes and concentrated on the feel. Her insides began to clench. As she moved against him, she asked, "Does that feel good to you?"

"Don't worry about me."

She opened her eyes. "I have to."

"Not this time."

"I want to."

He changed the way he touched her, sliding between her lips and just barely touching her opening. "Tell me when you're ready." He moved his hand, positioned it between them so she couldn't take him into her, and touched her again.

The feel of him, barely inside her. The way he touched her, making her tighten, the pleasure building, building... He began to move

237

beneath her. It was perfect, and suddenly she knew it was going to happen. Gasping, she begged, "Now. I'm coming now."

He grabbed her hips, pulled her down onto him. He felt huge, the pressure of his entry radiating out from where he pulsed deep into her. She held onto his shoulders, ground down on him, desperately trying to get him deeper. She saw him, saw that he was watching her, but it didn't matter. All that mattered was more. Her insides clenched tighter and tighter. She could feel him, hard inside her.

He thrust against her, arched into her. She felt it, felt him throbbing inside her, filling her. His fingers dug into her thighs, pushing her where he needed. His eyes rolled back, the muscles in his neck strained as he groaned with pleasure.

The world was nothing but him, pushing wave after wave of intensity into her, forcing pure ecstasy into every fiber of her being.

Unable to hold herself up, she fell onto him. Finally, he relaxed under her. She trembled, squeezed him inside her. He pulsed back.

Wrapping his arms around her, he held her. She lay on him as she tried to catch her breath. Slowly, the feel of being held close, the scent of Talan, the steady rhythm of his heart, calmed her. Long minutes later, she moved off him.

Keeping her in the crook of his arm, he trailed his fingers over her bare shoulder. "Mace?"

"Hmmm?"

"Are you okay?"

"I'm not sure." She smiled into his side. "I think I might not ever be able to move again."

"That's perfect. Because I really want you to stay right here."

# Chapter 24

Macy snapped the truck's radio off and answered Talan's phone. "Hi, Gage."

Sounding surprised, he asked, "Macy?"

"Yeah?"

"Where's Talan?"

She looked at him and smiled. She couldn't help it, she loved the way his hair was pushed back behind his ears, his profile in the oncoming headlights, and the small smile that played over his lips every time he looked at her. "He's driving."

"Where are you?"

"On our way home." She wasn't actually happy about that. She and Talan had been working for the last two weeks, but they'd been together. Now he was dropping her off at her hotel and going home, to wherever he lived. Startled, she realized she didn't even know where that was.

"You're coming in tomorrow?"

"Yes."

"Talan, too?"

She relayed, "Gage wants to know if you're going to work tomorrow."

His fingers tightened on the steering wheel. "Yeah, where the hell else would I go?"

She told Gage that Talan would be in, not in quite the same words, answered a few more questions and hung up. She settled back into the seat and watched Talan, hating the tension in his jaw. She reached for his hand, pulled it from the steering wheel, and held it.

He squeezed her fingers and gave her a tight smile. "Sorry my brother's such a dick. He should have given you until Monday off, considering how hard you've been working."

"It's okay. I like working."

"You do, don't you." He glanced at her, gave her a more relaxed smile. "You have this look, when you're shooting certain cars." His smile grew, reached his eyes. "Like the Shelby."

Butterflies erupted in her stomach. Feeling awkwardly shy, she said, "Actually, that day it had nothing to do with the car."

"No?"

She smiled self-consciously. She didn't have to admit it, but she wanted to. "No. That day, all I could think about was you."

The last bit of tension in his posture melted away.

It was after ten when they got to her hotel. He parked the truck in a regular space, instead of in the unloading zone, and they pulled her bags out and carried them up to her room together.

She opened the door and he followed her in. "So, this is where you live, huh?"

"Yup."

"It's nice."

"Well, it's got coffee anyway."

He grinned. "Gotta have priorities."

"Can't be going to work in ogre form." She tried to laugh, but her heart hurt, knowing he wouldn't be there in the morning when she had her first coffee.

"I guess I better let you get to bed." He took her hands and looked into her eyes.

"I guess." She tried to think of a way to say she wanted him to stay, without sounding desperate.

He let go of one hand, pushed her hair off her shoulder, and kissed her neck. She closed her eyes and inhaled, saving the memory of his scent. She slid her free hand around his back and pulled him close. When their lips met she practically melted into his arms.

Then he was pulling back, walking out the door, and he was gone.

Trying to ignore that it was very quiet without him, she started unpacking. She plugged her camera and flash batteries in to charge, then put the bags of gear in a neat pile in the closet. She was forever dropping clothes all over the floor, never cleaned toothpaste up in the sink, but she took excellent care of her gear.

Considering doing laundry, she turned to her suitcase and unzipped it. On top of the pile, neatly folded so the logo on the front showed perfectly, was Talan's Tootsie Pop shirt.

She picked it up and held it to her chest. How had he done that without her seeing it? She buried her face in it and inhaled, the scent of him so strong it made her head spin. She pulled her own shirt off and put his on.

*** ***

Talan lay in bed, staring at the ceiling. He'd never minded being alone, often actually preferred it. Now the empty space next to him just felt wrong.

He got up, grabbed a pair of jeans off the floor, and dragged them on as he made his way to the kitchen. He stood with the refrigerator door open, staring at a few orphan bottles of beer from who-knew-when. He didn't want a beer. He shut the door and went back to his room.

He turned the light on and picked up a guitar. Sitting on the edge of the bed, he strummed a few chords. He started to play the song he'd been working on forever, but his heart wasn't in it. He set the guitar back down.

This was a stupid waste of time. Nothing there was going to distract him enough.

He picked up his cell, turned it over in his hands, thinking. He typed, "I wish you were here." That was completely stupid. He deleted it and tried again. "What's up?" Just as dumb— he deleted it. It was almost midnight, Macy was undoubtedly asleep. He shouldn't even be considering texting her. He typed, "Hey," and hit send. He mumbled to himself, "You are an idiot, Talan."

Almost immediately his phone dinged. He read her reply, smiled despite that it was only one word, as creative as his had been. "Hi."

"What r u doing?" *Stupid. She's in bed.*

"Nothing. What are you doing?" came the response.

He typed, "Thinking about you." He stared at the words, knowing that was so corny. He couldn't send that. Then he hit send anyway. Seconds ticked by, became minutes. He was a hundred percent sure she wasn't going to respond to something that lame.

Then she did. "It's weird with you not here."

He dug a shirt out of the laundry basket he'd kicked into the corner, pulled it over his head without looking at what it was. He didn't care; he already knew it wasn't his favorite shirt. He paused in the living room long enough to stick his feet in shoes, then he was running down the stairs two at a time.

*** ***

Macy had tried really hard not to say anything that sounded too much like "I miss you." Guys got weird if they thought you were getting attached. Apparently she'd gotten too close because Talan hadn't responded.

She watched the light on the smoke detector blink and hoped her phone would beep again. It had only been ten minutes, that wasn't long enough to decide he wasn't going to reply. Really, even if he didn't, it didn't mean anything. It had taken her a while to figure out what to say, now it was close to one in the morning and he was probably asleep.

When her phone did finally beep, she jumped. All it said was, "Mace?"

She typed back, "Yeah?"

"Are you sleeping?"

She smiled. "Yes. I'm sleep texting."

Instead of a return text there was a soft knock on her door. Her heart hammered in her chest as she made her way through the dark. She had to fight back happy tears when she looked through the peep hole in the door. She flipped the security lock and opened the door.

Relief swept over Talan's face when he saw her, replaced quickly with a smirk. He pulled the hem of her shirt. "Looks good on you." As she opened the door more to let him in, he added, "It'd look better on the floor."

She locked the door behind him, wondering if he'd just shown up at her room at one in the morning to get laid. Before she could formulate a way to ask that, he was wrapping his arms around her, whispering in her ear, "I couldn't sleep."

She held him, relief at having him there washing over her. Then he was kissing her, and she was trying to move them to the bed, and he was pulling off her clothes, his clothes, getting them both in bed. She was already thinking about how it felt to be with him.

Once they were there, though, he didn't take her. Instead, he held her against him, kissed the top of her head softly. "Do you text in your sleep often?"

"Only when I need to." *That makes no sense.*

He laughed, but not in a mean way. "Just make sure the only person you're sleep texting is me." He ran his hand over her skin, down her back, to her hip.

"There is no one else." In the dark, her head against his chest, she smiled.

# Chapter 25

The morning sun glinted off the windows at the front of Dawson's Auctions two-story building. Macy sat in her rental car, her stomach in knots. Talan had gone home to change and she'd come straight to work, so he wouldn't be there yet. But she knew that the moment she saw him she'd smile. And if Keira saw it, she'd be suspicious. Especially since by now she was sure to know Macy and Zack weren't a thing.

She took a deep breath, squared her shoulders, and got out. She'd faked enough things in her life, she could fake this, too.

As she opened the front door Gage was already coming across the foyer. "Macy, welcome back."

"Thank you."

"Everything went okay?"

"Yes, it was fine."

"Talan behaved?"

Her ears got hot and she prayed she wasn't blushing. "Yes."

"Good. The pictures looked good, the catalog is already at the printer, and you and I are going to start the next batch of cars." He led her out through the lot to a seafoam green Ford Crestline.

As she settled into the white vinyl seat her phone beeped. She glanced at the message and smiled; Talan had sent her a picture of an ogre captioned, "Me, on days it's not raining."

*** ***

Gage parked the last car of the day and headed to the garage to check on a Model T that had just come in. Macy made her way through the log, squeezing between cars packed in so tight she wondered how whoever had parked them had managed to get out of the drivers seat. Once the next auction was over, in just a few weeks, a big chunk of the cars currently on the lot would go to new homes. In the meantime, they were packed in with cars that had already arrived for the auction after that.

"Macy," Celeste stopped her in the foyer, "Nate asked me to send you to his office."

Her stomach rolled. The list of reasons Nate could have for calling her to his office was pretty long.

Her sudden panic must have shown because Celeste smiled encouragingly and told her, "I'm sure it's fine. He's very happy with what you and Talan did."

If Nate knew what she'd done with Talan she was in for a seriously embarrassing meeting. Instead of trying to respond she headed down the hall. She struggled to stay calm as she knocked on Nate's door. When he called for her to come in, she broke out in a cold sweat. As she sat across from him, she locked her shaking hands together.

Nate didn't seem to notice how nervous she was. "Macy, it's great to have you back."

It was like listening to someone else as she answered without a tremble in her voice. "It's great to be back."

"I heard there was an issue with the rooms. I'm so sorry about that."

"It was fine." *More than fine.*

Nate folded his hands on the desk and leaned forward slightly. "Macy, I'm very happy with how things are going. I appreciate all you've done for us, especially the last two weeks." He paused, seemed to consider what he was about to say. "Gage has been working on a number of big deals, similar to what you and Talan just did."

Macy had to force down a hysterical laugh. If Gage was working on something like what she and Talan had done she didn't want to know about it.

"He doesn't have time to dedicate to driving cars to be photographed. Talan's going to be busy with what's come in since you were away. I've decided to allow you to drive, to help take some of the pressure off them. It'll be newer cars only, and nothing rare."

Macy stared, speechless.

Nate continued, "But if anything happens, one single scratch on even the least expensive car, you're done. Not just with driving. If you damage anything at all, you'll never shoot for us again." He paused, then said, "I trust you won't do anything stupid, like drive a rare Mustang at a buck twenty-five."

She continued to stare, her stomach churning harder at the mention of the Mustang. Did he know about that? He must. If he knew about the Mustang, what else did he know? He was looking at her, waiting for some sort of response. Finally, she managed, "Thank you. I won't let you down." She stood to leave.

"Macy, one more thing."

She turned back.

"Are you really still driving a rental car?"

*Embarrassing!* "Yes."

"If you see something on the lot you like, let Gage know. We'll work out whatever you can afford."

That was nearly as surprising as being allowed to drive. "Thank you!"

She practically danced to her office. Not office, she corrected herself. Her desk. She still didn't have her own office. But that was a small thing, compared to being allowed to drive. She couldn't wait to tell

Talan. If she was lucky he'd be alone and she'd get a minute with him.

She wasn't that lucky. Keira was at her desk and as soon as she saw Macy she stood up, a look of grave concern on her face. "Macy, hey, welcome back. How is everything?"

"Fine." She was immediately on guard; Keira was way too concerned. She turned to her desk, her back to Keira.

Keira come over and leaned against the wall, making it impossible to ignore her. "I heard about Zack. I'm sorry, that it didn't work out between you guys."

She eyed Keira, wondering exactly what Zack had said.

"I was thinking, I have this friend, Elton. He may be more your… style."

There was no way in hell she'd go out with another of Keira's friends, even if she wasn't with Talan. She briefly considered saying she was seeing someone, but that would lead to a million questions, none of which she wanted to answer. Instead, she said, "I think I need a little time. Ya know, to recover."

"Yeah, okay. When you're ready, let me know."

"I will." It was kind of strange, but she appreciated the gesture. As Keira started to walk away, Macy added, "Thanks, Keira."

"No problem."

She settled into her seat, her mind a whirl of thoughts she couldn't wait to share with Talan. He was most likely in his office. As she started her computer she tried to think of some reason to go see him. It wasn't something she usually did, which would mean Keira would notice.

She slid her headphones on and started a randomized playlist. Arctic Monkeys started singing about that girl, the one the guy was into. Macy wondered if he'd tried kissing her yet. A smile stole over her face; that strategy had worked pretty well for Talan.

She scrolled through files, check marking each image as 'edit' or 'discard'. These cars weren't bad. Not as nice as the cars—

A robotic voice interrupted her thoughts. "Hey bea-ti-ful do you want a cup of cof-fee?"

Her head whipped around. Talan stood at the door, a cup of coffee in one hand and his cell phone in the other. He raised one eyebrow and gave her a cocky grin as the voice spoke directly into her ears, "Need to make sure the o-gre stays a-way."

She yanked her headphones off. The motion caught Keira's attention; she gave Macy a weird look. Macy smiled and Keira went back to whatever she'd been doing. Talan set the coffee on the desk and went to his office, just as he always did.

Macy put the headphones back on. Bob Dylan was singing about the Tanglewood Blues, but over it the voice said, "Nice shirt. It would look bet-ter on my floor."

She grabbed her phone and texted Talan, "How are you doing that?"

"I hi-jack-ed your blue tooth sig-nal."

Unable to respond to the voice in her ears, she typed back, "That's crazy." Then she sent a second text, "Can you hear what I'm listening to?"

"No."

She thought about that for a minute. She'd gotten used to sharing her music with him, and having him share with her. If he had headphones, synced with her computer, maybe they could share at work. It seemed like such a cool idea.

She searched "sync two sets of wireless headphones to the same computer" on her phone. She read a half-dozen answers before she finally had to admit that even if it was technically possible, she didn't understand how to do it.

Shelving that idea, she texted Talan, "Thx for the coffee ;-)".

✳✳✳ ✳✳✳

Macy dug through the pile of t-shirts in her suitcase. She hadn't done laundry yet and all her Beatles shirts were dirty. She didn't want anything that seemed like she'd picked it because Talan would like it, so The Lumineers was out. So was Metallica.

She pulled out a simple black shirt with that one word across the front; *Coffee.* That was perfect.

In the car she rolled the windows down and cranked the AC even though she was only going to the grocery store a few driveways down. Talan was making spaghetti and meatballs; she was supposed to pick up bread.

It had seemed like a simple enough thing when they'd texted about it. Standing in the bakery department it suddenly seemed anything but simple. She almost grabbed a loaf of Italian, but that seemed so basic. Not Talan's style at all.

Every night they'd been away he'd taken care of dinner. And he'd done an exceptional job of it. There had been the baked chicken with all the trimmings. Then one night he'd made salads in their room, with pre-washed lettuce, a bag of baby carrots, grape tomatoes, grilled chicken from the deli, and two kinds of salad dressing.

*He had a loaf of French bread that night. Not whole wheat. That's helpful.*

He liked garlic. He'd gotten it on pizza, had ordered garlic chicken when they'd gotten Chinese, so maybe the ciabatta with garlic cloves. Or maybe the plain ciabatta, and she could put butter and minced garlic on it like her mom did.

But what if that was too fancy? What if he wanted the basic Italian bread after all? One night he'd microwaved tomato soup and made grilled cheese with the hotel room iron. He'd told her he loved old-school white bread and American cheese.

*Just pick a loaf.* She picked up a loaf and turned towards the registers.

*** ***

The sauce was simmering, the pasta drained and waiting. Talan dried his hands off and threw the towel over his shoulder on his way to answer the door. As he opened it a smile broke over his face. Macy stood in his hallway, looking very nervous. The best thing he could come up with to greet her was, "Hi." Lame, but there was no way he was going to start off their night by making some comment about how he'd literally checked the parking lot for her car three dozen times since he'd gotten home.

"Hi." She smiled back.

He could breathe. He hadn't realized he'd stopped. She glanced around him and he felt foolish for still standing in the doorway. "Come in." He moved to the side, making room for her to move past him.

He watched her intently, wondering what she'd think of his place. He'd made sure everything was tidy, and he'd put The Lumineers on repeat because he knew she'd like it.

It was maddening that he couldn't tell what she was thinking as she looked around the open space, from the kitchen and eating area to the living room. He'd brought a few girls home before, and none of them had ever been impressed. He'd never cared. But Macy... she was different.

Her gaze settling back on him, she said, "I brought bread." She held up a bulging shopping bag.

He took it, brought it to the island and started pulling out loaves.

"I wasn't sure what you'd like. They had so many kinds, and they all looked good." She was speaking fast. Too fast. That meant she was nervous. "I didn't want to get the wrong kind, so you can maybe freeze the ones you don't want tonight?"

He set the last loaf on the counter. He looked at her, her face flushed and her eyes hopeful. He moved, closed the space between them, brought her to him. "How about if we have the rustic ciabatta tonight. Then tomorrow we'll have the garlic one with hummus, and we'll save the Italian for Sunday and make Panzanella."

He didn't care about the bread, but he silently prayed she'd agree to be there all those days.

*** ***

Talan hadn't laughed at her inability to make a decision, or made snippy comments about her not being capable of something as simple as buying a loaf of bread. She slid her arms around his waist. "That sounds perfect." Then her face got hot and she asked, "What's Panzanella?"

"It's a salad made with tomatoes, cucumbers, olives and stale bread."

"Oh."

He kissed her forehead. "I better stir the sauce." He let her go and went to the stove. Over his shoulder, he said, "Can you cut the bread? There's cutting boards in the island and knives in the drawer next to the sink."

She watched for a moment as he reached into the cabinet above him for a bottle of something, added it to the pot, and continued stirring. He looked completely at home at the stove. *He's cooking, you can manage to cut bread.* She opened the cabinet he'd indicated, grabbed a big green board. There were a slew of knives in the drawer. She picked one and went back to the island.

As she held the bread with one hand and got ready to saw into it, Talan said, "That's probably not the best knife." She jerked her head up as he pulled out a different knife and came over to her. "That's a fillet knife. It'll make a mess out of that bread. This," he showed her a knife with a jagged blade, "is a bread knife."

Embarrassed, she mumbled, "I didn't know."

He smiled, but not in a mean way. "My dad has this thing about knives and which ones are for what. So, what you want to do," he took hold of the bread, "is hold it on its side. That'll keep the loaf from being crushed. Then move the knife back and forth. You don't want to push down, let the blade do the work." He cut a few slices.

"Can I try?" He handed her the knife and let go of the bread. She imitated what he'd done. Her piece wasn't even the way his were. "It's not as easy as it looks."

"You just need practice."

She asked, "You cook a lot?"

"I can only eat pizza or Chinese take-out so many times before I start to feel vegetable deficient."

She cut another slice of bread, correcting the angle when she noticed she was making one end thinner. Instead of a flat slice she ended up with a wavy one. "How'd you learn?"

"After my parents got divorced my mom went back to work full time and I started cooking to help her out."

"I think if I'd had to cook when I was growing up, we'd all have starved."

He brought plates of pasta over and set them on the counter. "I'm sure if you had to, you'd learn."

"Most likely not. When I was in photography school there weren't dorms, so I lived in an apartment. I managed ten entire months without cooking more than easy mac and instant oatmeal."

"What's easy mac?"

"It's mac and cheese that you just add water to and microwave."

He leveled a look at her. "That's disgusting."

She smiled. "Yeah, it kind of is."

*** ***

After dinner, Macy wandered through Talan's living room. She ran her fingers over the albums he had lined up on top of a bookcase.

Old-school vinyl, like her grandparents had. She pulled a random album from the shelf, Lynyrd Skynyrd's *Second Helping.* Next to that was Michael Jackson's *Bad,* and next to that Nirvana's *Nevermind.* "I have never been able to get into Nirvana."

From the kitchen, he said, "They were the voice of a generation."

"Not my generation."

"No, but what happened in the generations before ours influenced what's happening now, so it's worth understanding."

"That's true. A lot of what's on the radio right now sounds like what my mom listens to."

"Everything old becomes new again."

She picked up *Led Zeppelin III* and turned the paper wheel that peeked from the inner sleeve, watched as the images in the cut-outs on the front changed. "There's a band out of Michigan, Greta Van Fleet, who sounds just like Led Zeppelin. Even their original songs sound like them."

"I'll have to check them out."

She slid the album back in its place. "Why do you have records?"

"Last year my mom got me a record player and gave me all her old albums for Christmas. She'd heard people were going back to vinyl, that they said the sound quality was better, and she thought I'd appreciate that."

"Do you?"

"I do. I also appreciate the history associated with albums. With music in general." He came into the living room and stood next to her, fingering the edges of the albums. "Music captures what's going on in the world in a way nothing else can. Like rap."

She involuntarily wrinkled her nose.

He smiled. "I know you don't like rap, but in the '80s, when it first hit the music scene, it captured the frustration of the Black community. And in the '60s," he pointed at the Woodstock poster on the wall, "it was all about love and freedom, because America was fighting a war that most people didn't agree with."

"I've always wished I could have gone to Woodstock."

"Me, too. But we don't choose when we live. And some day there will be people saying they wished they'd been around to do the things we've done. Like being able to see Metallica live."

"It's pretty amazing, if you think about it, that people are still listening to them." She turned to him, hoping her explanation would make sense. "I mean, they've been around for like twenty years, at least. You know how many bands I listened to in high school, just a few years ago, that no one even remembers?"

"Good music has no shelf life." He sat on the edge of the couch, picked up a guitar from the stand next to it, and began to play.

Macy knew the song, it was on the radio a dozen times a day at least. When he finished, she said, "That's not old."

"Nope. But it was inspired by Chopin's *Nocturne*."

"I don't know what that is."

He said, "It's classical music. It was written in the early 1800's, and it's still relevant today."

"Huh. I've never listened to classical music."

"You should try it. Some of it's really amazing." He grinned. "And some of it is so bad, it incited a riot."

She tipped her chin down and gave him an incredulous look. "You're not serious."

"Yeah, I am. In 1913 there was a ballet called *The Rite of Spring*, by a Russian composer named Igor Stravinsky. It was cutting edge, for the time. The elite who attended the opening night in Paris were not impressed with the break from tradition, and they got into it with the Bohemians in the audience. There was shouting, things were thrown at the orchestra, the police reportedly dragged forty-ish people out."

"How do you even know that?"

"I studied music. Part of that included learning music history."

"Is that what you went to college for? Music?"

"It was."

It was tempting to ask him what one did with a degree in music. She'd been asked so many times, though, what one did with a degree in photography that she knew the question was both rude and hurtful. Instead, she asked, "Is that how you know how to play so many instruments?"

"I only did two semesters in college, then decided it wasn't for me. Part of the reason I went, though, was because I can play so many instruments. It's not something I really had to work at, it's something I can just do."

His offhanded admission, that he hadn't finished school, was surprising. She never wanted to admit she'd been a failure in school. "Do you still play more than one instrument?"

"I can, but I don't."

"Why not?"

He shrugged. "I decided a long time ago to concentrate on being really good at one thing, rather than decent at a lot of different things."

"Why did you choose guitar?"

He smiled a little. "I thought it would make me look cool."

"Really?"

"Really. Or, at least, that's why I chose it initially. Of all the instruments I've played, though, it's my favorite."

Awkwardly, she asked, "Will you play for me?"

"Sure. Anything in particular you want to hear?"

"Whatever you want to play."

He adjusted his position, settled, and began.

Goosebumps broke out over her arms as notes drifted from his fingers, words joining the music, telling of a bird— broken, waiting, learning to fly.

As the last notes faded he met her eyes. "I'll never be able to hear that again without thinking of you." He held out his hand. "Why don't you come sit?"

She sat next to him and said, "I think of you every time I hear that line in 'Sweater Weather' about how fingers taste." Her heart beat harder at his smile. Or maybe it was being close to him that had her blood hammering through her veins. Gently pulling his hand to her lips, she kept her eyes locked on his. She took his index finger into her mouth. And sucked.

He pulled his finger from her mouth, put the guitar on the floor. He took her face in his hands and leaned forward. He brushed his lips across hers. "Macy." He put his forehead against hers, looked into her eyes and whispered, "Will you stay tonight?"

Instead of saying yes, which was what she really wanted, she said, "I didn't bring a change of clothes."

"Clothes are highly overrated."

She whispered, "I'll stay, if you want me to."

"I want you to."

# Chapter 26

As he had every morning since Macy had moved in, Talan tried to ignore the alarm.

Macy mumbled from under the covers, "Make it stop."

He hit snooze then reached for her. "Come here."

"We have to get up." She moved to lay on him anyway.

"Just a few more minutes." He held her closer, knowing they weren't going anywhere until he hit snooze at least two more times. "We'll skip showers."

"'Kay."

When the alarm rang for the third time they got up. He left her digging for clean clothes in the pile of laundry that seemed to spontaneously re-spawn in the corner of their room no matter how many times they put it away. On his way from the bathroom to pour their first coffees he called, "Mace, can you find me something to wear?"

"Yeah." A few seconds later, she stepped into the doorway. "Do you know where I left that change of address form from DMV?"

"From what?"

She laughed. "Sorry, I forgot. Here you call it the DOT. I need to transfer my license."

"You're doing that today?"

"If I have time. Your dad was giving me shit about driving around on dealer plates. I can't avoid registering the car in my name forever, and I can't register a car in Arizona with a Connecticut license." She disappeared back into their room.

He stared at the space she'd just vacated, trying to get his thoughts in order. He'd known all along the day would come when they'd have to tell his father they were together. Now that it was staring him in the face, though, he wasn't ready.

There were things about it he looked forward to. Being able to introduce Macy to his mom, to his sister and her kids. Not having to worry all the time that one of them was going to slip up at work.

But he was not looking forward to questions he was sure to face from his mom and sister. And, the biggest reason he was keeping this a secret in the first place, he was terrified his dad was going to fire Macy.

She brought him a pair of jeans and a polo shirt and kissed his cheek. "Can't find khakis."

"Babe, I'm not supposed to wear jeans to work."

"I do."

"I know, but you're," he smiled, unsure why she didn't have to follow the same rules as everyone else. "Special."

She rolled her eyes. "I'm sure. Today you can be special, too. Or you can go to work naked."

"I'm sure that'll go over well." He took the clothes she'd brought. *She is special. Maybe special enough to not get fired?*

"Did you find that form?"

"Looking now." He set the clothes on the stool next to him, opened the drawer where he stuck things he didn't know what to do with, pulled out a stack of papers and started going through them. Bank statements, concert ticket stubs, expired coupons. The business card that guy who'd gone to school with Gage had given him.

He stopped, read the card. *James Camp, Talent Manager.* That had been months ago, before he'd known Macy. He hadn't forgotten about the offer James Camp had made, but he'd stopped thinking about it. *It's too late.* He shoved the card back where it'd come from, piled the bank statements and whatever else was in the stack on top of it, and shut the drawer.

When Macy came out of the bathroom, he told her, "I can't find that form."

"I'll just print a new one." She continued back towards the bedroom. "Mace?"

She stopped and turned to him. "Yeah?"

He tried to figure out how to tell her about his dad's rule. "Macy..." *What the hell am I supposed to say? That she doesn't really get it, that we can't tell anyone about us?*

She stepped closer. "What?"

"Nothing. Forget it."

Looking worried, she came all the way to him and took his hands. "Hey, what's wrong?"

He brushed her hair back and kissed her. "I was just thinking how much I love you."

"I love you, too." She smiled and stood on her toes to kiss him. "We have to go."

He let her go, knowing she didn't want to be late.

*** ***

By the time Talan got to Dawson's, Macy had gone out with her first car of the day. There were fewer and fewer cars she needed help with, and her being gone already was their new normal. *Because Dad trusts her.* It was an odd thing, for his father to trust anyone like that, and Talan couldn't help wonder what would happen when his father found out about them. He probably wouldn't trust either of them anymore.

As he walked to his office, he tried to imagine what it would be like if everyone knew he and Macy were together. *Easier, maybe. But Keira would have a field day with it. And once Vanessa knows...* He remembered vividly how nasty she'd been about Macy's tattoo and could imagine the kinds of things she'd say about their relationship. He didn't want to put Macy through that. *Assuming Dad doesn't fire her immediately.*

The issue wasn't Talan and Macy, per se. He very much doubted his father cared who he dated. It was that employee dating at Dawson's was prohibited. *But if I quit...*

The memory of James Camp's business card flashed through his mind. *It wouldn't hurt to call. Tell him my circumstances have changed.* Although the position he'd offered would have been filled, there was always someone, somewhere, putting together a band.

He dropped into his chair and looked at the stack of files on his desk. Since the last auction, and the catalogs that had gone with it, Dawson's business had increased considerably and there was always a stack of folders that needed his attention. He ignored them as he settled at his computer and instead considered how to phrase a search. "Guitarist wanted" seemed too simple. Unable to think of something better, he typed it anyway.

The search returned a bunch of websites dedicated to helping musicians find each other. He chose one and began going through drop-down fields to narrow what he wanted. *Accordion? Huh. Are there really so many bagpipe players around that they need their own category?* He clicked "lead guitar" and entered his zip code. He nearly choked on his coffee when the search returned more than five hundred ads. He scanned the descriptions under pictures of bands. *Jazz, nope. Punk, eeehhhh, no. Rock, maybe.* He clicked and began reading the requirements.

"Talan."

Startled, he jerked his head up and snapped at Gage, "What?"

Gage stepped further into the room. "I need everything you can find on Thunderbird convertibles."

Trying to cover that he'd been doing something completely unrelated to work, he said, "You're going to have to be more specific."

Annoyance flickered over his face. "Roadsters."

"Year?"

"Put together whatever information you can find on Thunderbird Convertible Roadsters."

"Why don't you have Keira do this?"

"Because I want you to do it."

Talan glanced at his screen, considered his brother, then said, "What are you going to do when I'm not here anymore?"

"You planning on leaving?"

"I was never planning on staying."

Gage stared at him for a long moment. "Thunderbirds. Convertible Roadsters. Everything you can find." Then he left.

*Absolutely no reason to stay here.* Talan sat in his chair, looking at the door, for a long time.

*** ***

In Macy's opinion, the 1987 Corvette wasn't a classic. This particular one also wasn't any fun to drive. She gripped the wheel, working to keep it under control. It was an embarrassment to be driving a Corvette at 55 miles an hour, but the car shook so bad she couldn't go faster. It wasn't a flat tire; it didn't have that feel. It was more like it needed air in all four tires. *Maybe just an alignment.* It didn't really have that feel, either.

She had intended to take it someplace cool, like maybe to the top of the nearest plateau so the city would be in the background. Instead, she took the first exit and headed to the commuter lot.

As soon as she parked, she checked the tires. All four were shot, covered with hairline cracks, like spiderwebs, over the sidewalls and into the treads. It sucked to drive, and it annoyed her that the car hadn't been fully inspected before she'd taken it, but she was already there and dry rot wouldn't show in the pictures so she started shooting.

She took her time, turning the car as often as she wanted, getting the lighting just right. Classic or not, someone would appreciate this particular model. It did have some pretty cool features. The electronic dashboard made her think of that 80's movie, *Back To The Future*, and there was always a market for convertibles no matter what year they were.

Driving back to the shop with the radio on, she smiled to hear that song about fingers in mouths. It still made her think of Talan, and thinking about Talan, and his fingers, always made her smile.

Gage was outside the warehouse, waiting for her. She parked the Corvette, slung her camera bag over her shoulder, and told him, "That car needs four new tires."

"Yeah?"

"Either that, or we need to have Talan add that it has to be towed away. Those tires are so rotted the car's barely drivable."

"I'll let my dad know." He pointed at a Rolls Royce. "Ready for this?"

"Sure." She knew she wouldn't be allowed to drive anything that nice.

Once they were on the road, he asked, "So, Macy, what'd you do this weekend?"

Gage never made small talk. Her defenses suddenly up, she answered as casually as she could, "Nothing much. Saturday night I went out with a friend to see this new local band."

"Oh yeah? Where was that?"

She figured it was safe to be honest; Talan wouldn't have told Gage anything about his weekend. They only talked when Talan couldn't avoid it. "Foundry 41."

"What kind of band?"

"Alternative."

"Is that what you like? Alternative?"

Not wanting to give too much away, or seem like she was avoiding by saying too little, she said, "I don't put labels, or limits, on what I listen to."

He nodded. "My brother's like that, too. I've heard him play Bach then immediately after play Metallica."

She didn't respond. She wasn't sure where this was going and she was terrified she'd give something away on accident. It was already bad that he'd associated what she'd said with Talan.

They came to the end of the exit ramp and he looked at her. "Do you have siblings?"

"I have two brothers."

He turned back to the road. "Do you have a good relationship with them?"

"We get along okay."

"You're lucky."

They lapsed into silence.

By the time they got back to Dawson's, four cars later, Macy was dusty, tired and looking forward to going home. She dropped into her chair and reached for her headphones.

Before she had the chance to slip them on, Keira said, "Macy, remember that guy I was telling you about? Elton?"

"Yes." It was impossible to forget; Keira mentioned him every chance she got.

"He's having a party this weekend. You should come. Vanessa and Sandra will be there. And Hailey, who you met last time you went out with us."

"That's really nice of Elton to invite me, but I'm going to pass."

Keira gave her a sympathetic smile. "Macy, it's really important that you get out and meet people."

They'd had this conversation, in one form or another, too many times to count. She was tired of it. "I am, actually. I've got tickets to a concert this weekend."

"Really." Keira immediately swiveled her chair and leaned forward, her elbows on her knees. "With who?"

"A friend."

Keira smirked. "Ah, I see. What band is it?"

"It's indie alternative. I'm sure they're not anyone you'd have heard of."

"Well, I'm glad to hear that you're making friends." Seeming satisfied, Keira turned to her computer. "And I look forward to hearing all the details Monday morning."

Macy's blood chilled, realizing she'd probably just made a huge mistake.

*** ***

It had taken Macy hours to get through all the editing she'd had to do. She'd been the second to last person out of the office; only Gage was still there. She trudged up the stairs towards the apartment she now shared with Talan looking forward to a hot shower and an evening of doing nothing. She paused in the hallway and listened through the door. If she hadn't known better, she'd have thought Talan was listening to the radio. The absence of drums and bass gave it away, though. Plus she recognized the song, and it wasn't something that the radio played. It was one of the songs Talan had written, one she'd become familiar with, about standing outside a window looking in. It was very sad, but she loved it anyway.

She opened the door as quietly as she could. Talan was on the couch, eyes closed, head down, as he sang. She loved the way he looked when he played. Hoping he wouldn't notice her, she closed the door and slipped off her shoes. She pulled her camera out and set the bag on the floor before tiptoeing closer to the couch.

Afternoon light, diffused by the white sheets Talan used for curtains, fell on his face. Macy squatted, held the camera to her eye and framed her shot to cut out everything except Talan and his guitar. She adjusted the settings, looking for a very shallow depth of field. She wanted his face in focus, nothing else.

Out of habit she bracketed exposures, then changed the settings. It didn't hurt to have a version where everything was in crisp focus. There was no telling what she might decide to do with these pictures and she wanted options. Satisfied, she refocused on his fingers and shot another set.

She zoomed out, including the room around him. Against the wall to her right were his other guitars. If she moved a little she could get his profile, with the guitars in the background. Trying to be super quiet, she shifted. The song was coming to the end. She framed, made sure it was what she wanted, changed the settings, and shot. *Plenty of space on the background for a title.* She smiled behind the camera as she pictured it. *The Talan Dawson Band.*

Talan looked at her. "Satisfied?"

She lowered the camera. It wouldn't be the same if she posed him. "Yes."

"I can keep playing, if you're not."

"You knew?"

He smiled a little. "I always know when you're in the room with me."

Her face got hot. "Oh."

He set the guitar down and asked, "Can I see the pictures?"

She moved to sit next to him and showed him the back of the camera.

He said, "This is how you see me."

"Yes."

"They're fantastic."

"You're fantastic."

He took the camera from her and set it on the coffee table before leaning back and bringing her with him. "I don't know that I'd go that far."

"I would." She turned to see him better. "Your songs are twice as good as half the crap they play on the radio."

Laughing, he said, "Twice as good as half the crap, huh?"

"Yes. I love that song, that you were just playing." She snuggled against him, the exhaustion from the day already easing. "Is it about you?"

He brushed his fingers over her hair. "Does it matter?"

"Yes."

"Why?"

She slid her arm over him. "Because you know I always want to know what songs are actually about."

"I do know that about you."

"And it's really cool that I can actually ask the person who wrote it."

He said, "It is about me."

She squeezed him. "I don't want you to feel lonely, watching other people live their lives. I want you to live your life."

"I wrote that a long time ago. My life then was very different."

She traced random patterns on his arm. "I always wonder if that guy from the Arctic Monkeys ever kissed that girl."

Talan laughed softly. "I'm sure you do."

Defensively, she said, "Don't tease me."

He tightened his arm around her. "I'm not. The things you think are fascinating."

She snorted. "Thanks."

"I'm serious."

"Okay, then I think it's time you wrote something new." She looked at him out of the corner of her eye. "Unless you're still sad."

He kissed her forehead. "As long as you're with me, I'm never sad."

"Then maybe you should write a song about me. A happy, singable one."

"A singable song about you. Hmmm." He pushed her gently off him, picked up his guitar and played a few chords. Then, grinning, he sang, "Macyyyyy you're a little bit spaceyyyyy, but I love you anywayyyyy."

She laughed. "Talan, not like that!"

"What's wrong with it?"

"I don't want all your groupies to think your girlfriend's a ditz."

"My groupies?"

She loved the smile he was giving her. It made her heart beat harder, and she hoped this never ended. "Yeah, your groupies. Because as soon as the radio stations get a hold of what you were playing when I came in, you're going to be at the top of the charts."

The smile faded a bit. "Macy, you know how unlikely it is that I'd ever have anything on the radio."

She hadn't actually thought about the possibility, she'd just been caught up in being silly. But it wasn't a completely outlandish idea. "How do you know, unless you try?"

He brushed her hair off her shoulder, all traces of the smile gone. "If I have a song on the radio, I hope it is about you."

There was nothing silly about this. She swallowed, whispered, "That'd be so cool."

He slid his hand to the back of her neck, leaned to kiss her.

She let him draw her into the kiss.

"Babe, I don't want groupies." He touched her cheek. "I just want you."

# Chapter 27

The shuttle bus from the parking lot to the camping area at Sounds In The Sand came to a jerky stop. Talan handed Macy two sleeping bags and hoisted a giant backpack over his shoulders. "Ready?"

"Yup."

They made their way off the bus and joined the line of people looking for an open area to set up camp. Tents were staked side by side, in loose rows, with as little room as possible between them. Talan asked, "Any particular place that looks good?"

Macy shrugged. "It's about the music. I'm not picky about the site." Laughing, she added, "Plus, from where I'm standing all I see is sand."

By the time they found an open space and dropped their gear, Talan was sweating profusely. He pulled a bottle of water from a backpack pocket, drank, and handed the bottle to Macy. "I'm sorry we don't have car camping passes."

She drank, then said, "It's okay. This is just part of the experience."

He kissed her forehead, ignoring the sweat dripping off her. "Camping in the desert in June is definitely an experience."

"I thought dry heat was supposed to be better than humidity." She wiped sweat from her face with the bottom of her shirt.

"It'll be better when the sun goes down." He unzipped the backpack he'd dropped. "Let's get the tent up, then see if we can find someone selling iced coffee."

"I don't like cold coffee."

Smiling, because that was so Macy, he said, "Have you ever tried iced coffee?"

"No, I don't *like* cold coffee."

"Iced coffee isn't like cold coffee. But I'll get you whatever you want." He stood and brought her to him. "Because I love you, and I want you to be happy."

She smiled sweetly. "I love you, too." Then, her smile grew. "Now, can we set up the tent? Because I can hear music already and I want to go *see* it."

"You can't *see* music." He teased her, but really he loved that she was as into this as he was. "But if you want to get there quicker, you can lay out the sleeping bags while I stake the tent."

She made a face, kind of smirking and puzzled at the same time. "Don't we need to set the tent up first?"

Talan pulled the tent from the carrying bag and it popped open, fully assembled. He set it on the ground.

Macy stared in awe for a moment. "Holy shit! That's cool!"

He laughed. "Wait, though, until we have to put it away. Easy-ups are not easy downs."

Once they had the tent and sleeping bags set, Talan pulled a pole from his backpack, extended it, and let the flag on the end unfurl. He jammed it in the sand next to the tent and said, "First time I came here, I didn't pay attention to where I set up. After the last band the first night, I wandered around for hours looking for my tent, which I didn't find until the next day."

"Where'd you sleep?"

He took her hand and started off in the direction the music was coming from. "Some random spot on the ground." After they'd gone a ways he paused and looked back. A guitar-playing dragon graced the bright red flag indicating where they'd set up. "I'm going to have to get a new flag made."

"Why?"

He squeezed her hand. "It needs to have a blackbird on it, too."

*** ***

Music, and ten-thousand other people, surrounded Macy and Talan. She leaned into him, swayed in his arms, felt the rumble of his voice against her as he sang. Squirrel Dog, the biggest name playing the main stage that night, was *on*.

Goosebumps covered her arms, despite the lingering heat.

Talan rubbed her skin. "Babe, are you cold?"

"Music."

He kissed her neck before joining back in with the lyrics. She was glad he understood that there was no unnecessary talking during songs.

They'd gotten there so late, they'd ended up towards the back of the crowd. That was cool, it meant there was more room to move. She didn't need a lot of room, but this was where the people who did need room hung out, and they were fascinating.

There was a guy a few feet away swinging glowing sticks tied to strings in an intricate pattern. And a little way past him were two women with lighted wings extending from their shoulders to their fingertips. They twisted and spun so the rainbow of lights swirled hypnotically. A girl came by with a hula hoop, managing to walk and twirl the hoop at the same time while lights chased each other around the circle.

As the next song started, Macy stopped looking around and closed her eyes. This was one of her current favorites and she needed to be completely immersed in the music, with no distractions.

271

*** ***

The early morning sunlight was bright even through the blue nylon of the tent. Macy pulled the sleeping bag over her face, tried to pretend she wasn't awake yet. The last band had exited the stage at two that morning, and it had taken her and Talan a long while to get back to their tent. Not that they'd rushed. It had been more of a meander through the crowd, past booths selling shirts and hats and stickers and all kinds of stuff by the light of battery powered lanterns, and eventually through the sprawling tent city until they saw their flag fluttering in the solar power light at the top of the pole.

They hadn't been able to sleep for a while. They'd talked, rehashing what songs had been particularly good. Then, they'd lay quietly, listening to people outside still partying.

She'd been to festivals like this before, and she'd never been one of the people out there laughing and drinking and calling to friends all through the night. Sometimes she wished she was, but she'd never had a big group of friends like that. Since kindergarten it had always been her, Emma and Logan.

But Emma didn't like the same music Macy did; any time she'd gone to concerts or festivals it'd been with Logan. Until he'd hooked up with Jennifer. After that, she hadn't gone to anything.

"You okay?" Talan mumbled, pulling her to him.

"Yeah. Why?"

"You're up."

"So are you."

He kissed her shoulder.

"Talan?"

"Hmmm?"

She was glad she was facing away from him. It was always easier for her to ask questions when she didn't have to look at him. "How come you never hang out with anyone besides me?"

"Why would I want to?"

She rolled over and looked at him. Her heart pounded at the sight of him next to her. She ignored the swirl of good emotions she felt and continued on the path she'd chosen. "I'm serious."

He ran his hand over her hair. "Because, Macy, you're the only person I want to spend time with."

"Don't you have friends, though?"

"No."

"Why not?"

"The people I was friends with growing up all moved away."

"How come you don't make new friends?"

He was silent for a long while before he said, "When I moved back I needed time alone." He kissed her. "Then I met you."

"So, you're not averse to having other friends?"

He smiled. "No."

She snuggled into his arms and tried to imagine what it would be like if she had a big group of friends to hang out with. They'd see bands at bars on Friday nights and go to each other's houses on the weekends. They'd set up tents together at festivals so they could sit around and talk after the last band. They'd text each other, just to check in.

*It wouldn't be anything like Logan and Jennifer. Talan and I would have the same friends.* She liked that idea. She pulled his arms tighter around her as she drifted back to sleep.

\*\*\* \*\*\*

The second time Talan woke it was because someone was throwing up next to the tent. He wasn't surprised, considering how rowdy the people next to them had been the night before, how their voices had gotten louder and more slurred the later it got.

He watched Macy, her face peaceful in sleep, and thought about her question a few hours before. Why didn't he have other friends? What he'd told her was true. There was no one else he wanted to spend time with. But there were moments when he missed being around other musicians. Missed having band mates.

If he was honest, he knew he'd purposely cut himself off from the rest of the world. Used Gage and Dawson's as an excuse not to open himself up to the possibility of being fucked over again. And for a while it had worked.

But lately, even before Macy had come into his life, it had become harder to ignore that he missed what he'd had. Creating. Being part of something. Allowing himself to be the person he really was.

He pictured band practice, the way it had been. How there had always been girlfriends around, hanging out together. If he joined a band, Macy would be one of those girls. She'd have other friends, and so would he. She deserved that. Late night practices. Traveling to gigs. If they actually made it, they'd have to go on tour. She'd have to stay home and work.

Macy's eyes fluttered open and soft smile spread over her face. "Hey."

"Hey."

"What are you looking at?"

"You."

A light blush rose in her cheeks. "Why?"

The now familiar feeling of crushing love filled his chest. "Macy?"

"Hmm?"

*Can I leave her for months at a time? Doesn't matter. I'm not in a band.* "You want to go get coffee?"

"Talan Dawson, I always knew you were my one true love."

They dressed and headed towards the vending area. The people they passed, walking to or from the tent area, standing in line at food trucks to buy breakfast burritos or power breakfast bowls or organic oatmeal topped with local honey, were mostly quiet this early in the day.

Talan stopped at the events board. Macy asked, "Is there anyone specific you want to see?"

"Yeah, actually." He pointed to a name. "This band, Shuffle? I saw them at Foundry 41. They're really good."

"Cool." She glanced at the clock above the board. "They don't go on for a while, let's go find that coffee truck."

"Gotta make sure you don't transform into your ogre form."

"Ha ha." She was smiling, though. "Why is it that no one out here can get my coffee right? I mean, it's pretty simple. Coffee. Regular. Cream and two sugars."

He grinned, remembering the very first day he'd met her and she'd looked at him like he was an idiot for asking what she wanted in her "regular" coffee. "Babe, 'regular' only means cream and two sugars in New England. Everywhere else it means you want regular coffee, not decaf."

She stopped walking and turned to him, a look of sheer disbelief on her face. "Oh. My. God. Are you serious?"

"Yeah, I am."

She began walking again. "That explains so much."

Once they'd had coffee they wandered through the vending area. As they passed the tattoo booth, he kidded her, "You should get 'coffee' tattooed on your...somewhere."

"My somewhere?"

"Yeah. I don't know where. 'Macy' and 'coffee' are just kind of the same thing in my mind."

"Oh yeah? I think 'Talan' and 'that was a totally goofy thing to say' are pretty much the same thing in my mind."

He squeezed her to him. "I'd agree with that."

275

"I could get Talan tattooed on my...something."

"That's bad luck, you know. To put someone's name on you."

"I know." She slid her arm around his waist as they continued down the aisle. "I'll just content myself with having Talan himself on me."

"That sounds like a fantastic idea."

She pointed at a rack of shirts in front of a booth. "We need to get shirts." She glanced up at him. "Have to support the bands, right?"

"We should definitely do Sounds In The Sand shirts."

"And Shuffle."

Surprised, he asked, "What if you don't like them?"

"Do you think I will?"

"Yes."

She squeezed his hand. "That's good enough for me."

He told the girl behind the table what they wanted and paid for their shirts. With his free hand, he intertwined his fingers with Macy's, turned to leave, and came face to face with James Camp.

Recognition crossed his face and he smiled. "Talan Dawson. How've you been?"

"Hanging in there." He turned to Macy. "This is my girlfriend, Macy. Mace, this is James. He went to school with Gage."

Macy said, "Nice to meet you."

James nodded to her before turning back to Talan. "What are you doing these days?"

He wished he could talk about this with Macy first, but with James right there this opportunity was too good to pass up. "Actually, I was just thinking about calling you. I've been working on solo material and Macy," he glanced at her, "seems to think it's twice as good as half the crap on the radio."

James laughed. "Yeah? I don't usually consider unsolicited material, but for *Talan Dawson* I think I can make an exception." He turned to Macy. "Especially since it comes with such a ringing endorsement."

She blushed. "He's really good."

"I know." To Talan, he said, "Email me a sample."

As soon as James had disappeared into the crowd, Macy asked Talan, "What was that?"

He pulled her gently away from the shirt booth and back towards the camping area so they could stash the shirts in their tent before the first band went on stage. "That was possibly a way to get that song you like on the radio."

She stopped in the middle of the path, ignoring the people walking past them. "What?"

"James is a talent manager, which is sort of like an agent, for bands."

"You know, like actually know, someone who manages bands?"

"Kind of. He was Gage's friend."

"But he knows you."

"Macy, a lot of people know me. Before I came to work with Gage, I had was in a band called Cyanide Suicide."

"Nice name."

He grinned. "Yeah, well, it was death metal. Anyway," he wished they weren't doing this here, surrounded by thousands of people. "Mace, this is complicated, and it's not something I talk about."

She squeezed his hands. "You don't have to."

"I think, actually, I do." He paused, considered where to start. "When I was in college, I joined a band that eventually became Cyanide Suicide. We were *okay*, until our bassist left. We replaced him with my girlfriend, who was, hands down, the best bassist I've ever met. And it was like magic." He could still feel that excitement that had gripped him the first time they'd all played together, when he'd known everything was perfect. "We wrote all original music, worked night and day, built up a following.

"But I was young and naive and I didn't see what was really going on around me." Uncomfortable, he had to force himself to continue.

"That my girlfriend had her own agenda. The band replaced me, and right after that they signed a recording contract."

"Oh, Talan. I'm sorry."

"I'm not. If I'd still been part of that band, I never would have met you." He smiled crookedly, "Plus, they changed all the songs I'd written, put their own spin on them, and their record tanked."

A crease formed between her eyebrows. "So, what does that have to do with Gage's friend?"

"I never paid attention to Gage's friends, I barely remember James. But guys like him are always on the lookout for new talent. He knew my name, and he followed my career. Including when I dropped out of music. I ran into him the night Shuffle played at Foundry 41. He knew I used to play piano, and it just happened that they were looking for a pianist. So he offered me an audition."

"You mean with Shuffle? The band whose shirts we just bought? That's playing the main stage in a little while?"

"Yes."

Dismay filled her voice. "He's the manager for Shuffle?"

"Yes."

"Wait. Shuffle wanted you to join their band?"

"James wanted me to audition. But they were looking for a pianist, and I don't play piano anymore."

Her brow creased. "Yeah, but Talan, you'd have been in a band. Doing what you love."

"Not really. I don't love piano." He smiled slightly, "It would have been like asking you to spend all day photographing used minivans. It's doing photography, but not what you love."

He watched her face as she processed that, saw her expression go from dismay to understanding. "Okay, I get that. So, then, exactly what just happened?"

"James is willing to listen to what I've been working on."

"And that's a big deal."

He didn't want to get her excited over nothing, but he also didn't want to lie. "Maybe."

# Chapter 28

Being at a festival, dancing in the sand with Talan, was the best thing. Being home, showered and clean for the first time in three days, was a close second. Macy stood at Talan's dresser, the dresser they now shared, and combed her hair. She smiled when he came up behind her. "Thank you for taking me this weekend."

"I wouldn't have it any other way." He took the comb, reached around her and placed it on the dresser. With both hands on her hips, he whispered against her neck, "You're beautiful."

She leaned back into him, feeling his warmth against her back. "So are you."

He smiled as he kissed her neck. "Guys aren't supposed to be beautiful."

She closed her eyes and concentrated on feeling him. "I don't care. You are." She loved the pressure of his fingers, squeezing her lightly.

He slid a hand up under her shirt. "You look good in my shirt."

"Thanks." She knew what was coming. Rather than diminish what he said, the predictability made her feel good.

"It'd look better on my floor."

She smiled, still with her eyes closed. He pulled at the shirt and she moved so he could get it off. She opened her eyes and watched in the mirror as he slid his hands across her stomach, cupped her breast, kissed the tanned skin of her shoulder. She began to move against him, a soft moan escaping from her lips. He slid his hand down to the blue lace at the top of her panties.

In the mirror their eyes met, and held, until he slid his hand lower. Her gaze moved, to watch his hand slip into her panties. He began to touch her, moving his fingers against her. She spread her legs a little, wanting him to be able to touch as he pleased. She could feel him pressing against her back, hard and needing. She reached behind her and touched his hip, trailed her fingers down bare skin to his ass, then around to try to touch him.

"Just relax."

She couldn't. Her mind was too fixated on the way his hand made the blue satin move, with the idea that she could feel what she was seeing.

She wanted more. To see more. She bore down on his fingers, needing him.

He slipped his hand out. She sighed, "More."

He hooked his finger in the top of her panties and slid them down, moved his hand up her leg, picking it up to set her foot on the edge of a drawer that was too full to close correctly. Then, he began to touch her again.

She stared at his fingers, fascinated at being able to see him touching her. She moaned, feeling him, the want inside her growing to hot need. He pushed from behind, his tip between her legs, rubbing her opening. She was throbbing, desperate. "Talan, oh god…"

He kept her against him with one hand on her hip and touched her with his other hand.

She rocked against him, reached between her legs and touched his cock, pressed it between her lips, rubbed her clit with his head, watched where they touched.

Then he was insider her. She gasped, the fullness satisfying in itself. It took effort to kept her eyes open, but it was worth it to see him moving in and out, his hardness wet with her, her wrapped around him.

She moved harder against him, wanting him deeper. She couldn't take her eyes off where they joined, even as her body trembled with release.

*** ***

Seeing her quiver around him, feeling her tighten, was so perfect, Talan needed to keep Macy moving exactly the way she was. He pulled at her, making her slide onto him hard and fast as he pushed into her. His cum burst into her, splashed back onto his head. He groaned as his wet combined with hers and he pushed into her again and again. And the whole time, he kept his eyes on where they were together.

Her legs buckled. He held her, slipping from her but not letting her fall. He moved them to the bed, lay down with her and held her.

*** ***

Macy woke to the feel of Talan holding her close. For a moment she thought he'd kept his arms around her since they'd made love, but that couldn't be right. The lights were off, he had to have gotten up after she'd fallen asleep.

"Are you okay?" His voice was soft, and there was no hint of sleep.

"Mm hm. Why?"

"Because I worry about you."

She laced her fingers with his and pulled his arm tighter around her. "I'm fine."

"Why are you awake?"

"I don't know." She let go of his hand, rolled over and smiled. "Why are you?"

He brushed his hand over her hair. "I was thinking about you."

In the mostly-dark of the middle of the night she couldn't see his eyes, the way the gold flecks gave warmth and depth to the darker brown. She couldn't see the shape of his nose or the way he smiled when he looked at her. But she didn't need to. She knew every part of him by heart. "What were you thinking about?"

"Macy," he traced circles on her shoulder. "I love you."

She was glad it was too dark for him to see the tears that sprang to her eyes; she'd have felt like a total idiot if he knew how much his words affected her. She remembered when she'd worried that she was imagining things, reading into the looks he gave her and the things he said. Now she knew she wasn't, that he felt about her the same way she felt about him.

"Babe?"

"Hmm?"

"Your camera can do video, right?"

"Yeah."

"Will you help me record something to send to James?"

"Yeah, of course." After a minute, she asked, "Do you have a song in mind for this?"

"I'm going to do the one about watching through the window, because you like it."

The lyrics of that song drifted through her mind, an idea already forming. *Talan at the window with his guitar, with the white sheets pulled back a little so he can look outside. That lighting'll be great. And I can go down to the parking lot and shoot some footage of him from outside. And when it gets dark we can do more, with the lights of the city showing through the window, and from outside with him lit from behind.*

"Mace?"

"Yeah?" She pulled herself out of her thoughts.

His arms tightened around her. "What do you think about me

quitting Dawson's?"

She didn't answer right away because, for entirely selfish reasons, that wasn't something she really wanted to happen. At the same time, she didn't want to hold him back. She briefly considered pretending she was completely okay with it. That would be a lie, though, and she wouldn't lie to him. "I'll miss you. I mean, the idea of going to work and not seeing you is pretty awful. But you being there and miserable is worse. I definitely don't want you to pass up an opportunity to follow your dream."

"I was thinking, if this thing with James doesn't work out, I'm going to try to self-produce an album." He ran his fingertips over her arm. "If you'll help me."

"Of course I will." She squeezed him.

"And, Macy, I don't want to keep this, us, secret anymore." His voice dropped. "We never should have in the first place."

It didn't matter that she'd been thinking about that herself just a few days ago, the idea of everyone knowing made her tense. It was too easy to imagine the looks, the way Keira and the other girls would talk about her behind her back. "Can I think about that?"

"How about if I just tell Gage and my dad." He ran his hand over her hair. "Because I want you to meet my mom, and my sister and her kids. And I can't do that if Gage and my dad don't know about us."

She mulled that over, nerves churning harder in her stomach. "Do you think your dad's going to be mad? That we've been together all this time and haven't said anything?"

"I don't know." He sounded worried. "It's a possibility that he'll fire us both."

Although she hadn't wanted to face it head on, she'd known that was a possibility. She let his words sink in, moved them around and tried them out. *I could lose my job because I fell in love with Talan.* It was an almost ridiculous thought. And one she found, now that it was out in the open, that she could deal with. "Talan, if your dad fires us for being together, he doesn't deserve us anyway."

He wrapped his arms around her and held her tight to him.

# Chapter 29

Macy jumped up, realizing she'd overslept. "Shit! Talan! We have to get up."

He rolled over and watched her throwing clothes haphazardly from the laundry basket. "Fuck it. Let's call in sick."

"I can't. I'm starting on that lot that just came in. Gage wants *all* those cars done by tomorrow." She headed for the bathroom.

She didn't have time to shower, so she tied her hair back in a loose ponytail in an attempt to keep from getting toothpaste in it. After she finished brushing her teeth, she re-did the ponytail more neatly, deciding she wanted her hair out of her face all day.

Talan brushed past her to use the bathroom. "Hon, go to work. I'll pick up coffee."

She kissed him lightly. "Thanks." She grabbed her gear and headed out, wishing she was back at her hotel. There she'd have been able to grab a coffee on the way through the lobby. She hoped maybe she'd have time to brew a cup once she got to the office.

It didn't work out that way. Gage was standing in the foyer, pacing, when she rushed in. "You're late." He stalked through the front door.

She turned around and followed him, trying to think of an excuse. By the time they got to the first car, she'd decided to say her alarm hadn't gone off. That was possibly true. Either that, or Talan had hit dismiss instead of snooze. Either way, she didn't remember hearing it at all.

There was no chance to tell Gage anything, though, because as she got in the passenger seat of a lime green Hemi 'Cuda he said, "I'd let you drive this one, but my father seems to think that's a bad idea."

Shame filled her and she spent the ride to the commuter lot staring out the window in silence.

By the time she was done with the car and headed back to the office her head was pounding. She needed that coffee. Gage had other ideas, though. Once he'd parked the Hemi 'Cuda, he handed her the keys to a '78 Cadillac and told her to find him when she was done with it.

There was nothing spectacular about the Cadillac, but the freedom of taking a car out on her own was still appealing. Macy drove through town, looking at buildings for something promising. There had been one that would have worked— it was avocado green, which would have looked great with the canary yellow car— but there had been too much traffic in the parking lot. She continued driving.

What she really needed was coffee. She pulled into McDonald's and got in line at the drive-thru. It wasn't Dunkin' Donuts, but it was caffeine. *God, I miss Dunkin'.* Apparently that was a New England thing.

There *were* still moments when she missed Connecticut, but as she inched towards the speaker she realized she didn't really consider that home anymore. "Home" was with Talan.

Despite the caffeine withdrawal headache, a sense of peace filled her. *Even if Nate fires me, I'm staying here.*

She knew in her bones it was time for them to come clean. Especially since Keira was going to want "all the details" of her weekend when Macy got back to the office, and she had no idea how to do that without mentioning Talan.

As soon as she had her coffee, she pulled into a parking space and dug in her camera bag for her phone.

After a solid minute, she sat back. *Shit.* Her phone was at home, on the dresser. Resigned to having to wait until she was back at the office to talk to Talan it was time to come clean, she decided to give up on finding a cool place to shoot the Cadillac and go to the commuter lot.

As the coffee kicked in and her headache receded, she began to pay attention to the car. Cold air blew from the vents. She'd have to make sure to let Talan know the AC worked. That was the first thing most of Dawson's Arizona clients asked about.

It was a huge boat of a car, but easy to drive. With an automatic transmission, power steering, and power brakes. The light at the next intersection was yellow. The brakes were fine, she had no problem stopping behind the white line. There was a slight jingling noise, maybe the muffler bracket—

The rev of an engine over the screech of tires broke into her thoughts. It seemed to happen slowly, allowing her to take in every detail. The driver was young, his hair short and dark, and for a split second he looked ecstatic. Drifting, in a tiny Japanese import with a white skull painted on the black hood. She had enough time to think he was an idiot. Then he was coming straight for her, and the delight on his face turned to panic. She could see him desperately yanking the steering wheel, trying to turn sharper, to avoid the yellow Cadillac in his path. Then, his face became a mask of terror as the compact car slammed into the Cadillac.

The impact forced Macy towards the passenger side. She was held in the driver's seat by the safety belt, pulled back with enough force to slam her head into the window.

Dazed, her head screaming with pain, she tried to shut the car off. She knew you were supposed to do that, because if you didn't something could happen. She remembered her dad telling her that when he was teaching her to drive. He'd be so proud that she remembered. She lifted her arm just as the passenger door opened.

Some guy stuck his head in and asked, "Are you okay?"

"Yeah." She tried to get to the keys again.

"Don't move. We're getting help."

She had to get out of the car. Had to see the damage. Nate was going to kill her. She started trying to unbuckle. No, not kill her. Fire her. Her heart beat hard, making the blood pound in her ears as she fumbled with the buckle, pushing glass off her lap and not caring that it landed on the floor. *I'm gonna be fired anyway, when he finds out about me and Talan.* She forced down a hysterical laugh.

The guy was standing at the passenger door yelling to someone else, telling them to relay one occupant, lacerations, possible concussion. The engine wasn't running. That was good, although she was sure she hadn't shut the ignition off. Maybe there was an emergency shut-off, like a kill switch or something. She'd ask her dad, next time she saw him. *Did the Camaro shut off?* She couldn't remember.

That guy leaned back down and asked, "What's your name?"

"Macy." *Duh, give him your whole name.* "Macy LaPorte."

"Macy LaPorte, how old are you?"

She started on the buckle again. "I have to get out. Can you help me? I can't get," she yanked at the belt, "this" she yanked again, frustrated, "undone."

"Just wait. The ambulance will be here in a minute."

She had to make him understand, she needed to know how bad it was. "I can't wait. I need to see it."

"See what?"

Wondering why he didn't understand, she said, "The car. How bad is it?"

The guy's features softened. He was probably as old as her dad, his hair mostly grey, his eyes alert behind his glasses. Maybe he knew why the engine had stopped. Before she could ask, he said, "I don't think you'll be driving it home."

"Fuck." She tore at the belt, desperate to get out of the car. Blood splattered on the belt. "That kid, the one who hit me." She glanced at the guy to make sure he was listening. "How is he?"

"He's fine. Those compact cars have crumple zones, airbags, that kind of thing."

She stopped pulling at the belt. Instead, she pushed gently down on the buckle, pressed the button deliberately, and heard the satisfying "click" as it released. "I need to call my boss."

# Chapter 30

Although her head was still pounding, Macy wasn't confused anymore. She knew what would happen next. The car would be towed, insurance companies and clients would be contacted. And Macy would be terminated.

At least this time there would be no question. No wondering if she'd be forgiven.

And this time, she was going to take responsibility right up front, beginning with making the call to Nate herself.

She sat on the stretcher and stared at the phone. Since she'd left her phone at home, the guy who reminded her of her father had been kind enough to let her borrow his. *Just do it. Get it over with.*

She wished she could call Talan first, to let him know she was okay. But since she didn't have her phone, she didn't know his number and there was no way to get him on his office line without going through Celeste. She used the man's phone to search for Dawson's and called the number on the website. She was just going to telling Nate and hope for the best. *Not that I even know what the hell the best is at this point.*

"Hello, Dawson's Auctions," Celeste's sunny voice answered.

"Hi, Celeste. It's Macy. I need to talk to Nate, please."

"I'm sorry, he's in a meeting."

"This is an emergency."

"I'm sorry, Macy. He left strict instructions not to interrupt him."
*The first time is the hardest.* "I just crashed the '78 Cadillac."

There was a moment of silence. Just as Macy started to wonder if they'd gotten disconnected, Celeste said, "Hang on, I'll get him."

Hold music started, some generic instrumental junk. She watched the cop talking to the kid who'd been driving the other car and thought she should be mad at him. He'd wrecked the Cadillac, and she was ultimately responsible even though she hadn't actually done anything wrong. She couldn't conjure anger, though. Just resignation.

"Macy?"

Nate's rough voice startled her and suddenly all the calm was gone. Her words coming fast, she said, "Nate, I'm sorry. I know you're in a meeting, but the police are going to want to talk to you. I was in an accident. This kid, he was drifting. Who the hell drifts in the middle of a busy intersection? But he did, and he hit me. I'm so sorry, the Cadillac's wrecked." Tears welled in her eyes as the reality of everything hit her. "The police will tell you where the car is being towed to."

"Are you okay?"

Stifling a sob, she said, "Yeah. But the car, I'm so sorry. Hold on, here's the police." She handed the phone to the officer as he came over. One of the EMTs gave her a tissue and she wiped her eyes.

*** ***

Talan finished his coffee and eyed the other cup. Macy had already been out by the time he'd gotten there and her coffee was getting cold. She wouldn't drink it once it hit room temperature. He considered drinking it and replacing it with a freshly brewed cup from the kitchen. Except she took hers with cream and sugar, and he took his black.

He sipped hers, immediately set the cup back down and mumbled,

"That's nasty."

When she got back he'd microwave it for her. In the mean time he'd make himself a second cup.

He barely glanced at Vanessa as they passed each other in the hall. It had been months since she'd voiced her distaste for tattoos and people who had them, but Talan hadn't forgotten the glimpse of who she really was. Not that it mattered; they mutually avoided each other.

It was harder to avoid Keira, who happened to be in the kitchen.

She put a bowl of something in the microwave and leaned back against the counter. "So, Talan, how was your weekend?"

He stuck a pod in the coffee maker. "Fine."

"What'd you do?"

He pushed the start button and considered how to answer. He smiled involuntarily as he remembered Macy, her blonde curls flying as she danced in the sun.

In a knowing voice, she said, "Looks like it was good."

No point in denying that. "Yeah, it was."

"So, what'd you do?"

"I went to a festival."

She looked at him critically. "Like Holi?"

"What's Holi?"

"It's the Hindu festival of spring."

"No." He shook his head at the ridiculousness of that. He knew nothing about religion of any kind. "A music festival. Like Coachella?"

Comprehension spread over her face and she laughed. "That makes more sense. Who was playing?"

"It was alternative music."

Her eyes narrowed and she tipped her head a bit. "Alternative?"

He didn't like the speculative look she was giving him. "Yes."

"Huh." The microwave beeped. Keira took her bowl and left.

Alone, he texted Macy and told her not to say anything to Keira about their weekend. Keeping this a secret was becoming increasingly difficult.

Back at his desk, he stared at a hand-written description of a Chevy Impala and thought about how to best approach his father. *Quit first. Then tell him about Macy. Since I no longer work here, I'd like to introduce you to my girlfriend. No, that's terrible. And it just highlights that I knew. Maybe ask permission? That's ridiculous. I don't need his permission. Probably best to just do it. Dad, I'd like you to meet my girlfriend. Then deal with whatever happens. Maybe I should talk to Gage first, give him a heads up. And to get a feel for how Dad might react.*

*Or I can just quit and never say anything about her. It's not like I see him outside of work. But she'll still see him, and I can't leave her here like that. It's going to be bad enough for her, once Keira finds out.*

He focused on the paper he'd been blindly staring at and sighed. It was Macy's job on the line, Macy who would have to live with the repercussions of this. And she wasn't ready. *Just hope she is before anyone figures it out on their own.*

"Talan." Gage stepped into his office without knocking.

He looked up from his computer, already thinking about saying something about Macy.

"Did you put together that information I wanted on Thunderbirds?"

"I'm giving notice." He nearly laughed, where the hell did that come from?

Completely ignoring that, Gage said, "Thunderbirds?"

*So fucking done.* "Gage, I'm quitting."

His face reddened, like their dad's did when he got mad. "I don't have time for this, Talan. Dad left to go deal with Macy, and I have to ex—"

"What happened with Macy?"

"Do you pay attention to anything that goes on here?"

Panic clutched him. *"What happened to Macy?"*

"She was driving that ugly yellow Cadillac and some kid hit her. Dad went to the hospital—"

"What hospital?" He stood up. "*What hospital, Gage?*"

"I don't know. Memorial, I guess."

"*You guess?*"

"Yeah. She was downtown when she got hit. That's the closest—"

Talan didn't wait for him to finish before he was running down the hall, out the front door. Then he was in his truck, starting the engine, barely looking behind himself as he backed out of the parking space way too fast.

He planned his route as he waited to turn left out of the lot. He wanted the quickest, easiest way, with the least lights. He chirruped the tires as he turned onto the road, not caring that he cut off an SUV.

*** ***

By the time the doctor was done stitching the gash in Macy's temple Nate was there. She sat on the hospital bed and recounted exactly what had happened. He stood in front of her, his expression stony, and listened.

She refused to look away, no matter how uncomfortable this was. When she was done, she said, "I understand what this means. I don't have anything personal at the office, but I'd like to say goodbye to everyone. If that's okay."

"Why don't you give it a few days. Then we'll talk."

For the first time she broke her gaze and looked down at her hands, clasped tightly in her lap. She nodded without looking up. "Yeah, that's probably a good idea."

"I'm going to go make some calls, get things rolling to take care of this. I should only be a few minutes."

"You can go." She smiled as much as she could. "It was nice of you to come."

"I had to. You need a ride home."

"I'll Uber. As long as it's okay to leave my car at Dawson's until tomorrow. I'm not supposed to drive today."

There was a flicker of something across his face. Concern? She dismissed that. Nate didn't have it in him. "Macy, I'll get you home. And don't worry about your car. It's fine where it is."

She couldn't let him drive her home, because that would be to Talan's. Before she could figure out how to get out of this, he said, "I'll be back in a few minutes."

She lay back on the bed. Her head really did hurt, and there was blood all over her brand new Shuffle shirt. That pissed her off. Maybe she'd call her mom and ask about how to get blood out of cotton. If it was cotton. She'd have to ask her mom how to tell.

The thought of calling her mom, telling her she'd wrecked another car, wasn't all that appealing. Worse, this time she knew she no longer had a job, so her mom was going to want to know how she was going to pay her business insurance, which was sure to skyrocket now that there were two totaled cars on her record.

Her mom would probably tell her to come home, to take that job with Aunt Holly. *Going to have to explain Talan.* She hadn't kept him a secret on purpose. It had just seemed easier to avoid the conversation. Until now.

She sat up, unable to relax, and instantly regretted it. Her head spun, making her nauseous. She lay back, closed her eyes and willed the feeling to pass.

"Macy."

Her eyes popped open.

"I got here as fast as I could." Talan rushed to her, taking her face in his hands, kissing her forehead. "Jesus, Macy." He spoke softly, "Please don't ever scare me like that again."

She wrapped her arms around his waist, put the undamaged side of her head against him and held him tight, the feel of being with him soothing her. "You shouldn't be here."

"Yes, I should." He held her close, kissed the top of her head. "I want to always be wherever you are."

Moving back so she could see him, she said, "Talan, your dad's here."

"I don't care."

"But—"

"Shh." He ran his thumb over her lips.

"But—"

"Macy, stop. I don't care about my dad, or Gage, or anyone but you."

"Did you talk to your dad?"

He shook his head. "Not yet. I was waiting for you to be ready."

"I'm ready."

He nodded. "That's good, because I'm pretty sure after the way I left just now that everyone's going to know."

*Guess that's that.* Changing the subject, she pulled at the bottom of his shirt. "I got blood on your shirt."

"I don't care."

"Actually, I was kind of hoping you knew how to get it out. Because there's a ton on mine, and I really like this shirt."

He stepped back a little and looked at her. "It is kind of a mess. I'll make it look better, though." He gave her a devilish grin. "When we get home, I'll drop it on the floor."

Unexpectedly, tears obscured her vision.

Panicked, he said, "I'm sorry."

Through the tears she said, "No, don't be. I'm just, I guess, more freaked out than I realized."

He kissed her softly. "Are you okay? Really? I mean, not to scare you, but that is a lot of blood."

"I'm okay. The doctor said head wounds bleed a lot."

297

He touched her head, peering at the bandage. "What's under this?"

"Fourteen stitches."

"Jesus. What happened?"

"I was at a red light and this dumb-ass kid drifted around the corner and smashed into me. The side window blew out and I guess my head hit a piece of glass that was stuck in the frame."

"Who the fuck drifts on a public street?"

She snickered. "That's exactly what I said."

Concern crossed his features. He glanced at the bandage. "I thought windows weren't supposed to break."

"That's only windshields, because they're laminated. Well, actually, all the side windows in cars older than mid-'50s are, too. Since then side windows are tempered but not laminated. So, yes, they do break."

He smiled at her. "How the hell do you know that?"

She shrugged, returning his smile. "I'm a car person, remember?"

"How could I forget?" He took her hands and squeezed them. "How long do you have to stay here?"

"I don't think long. The doctor said he was going to send a nurse with my discharge papers."

He looked into her eyes. "Macy—"

From behind them, Nate cleared his throat. They both turned to see him at the door. "Macy, I'm going to head out. Call me tomorrow and let me know how you're feeling."

"I will." Her face burned, knowing they'd been caught. "Thank you."

Nate shifted his gaze to his son. "Talan."

"Dad."

"Make sure she gets home okay."

"I will."

There was an odd, uncomfortable moment of silence. Then Nate turned and left.

Talan shifted back to Macy. "That wasn't exactly how I'd planned that." He sat on the bed next to her, slipped his arm around her waist and pulled her to him, "But damn am I glad it's done."

She whispered against him, "Me, too."

*** ***

Talan eased Macy's shirt over her head. His stomach turned to see that blood had soaked through, staining her bra and coating her skin. "Hon, get in the shower. I'll get you a towel and something to wear."

"I'm not supposed to get the stitches wet."

He traced her collar bone, more relieved than he could believe that she was standing there. "How about if I give you a bath?" He pushed strands of hair off her shoulder, thinking what a good idea that was. "I'll be really careful. And soaking in the hot water will make you feel better."

"'Kay."

The way she was looking at him, her chin tipped down just a bit, her eyes meeting his, a soft smile on her beautiful lips, had his heart hammering. He had to forcefully remind himself she'd just been in a car accident and it really wasn't the time to act on his impulses.

While the tub filled, he had her sit on the edge so he could take her sneakers off. He slid her socks off and she wiggled her toes.

Once he had her jeans off she reached for him, taking his shirt and sliding it up. He didn't, couldn't, resist as she brought it over his head and dropped it on the floor.

"There. Now it's perfect." There was no teasing in her voice. Rather it was soft, making his heart melt. She undid his jeans, pushed them off his hips, until he took over and yanked them completely off.

She gave him a devilish smile. "Talan Dawson, do you ever wear underwear?"

"Guys underwear are stupid looking." He wished he was wearing

299

them, though. He was totally hard, and there was nothing he could do to stop from poking her as she brought him against her. He kissed her, being very mindful of her injuries. He sank his fingers into her hair, just above the back of her neck and far from the stitches in her temple, reveling in the feel of her curls. Her lips on his, the way she sucked gently to taste him, had him drooling down her leg.

They had to stop. "Let's get you cleaned up." He held her, keeping her steady, as she stepped into the water. He expected her to sit, but instead she pulled on him. He stepped into the tub with her. She smiled a little and he knew it had been the right thing to do.

He sat first, then helped her sit between his legs as he leaned back against the porcelain. "Oh shit! That's cold."

She leaned against him. "Feels good to me."

He wrapped his arms around her and let her relax against him, closed his eyes and concentrated on the feel of her.

When the water reached the overflow drain, he shut it off with his toe and picked up a washcloth. "Tell me if anything hurts." He dipped the cloth in the water and began to slowly rub it over her stomach, her chest, and her shoulders.

She flinched as he touched above her left breast. "That's tender."

"Probably from the seatbelt." He dipped the cloth in the water again and instead of rubbing her skin he drizzled water over her. A lump formed in his throat as he thought about her being tossed around in that car, and about how much worse it could have been. "Macy, I love you."

She twined her fingers in his, held his arm across her stomach. "I love you, too."

*** ***

Macy stood in the middle of their bedroom and let Talan towel her off. It was nice to be pampered like this. Her heart seemed to grow too big for her chest when he handed her the Tootsie Pop shirt. She held it to her face, savoring his scent.

"Here, I'll help you." He took the shirt back and carefully held the neck open so she could get into it without disturbing the bandage covering the stitches. Then he brought her to his bed and held the covers back for her.

"It's only like four o'clock."

"I don't care. You need to rest."

She wasn't up to arguing. She slid between his sheets. "Can you get me a glass of water?"

"Anything else? Are you hungry?"

It was the first time she'd thought of food all day. "I don't know. I feel kind of nauseous, actually."

"Have you eaten anything today?"

"Just crackers in the ER."

"That's probably why you feel that way. Rest, I'll bring you something to eat." He kissed her forehead and left.

She snuggled down into the pillows, inhaled the scent of Talan. Talan, who was taking care of her. Who had come to her even though she hadn't been able to call him. A smile spread over her lips as she drifted to sleep.

# Chapter 31

Early morning light filtered through the sheets tacked over the bedroom windows. All through the night Talan had drifted in and out of sleep, worried that Macy was going to need him. That she'd wake in pain, or that there was some latent injury that would require immediate intervention. He knew she'd been fully examined, that there wasn't any evidence of internal injuries, but knowing didn't help at 3AM.

Now he stayed as still as possible, listening to her slow, even breathing, and wished she'd wake up. He felt ridiculous for it, but he wanted to talk to her. Just to hear her voice, to see the sparkle that lit up her eyes when she got excited about something.

He lay his hand on her side. It was a mistake; her breathing immediately changed.

She rolled towards him, failing to suppress a grimace. "Morning."

He pushed her hair away from her forehead. "How do you feel?"

"Sore." She gave him a weak smile. "And I need coffee." Her smile became a bit more natural. "Can't be starting the day in ogre form, right?"

He kissed her forehead, next to the bandage. "I'll start coffee, then be back with aspirin."

"Kay."

In the kitchen, as he scooped grounds into the filter, his mind wandered back to the day before. The twenty minutes between when Gage had said 'hospital' and when he'd walked into Macy's room and seen her alive had been the longest minutes of his life. He'd dialed her cell over and over, listened to her outgoing voicemail message at least ten times. Every red light had seemed to last hours. Explaining to front desk who he was there to see, trying not to drum his fingers impatiently while the woman looked up where to send him, had been torture.

Then he'd seen Macy laying there, covered in blood, her freckles standing out against the unusual paleness of her skin, her face peaceful. Panic had exploded in his brain. He'd managed one strangled word, *Macy*. And she'd opened her eyes.

He stood at the counter, staring at the coffee maker, and forced himself to breathe evenly. Everything was fine. Macy was home, in bed.

The bedroom door opened. *Or not in bed.* "Mace, what are you doing?"

"Gage texted you like twenty times. And I have to pee."

He didn't care about Gage, but he did care about her getting to the bathroom safely. He started towards her. "Hold on, I'll help you."

She waved him off. "I got it."

It took all his self-control to stay where he was. After the bathroom door closed, he finished the coffee and turned to the refrigerator. Macy had to be hungry. She'd barely touched the chicken soup he'd made the night before. Usually she ate yogurt for breakfast but he wanted to do something more for her. Something special. He pulled milk and eggs out, got a bowl and a cookbook, and looked up how to make pancakes. By the time she was out of the bathroom he was ladling batter onto a skillet.

"Babe, go back to bed. I'll bring you breakfast."

"I don't want to be in bed alone." She settled onto a stool at the island.

"Did you take aspirin?"

"I did." She touched his hand as he set a cup of coffee in front of her. "I'm okay, Talan."

The lump in his throat was embarrassing. Not wanting her to see him choking up, he turned back to the stove. "I hope these are as good as the ones the automatic pancake maker at your hotel spit out."

"They smell amazing."

He stacked pancakes, gave the plate to her and watched her pour syrup and take a bite before turning to the pan. "I put together music to send to James. I was hoping you could listen to it."

"Oh, shit, Tal. I was going to do that video for you last night after work."

"It's okay. I just want to send him something before too much time passes."

He brought his plate to the island and sat across from her. He opened a file on his laptop and watched her face as the song started, wanting to see if she approved.

Macy closed her eyes. Her lips moved to the lyrics. It felt odd, that she knew all the words to a song that hadn't been played anywhere outside his apartment. The guitar solo began and she smiled; Talan released the breath he hadn't realized he'd been holding.

When the song ended, she opened her eyes. "That's perfect. Send it."

"Are you sure?"

"Yes." She took a bite of pancakes.

He had the email all set to go, he'd just been waiting for Macy to approve. He clicked send before he could change his mind. Immediately he regretted it. "Shit, Macy. What if that was the wrong song?"

"It wasn't."

"What if that was the *right* song?"

She set her fork down and considered him for a moment. "Are you afraid of that?"

"Yeah, a little."

"Why?"

"Because," he took her hand and held it, "I like where we are and the idea of things changing is scary."

She squeezed his hand. After a moment, she let go and picked up her fork.

There were a thousand things she could have said; she'd always be there for him, they'd get through it together, nothing could ever change them. Somehow, her not saying anything was the best response. Feeling much more settled, he took a bite of pancakes.

*** ***

Talan washed the breakfast dishes while Macy watched a You-Tube tutorial on how to use the video editing software that her computer had come with. He'd wanted her to go back to bed, but she'd been resistant. They were going to need to make videos, and since she was stuck at home recuperating she might as well do something productive. They'd finally made a compromise- she could watch videos but only if she stayed put on the couch.

It made him feel good that she was supporting him. Growing up, the only person who had ever encouraged him was his mom, and he was sure that was because moms pretty much had to encourage their kids. Whereas Macy wasn't obligated in any way.

The doorbell rang, interrupting his thoughts. He shut the water off and dried his hands on the way to answer it.

Gage stood in the hallway holding Macy's camera bag. "I tried calling, but you didn't answer."

"That's because I'm busy."

"Can I come in?" Talan moved to the side and Gage glanced around as he came through the door, zeroing in on Macy.

She nodded. "Morning, Gage."

"How are you?"

"Fine, thank you."

"I tried texting you."

"My phone's off. I'm supposed to be resting."

Talan added, "She *is* resting, Gage. That's why she's not at work."

"I don't want to disrupt her resting. I just came to check on her and to drop this off." He held out the camera bag.

Macy set her laptop on the coffee table and started to stand. Talan immediately said, "Sit, Mace." He took the bag from Gage and brought it to her.

She opened it and checked the contents. "Thank you."

"No problem." He shoved his hands in his pockets. "I'm glad you're okay."

Talan wanted him gone. "Thanks for bringing the camera."

Gage took the hint and headed towards to door. On his way past Talan, he said, "Can I talk to you in the hall?"

"Sure."

As soon as they were out of the apartment, Gage asked, "Is she really okay?"

"She's got fourteen stitches in her head, she's sore, and she's shaken. But she'll be okay."

"That's good. I gotta tell you, Dad was pretty upset when he got back yesterday. He said there was a lot of blood."

"Head wounds bleed a lot."

Gage nodded, looked around the hallway, then asked, "Talan, why didn't you tell me about you and Macy?"

He'd thought about telling Gage, and maybe he would have if things had been different. But it wasn't like they were close. There had really not been a reason to before this. "When Macy and I started seeing each other we kept it quiet because she already deals with a ton of shit from Keira and Vanessa. She didn't want to give them anything more to talk about."

"That's it?"

"No, that's not it. We also didn't say anything because Dad has that ridiculous rule about no employee dating and I didn't want to risk Macy losing her job. Because, for some reason I can't fully understand, she likes working for you."

"Is that why you told me yesterday that you were quitting?"

"I told you I'm quitting because I am. I never wanted to work for Dad in the first place. I did it because you asked me to. It was supposed to be temporary, remember? Just to help you get the shit with Travis's cars straightened out. So you didn't end up in jail with him." Bitterly, he finished, "That was four years ago, Gage."

"Yeah, I know."

"You know? That's it?"

"I appreciate that you came when I needed you, and that you've stayed all this time. I can't do anything about the last four years. And I need to ask you to stay a little longer. Please."

"No."

"Talan, we're being sued."

"You're being sued. I'm quitting."

There was a flicker of something- fear?- across Gage's features.

"Who's suing us?"

"Remember the Thunderbird Roadster?"

"It's not a Roadster. It's a convertible."

"I know. The problem is, the seller didn't know when he bought it. He thought it was worth ten times what we sold it for and he's pissed."

Talan narrowed his eyes at Gage. "Didn't you call him and explain after we talked about it?"

"I did. I got him to sign new contracts and everything. But then a lawyer got involved and now it's a big mess."

"So what am I supposed to do about that?"

"Just explain to our lawyer what happened. Most likely, we're going to push back. Say the seller tried to screw us, and he's lucky we found out before we sold the car otherwise he'd be facing fraud charges."

"Is that true?" Talan knew nothing about the legality of this particular situation.

Gage shrugged. "No idea, but our lawyer seems to think this is frivolous and all it'll take is incontrovertible evidence that we listed the car accurately. Especially since the seller had the option to take the car back and he didn't. Seems like this is sellers remorse."

Talan knew he was going to help Gage. But he wanted to be very clear that it was the last thing he was going to do. "I really am quitting."

"I know. I started looking for a replacement for you this morning. And, Talan, I think I can smooth things over for Macy. Actually, I already have an idea. And I think it's one she'll be very happy with."

"Yeah?"

"I loved what she did with the Barker's cars. I think I can talk Dad into paying her as a subcontractor, which means she'd be able to photograph cars the way she wants. And she'd be able to go to them, so she wouldn't have to come into Dawson's at all." He smiled awkwardly. "Keira put two and two together yesterday."

"I figured."

"You need to call Dad and set up a time to go talk to him, though. The amount of blood wasn't the only thing he was upset about yesterday."

"Is he pissed that we didn't tell him?"

"More hurt, I think."

It was, he supposed, a possibility. "I'll call as soon as I talk all this over with Macy."

Gage had only gone a few steps down the hallway when Talan stopped him. "Gage?" He turned back. "Thanks."

# Epilogue

Epilogue

Macy took a second to orient herself, to pinpoint where the ding had come from. At home she charged her phone on the dresser, but in a hotel it depended on where there was a plug and every hotel was slightly different. Her phone dinged again, from behind her. She rolled over and picked it up, read the text from Gage, and considered it. "Talan? Do you think we can make a detour?"

"Where to?" He tried to look at her phone but she had it against her chest.

"Jessup?"

"What's there?"

"A Hemi 'Cuda."

Suppressing a smile, he said, "Let me see it."

She handed over her phone. "If it's too far out of the way Gage said they'll have it shipped and wait to do pictures until we're back home."

"That's not for three more weeks."

"There's plenty of time. And he promised, remember? That your tour came first."

"And you promised you'd be reliable, remember?"

Indignant, she said, "I am totally reliable."

"Yeah? Like that time you pushed a client's Shelby to 120 miles an hour?"

"I didn't push it." She crossed her arms over her chest. "That car could go so much faster than that."

Grinning, he said, "Babe, we're going to Jessup."

"We don't have to."

"Actually, we do." He handed her the phone back. "Because until you get your hands on it, you're not going to be able to think about anything besides getting behind the wheel of a Hemi 'Cuda."

Setting the phone safely on the nightstand, she snuggled against his side. "I don't know that I'd go that far."

He laughed. "No? I'm pretty sure I heard you whispering about how much you wanted to run your fingers down the side of that Camaro last night. Ya know, when you were running your fingers down my side?"

Red crept into her cheeks. "Well, it's a pretty hot car. And you're a pretty hot guy. I can't help it if I get confused sometimes."

He grabbed her and tickled her. She shrieked and squirmed, trying to get away. After a minute he stopped and they settled back down. "It figures, I spent my whole life avoiding cars like the plague, and I fall for the one girl in the world who thinks about nothing but cars all the time."

"Hey! That's not true." She grinned as she finished, "Sometimes I think about coffee."

"Lucky for you, I'm self-confident as fuck. Otherwise I might be offended by that."

She traced her fingers over his shoulder, absent-mindedly following the curve of the dragon. "Talan, I think about you all the time."

"I know."

"Are you sure it's okay if we go to Jessup?"

"Yeah, of course. Gage is counting on us." He traced the birds flying over her shoulder. "I should have known, when I saw that Mercury on your hip, that this is what life with you would be like."

"Probably."

He didn't care, really. Macy without cars would be like water without coffee. He smiled to himself as he thought, *or Macy without coffee.*

"What are you smiling about?"

Not about to tell her the truth, he kissed her. "Nothing. Just what I'm going to do to you." Her grin was all the encouragement he needed. "You—" his phone dinged. She tensed. He tried to ignore the ding, and the fact that she'd reacted. "You are the most—" his phone dinged again.

"You should get that."

"It's just Gage. He wants to know if we're going to Jessup."

She pulled back a little. "How do you know that?"

"Because no one else in the world has such perfect timing."

She traced his hip. "Tell him yes, so he'll leave us alone."

He reached behind himself, keeping one hand on her, and grabbed his phone. He read the messages- twice. Then, slowly, set the phone down. He ran a hand over her hair, let his fingers caress her cheek, avoiding her temple out of habit. "Hon?"

"Hm?" Her eyes were half closed and she had a dreamy look on her face.

"Do you want to go to a festival?"

Confused, she opened her eyes. "Gage wants to know if I want to go to a festival?"

"No." He had to work really hard to keep his voice steady. "James does. He wants to know if we're interested in Sounds In The Sand."

The smile that spread over her face would have been answer enough, if he'd actually been asking what she thought he was. "Yeah. Of course."

"That's good. Because I'm playing the main stage."

The stunned silence only lasted a second, then she was screaming,

"Holy fuck! Talan! Holy shit!" She grabbed him, hugged him tight, buried her face against his chest. "I always knew you'd make it."

"Babe, it's one show."

She pulled away, sat up and leveled a look at him. "That's what you said when it was Foundry 41. And when the video for 'The Dragon and the Blackbird' hit a hundred-thousand views. And again when your name was printed on actual tickets."

"I headlined a show at a college. The place only held five thousand people, and they had to print their own tickets from an email."

"And you sold out three nights." She grinned. "You did it, Talan. Admit it. You're a star."

"I don't want to be a star."

She raised a disbelieving eyebrow at him. "No?'

Sitting up and draping his arms over her bare shoulders, he put his forehead against hers. "No. All I want is to play for you. Every night." He kissed her softly. "And that's exactly what I do."

Her voice dropped in response to his. "I know. And that's why the audience loves you." She smiled a little. "And why they can't have you."

"Nope. The only person who can have me is you." They sank back down into the bed. His phone beeped again.

"Ignore it. I don't give a shit who it is." She wrapped her arms around him, needing to feel him against her.

"Ignore what? The only thing I hear is you."

Made in the USA
Middletown, DE
09 February 2021